Love,
Meg

Love, Meg

C. LEIGH PURTILL

razor
bill

Love, Meg

RAZORBILL

Published by the Penguin Group
Penguin Young Readers Group
345 Hudson Street, New York, New York 10014, U.S.A.
Penguin Group (USA) Inc., 375 Hudson Street, New York, New York 10014, U.S.A.
Penguin Group (Canada), 90 Eglinton Avenue East, Suite 700, Toronto,
Ontario, Canada M4P 2Y3 (a division of Pearson Penguin Canada Inc.)
Penguin Books Ltd, 80 Strand, London WC2R 0RL, England
Penguin Ireland, 25 St Stephen's Green, Dublin 2, Ireland
(a division of Penguin Books Ltd)
Penguin Group (Australia), 250 Camberwell Road, Camberwell, Victoria 3124,
Australia (a division of Pearson Australia Group Pty Ltd)
Penguin Books India Pvt Ltd, 11 Community Centre, Panchsheel Park,
New Delhi – 110 017, India
Penguin Group (NZ), Cnr Airborne and Rosedale Roads, Albany,
Auckland 1310, New Zealand (a division of Pearson New Zealand Ltd)
Penguin Books (South Africa) (Pty) Ltd, 24 Sturdee Avenue, Rosebank,
Johannesburg 2196, South Africa

Penguin Books Ltd, Registered Offices: 80 Strand, London WC2R 0RL, England

10 9 8 7 6 5 4 3 2 1

THE LIBRARY OF CONGRESS HAS CATALOGED THE HARDCOVER EDITION AS FOLLOWS:

Purtill, C. Leigh.
  Love, Meg / by C. Leigh Purtill.
    p. cm.
  Summary: High school sophomore Meg longs for a "normal life" instead of constantly
moving whenever Lucie, her older sister and guardian, finds a new boyfriend, but after Meg
discovers a family secret, she leaves Lucie and Hollywood, California, for Queens, New
York, in search of answers and loving relatives.
  ISBN 978-1-59514-116-3
  [1. Family--Fiction. 2. Family problems--Fiction. 3. Parent and child--Fiction. 4. Moving,
Household--Fiction. 5. New York (N.Y.)--Fiction.] I. Title.
  PZ7.P9793Lo 2007
  [Fic]--dc22
                                                        2007001941

Razorbill paperback ISBN: 978-1-59514-147-7

Printed in the United States of America

Chapter
ONE

Dear Jen,

    How are you? I am fine.

    So, another move, another school: "Hi, I'm Meg! I'm a sophomore at Hollywood High!" That sounds both lame and cool at the same time, doesn't it?

    Up until the last minute, I thought for sure Lucie would let me stay in RC with the Heffernans. Why did she have to tear me away from my friends like that? Okay, friend, but still. Plus, it's almost the end of Sep-tember and school is practically over, right? Despite my arguments, here we are—in Hollywood—together.

    Lucie has been really moody since our move. She got all pissy when I asked her about shopping for school clothes. Worried about her new job, maybe? She says she's an assistant this time, not a secretary, which I hope translates into her holding onto a job for more than a year. Maybe this time we'll finally sign a lease and buy some real furniture instead of the Wal-Mart specials we drag around with us.

At least in this place, I have my own bedroom. I've got your picture right next to my bed so your smile shines on me while I sleep. It's very comforting.

God, Jen, why can't Lucie be more like you? When things get bad, you rise above your problems. You deal. Lucie just moves.

Anyway, I hope Hollywood will be a good luck charm for Lucie and me and it'll be the place we'll live forever. It's scary and it smells like warm sweet pickles, but it can't be all bad. You live here, so maybe we'll get to visit all the time and have coffee and make cookies. I make the best chocolate chip with walnuts. You'll love them!

> *I'll write more soon!*
> *Love,*
>
> *m*

Meg wanted to add, *P.S. I'm totally freaking out. I've never lived in a city before!* But she didn't have to; Jen knew her so well.

She studied the sheet of pale peach stationery on her lap and considered her signature. An *m* made a statement: it said, "I'm confident enough not to need the rest of the letters," while the lowercase added, "I'm humble." Just like Jen herself.

"Margaret" was such an ugly name, "Margaret Shanley" simply hideous. And she'd rather have her eyebrows tweezed with the claw end of a hammer than have anyone know her as "Margaret Anne Shanley." Back in first grade, when she began her spelling lessons, she and Lucie came up with the easy-to-spell "Meg" so she could be the first in class to get the gold star—before the only other tri-lettered kid in class, Joe Pietro, who insisted on writing Joep Ietro, so it wasn't like he would have gotten the gold star anyway.

With each year came a different school and a different name: Meg at seven, then Maggie at eight, Margie at nine, Peget at ten, Mags at eleven, M. A. at twelve, Anne for thir-teen, a quick detour to Peggy for fourteen, and back to Meg at fifteen. Maybe next year she would be capital M. Just M. Or M. S.

Hmmm . . . maybe not.

She carefully folded the stationery into thirds, align-ing the bottom edge just below the salutation, creasing it sharply with her thumbnail, then tucking the top third inside.

This week she ought to send along a photo, she thought. Something to delineate past from present, Rancho Cucamonga from Hollywood. She rummaged around an old Skechers shoe box and found a handful of photos taken with Reggie.

She was a good friend, Reggie Heffernan was, and had been for the nearly two years Meg and Lucie were in Rancho Cucamonga (the longest for them in one place), but Meg doubted their friendship would last beyond that.

After a move, she had learned, old friends gradually fell away, established new relationships with people they had disliked in the past, discovered talents for sports or instruments or dating, and found less time to keep up with the kid who left.

Out of sight, out of mind. That's what happened, and while it certainly did suck, it was nothing that couldn't be gotten used to.

Meg had gotten used to it a long time ago.

But all this moving around and new schools and new teachers again and again and again was exhausting. Meg wondered, who would she be *this* time? What class would she do well in? What personality would work best at Hollywood High School?

For now, Reggie was attentive and called frequently and made plans to come visit. But she would most likely be out of Meg's life in a couple of months.

That was all right, but Meg hoped she could time Reggie's inevitable departure with New Friend's arrival, whoever New Friend might be.

Meg held up a fairly recent photo—one of her and Reggie's trip to Epicenter Stadium, home of the minor-league Quakes, one of the few cool things to do in RC. It had been taken at Reggie's house by Reggie's older brother, Billy, before they left for the game. Meg sat on the hood of her friend's brand-new navy blue Jetta, slender legs crossed daintily at the ankles, while Reggie leaned against the bumper, arms akimbo, caught in mid-scowl, her face contorted with pissed-offness because Billy wouldn't stop goofing around. Meg was laughing as the picture was being snapped—her strawberry blond hair falling across her face, blown by gusts of arid wind coming off the concrete driveway, her powder blue eyes squinting against the setting sun. The photo confirmed Meg's long-held suspicion that Billy secretly liked her: Reggie's entire right half was cut off while Meg was centered perfectly in the frame. At least the boy had gotten one thing right—he'd somehow made Meg look like she had more cleavage than the 34Bs Mother Nature had given her.

Meg sighed and turned the photo over, then scribbled across the back: *Meg & Reg, Reg's hse, RC* and the date. She carefully placed it in the envelope, wedging it beside the crisply folded letter. She licked the flap, sealed it, and flipped it over. *MS. JENNIFER ANISTON,* she wrote in thick capitals, followed by the address for Jen's manager in Beverly Hills. Meg didn't have to look it up; she knew it by heart.

Jen would understand what Meg was going through—she always did. She would read Meg's letter, and then, after careful consideration, she would tell Meg exactly what to do about her ridiculous, insane, absolutely chaotic existence.

Jen—unlike other people in her life—never failed her.

Chapter
TWO

The apartment building where Meg and Lucie lived looked like a concrete shoe box on stilts. The two floors of apartments, twelve units in all, had a long balcony running parallel to the road. Similar buildings flanked theirs, as if the builder had been given a twofer or, at the very least, a steep discount on additional materials.

The really cool thing about the place was its location: five blocks south of Hollywood Boulevard, a mere stone's throw from the Walk of Fame, the Chinese Theatre, El Capitan, and Pantages—not to mention the Capitol Records building on Vine.

But there was so much more to Hollywood than the tourist sites, Meg knew. There were movie lots and recording studios and famous restaurants and infamous bars. There were gilded mansions where celebrities lived and roach-infested apartments where they died. Meg wanted to see it all, and she really, really, *really* hoped her sister could hold it together long enough so that Meg could actually do it.

She stared out the kitchen window toward the towering palms on the sun-drenched boulevard, cradling a tiny Motorola cell phone against her ear while she stirred sugar into a mug of lukewarm tea. The microwave was somewhere under the junk here in the kitchen—or maybe the living room, she wasn't sure—but it definitely wasn't where she needed it.

"How did people used to heat their tea in olden times?" Meg asked into her phone.

Reg's voice answered on the other end of the line. "What do you mean, like, before we were born?"

"Before there were microwaves."

Reg scoffed. "How do I know?"

"I guess we could Google it." Meg took a gulp of the sweetened Earl Grey. No cream. Yuck. "What time is it?"

"Hang on, I gotta turn." Meg could hear Reggie's phone slide down her shoulder as she juggled her coffee mug and downshifted on the curve into RC High's parking lot. "It's eight-oh-seven," she said when she returned. "When do your classes start?"

"Eight fifteen, I think," Meg said. "Where the hell is she? She promised she'd drive." She shook her head. Lucie couldn't be trusted with anything, not even a simple little task like driving her own sister to school.

"I wish you could have stayed with us," Reggie said. Meg heard the same dispirited note in her friend's voice as she had a month ago, when she'd first told Reggie she was moving. "We could have driven together every day. You'd never have been late."

"I know, right?" Meg said. "That would have been amazing."

Reggie half laughed. "Billy said you could have the extra bed in his room."

"I'd have taken it, too." Meg would have loved living with Reggie's family—a normal family—even if she had to sleep in the garage.

But it was too late to bemoan what could have been, and Meg didn't want to dwell on the negative. She had awoken that morning full of hope and promise—had jumped into the shower, ignoring the tiny pellets of poop in the corner of the hallway that were the telltale sign of mice, had washed and dressed and lipsticked and rushed into the kitchen—only to find everything looking exactly the same as she left it when she went to bed last night.

No breakfast, no coffee, no Lucie. And no note.

"Meg?" A shrill bell whistled beneath Reggie's voice. "Class is starting. I gotta go."

"Call me at lunch?"

"Yeah. Keep your phone on."

"Cool." Meg smiled.

There was a sound at the door. Keys in the lock. "Who are you talking to?"

Meg shut her phone and saw Lucie entering the apartment. Her cheeks and lips were pale, her mascara smudged. And that outfit—was there a button missing on her blouse?—was definitely the same one she'd been wearing last night. Super–low riders and flip-flops, Lucie's after-work uniform of choice.

"Where have *you* been?" Meg asked. "I've been waiting for, like, an hour already."

"God, I'm exhausted." Lucie pulled out a chair and sat down heavily at the imitation-oak-topped kitchen table. "Get me some coffee."

"No coffee. I can't find the pot."

"What are you drinking?"

"Tea."

"Get me some of that."

Meg turned on the stove. "You're supposed to drive me to school, you know. It's my first day, and you promised. And what about work? You have to go to work."

"Work starts at nine. I have plenty of time." Lucie pulled her hair back with both hands and knotted it loosely against her neck. The two sisters shared a love of long, stick-straight hair, but where Meg's was flaxen with coral highlights, Lucie's was the opposite: a vibrant red with golden strands.

Lucie pointed toward Meg's phone. "Where'd that come from?"

Meg filled a saucepan with water and set it on the burner. "Reggie."

"Why is Reggie buying you—"

"If you haven't noticed, we don't have a phone."

Lucie frowned. "We *have* a phone."

"It's not working." Meg set a mug down in front of her sister. "We've been here a week and we don't have a working phone. What if we had an emergency? That's a bit dangerous, don't you think?"

"No." Lucie's gaze hardened. "I suppose I hardly *think* at all. Isn't that what you're saying? Don't talk to me like I'm a child, Meg."

Then get the damn phone working already, Meg wanted to shout. Honestly, you'd have thought Lucie was the one about to start high school.

Wait—high school! Meg glanced down at the clock on her phone. "I gotta get to homeroom, Luce. Let's go."

Lucie shook her head. "Sorry. Gotta shower."

Meg sputtered. "Shower? But—but what about me?"

"You're a big girl. Figure it out."

Meg stared at her sister, dumbfounded. "Are you kidding me? You told me you'd drive me to school. God, you are so self-centered."

Lucie stood. Pulled up to her full height, she was still a couple of inches shy of Meg's five-five. "*I'm* self-centered? What's self-centered is you expecting me to *drive* you to school. Maybe your little friend gets whatever she wants— has her own car and can give you a fancy phone—"

Meg felt heat rising in her cheeks. "My *little* friend?"

"—but that's not our life."

Meg took a deep breath. Whatever. She so didn't need to be having this conversation. What she needed was to be out of the house and in homeroom, having her name called and introducing herself to the rest of her classmates.

"Luce, I gotta go. Are you taking me or not?"

"Not."

"Fine."

Bitch, Meg added to herself. She poured warmish water from the saucepan over the tea bag in her sister's mug, then gathered her purse and backpack. "Give me some money for the bus."

Lucie shook her head. "No cash."

"Unbelievable!"

"You can walk."

"Walk? It's, like, a hundred blocks from here!"

"It's six."

"Luce, this is LA. I will look like a total moron walking to school."

Lucie blew air across the top of her mug and carried it with her to her bedroom. "Have a good day. There's a tape from last night in my bag."

Meg clenched her jaw, closed her eyes, and tried to remain calm. Of course. Lucie had been at Aaron's show last night. Maybe they had been fighting, Meg considered, maybe that was why Lucie was so grouchy lately. She rooted around in her sister's fake Kate Spade purse and found a blank-faced cassette.

For twenty bucks, Meg was supposed to type out the

audience's reactions to Aaron's show so he could see what worked and what didn't. The extra cash he paid for this service would come in handy. Especially if Meg was going to need bus fare.

Okay, she thought. This sort of made up for having to walk to school.

Sort of, but not really.

Hollywood High was a compact group of art-deco-style buildings on the corner of Sunset and Highland, surrounded by wide, flat banana palms and clusters of birds of paradise. Murals of old-timey movie stars covered the auditorium's exterior walls—no one the Shanley sisters recognized, but cool all the same.

Meg and Lucie had been awestruck walking up the front steps two weeks ago to register Meg for classes. They had driven the hour from RC—west on the 10, north on La Brea, east on Sunset—gabbing all the way about what they would see and who—and look how close their new apartment was to Hollywood Boulevard, which was *surely* where all the stars hung out.

"Yes, it is," Lucie had said. "But—"

"—stop calling me Shirley," Meg finished, which set the two to giggling as they waited in the principal's office. Outside, the cheerleading squad was practicing on the track.

"Look, it's your alter ego," Lucie had whispered as a blond, ponytailed girl jumped in the air, her legs spread in a wide, flat V. "Yay, rah-rah—"

"Shut up! Like I would want to," Meg had whispered back, but secretly, she believed that she might.

She was smart, sure, but it would be *infinitely* better to be popular. And was that such a bad thing—to want to be well liked and cool and, let's just say it, normal?

Lucie acted like being normal was the craziest idea in the world.

The principal had walked in then, a silver-haired man with a tired smile, who wanted to know about their parents, where they were, and why Lucie was Meg's guardian.

Lucie sobered up and delivered the speech Meg now knew by rote: mother's cerebral hemorrhage during delivery, overwhelmed father, car accident two years later, Lucie took over at seventeen, move, move, move, job, job, job, but stable now. Not to worry, Lucie's concern for her sister's welfare was foremost in her mind, hence the new and improved apartment and the new and improved job, and Meg would be at classes every day, Lucie would see to that, yada, yada, yada.

Actually, Lucie had come to Hollywood for Aaron, Meg knew, not for a job and not for Meg. Lucie had said as much on the drive out.

"It's serious this time," Lucie had told Meg in a cheerful voice. "We've been together for a year, and I really think it's going to happen."

It being marriage, obviously. Or at least settling down in one place. Meg didn't want to hold out too much hope because, God, disappointment was too much to take. But her sister's happiness was contagious, and besides, she wanted to believe.

"That's awesome, Luce," Meg had said sincerely.

In the administration office, after Lucie finished her tale, the principal's eyes softened, just as Meg knew they would, so she turned off her brain, watched the cheerleaders, and listened to the clamor of students in the hallway outside.

Would one of them be the New Friend? she wondered. Would she actually get to graduate from this place? Would their lives finally be normal like everyone else's? Two weeks ago, it seemed like a real possibility.

But now, at eight twenty-nine, the halls were quiet and Meg was sprinting through them, desperately searching for her locker. She thought the principal's assistant had shown her down this passageway and that there was a left turn involved and possibly a right, and then a glass case full of photographs, and then her locker. But so far all she had found was a girls' bathroom and a fire extinguisher.

At least she had managed to arrive at the school in less than fifteen minutes, which was surprising, considering the walk was eight long LA blocks, not six short ones, and required crossing two major intersections. Fortunately, she was able to distract herself by watching the cars sitting in traffic on Highland. Was Jen in one of those cars? she wondered. On her way to the big studios in Burbank? Or to Beverly Hills to visit her agent or her manager? She was certain Jen disdained limos; she was so much more down-to-earth than that. She was the kind of person who would drive a classy Saab or a Mercedes coupe, something reliable, not flashy. Jen was so not about flash.

"Meg?" she imagined she would hear. "Is that you?" And Meg would turn toward that mellifluous voice and see a delicate hand brush back a golden mane and lower a pair of sunglasses down a perfect nose.

"How did you know it was me?" Meg would ask as she walked closer to the curb where Jen's Miata or whatever would be parked.

"I recognized that beautiful hair of yours from your pictures, silly. Need a ride?"

And Meg would nod and smile at all the fans who had suddenly appeared around the car, all the jealous fans with their autograph books, shoving them toward Jen, who would ignore them and smile only at Meg.

"Let's skip school. You want to hang out on the set?" And Jen would pull the car away from the curb and wave to all her fans in her wake and the little car would whisk them up Highland, its road instantly devoid of traffic, and Jen and Meg would lift their hands like they were riding a roller coaster and laugh and laugh.

The bell rang then, stirring Meg from her daydream. Classroom doors slammed open and students poured out and around her.

She was pretty damn sure she had missed homeroom.

A few hours later, Meg was sitting on the school's front steps facing Sunset Boulevard, reading the same page of an

Anne Rice novel over and over. She flipped open her ring-
ing cell. "Nice timing, Reggie," she said. "You totally caught
me at lunch."

"So, how is it?"

"It's high school." Meg cast an eye toward a clique of
girls posing against the stone steps. "Just like in RC, but
with more smog and less grass."

"Got any good classes?"

"I guess. I'm taking an English class that looks all right.
Bio's gonna be gross, though, cutting things up."

"I took bio last year. It's not so bad." Reggie, a year
ahead of Meg, was now a junior. "I kinda liked dissections.
I can help you if you want."

"Yeah, all right." Meg's gaze wandered to one of the girls
on the steps who was shaking out a pack of Virginia Slims—
menthol, it looked like—and offering them to her friends.
One by one, each girl took a cigarette from the pack except
for one holdout who shook her head and mumbled something sly.

"Meet anyone as cool as me yet?" Reg asked.

Meg sneaked another glance at the clique. The non-
smoker looked familiar, from French, maybe? Or was her
locker nearby?

"You mean as lame as you?" Meg teased. "Dude, this
is Hollywood. Everyone is cool here. This is where they
invented cool."

"Well, you better get your ass on back to RC before they
find out about *you*."

Meg watched as the group of girls moved as a single unit up the stairs and inside the building. She knew without even finishing out the day how the rest of the year would unfold. By the beginning of next week, she would have scoped out everyone in her classes and earmarked the two or three girls she had a chance of befriending: one of the lonely girls sitting at lunch by herself, one of the semi-popular girls who would need help in math class, or possibly one of the goth girls who would want to dye her hair. It always went that way.

She would excel in her classes at first, impressing all of her teachers with her intelligence and dedication. Then she would slack off around Christmas and begin a slow decline through spring, culminating in a solid C-plus average.

She wanted to remain optimistic. She was, by nature, a positive person. But why bother to try so hard when she and Lucie would just move again anyway?

A buzzer sounded over the loudspeakers.

"I'll call you later," Meg said to Reggie, and then closed her phone. She slung her backpack over her shoulder and retreated inside the building.

Dear Jen, she heard in her head, *this new school bites too.*

Chapter
THREE

The Durant public library was on Sunset Boulevard across the street from a liquor store and kitty-corner to a Fantastic Sam's. It was brand new, with skylights and a machine where people could check out books by themselves. It had, nevertheless, acquired a bum stink from all the homeless people who slept on its steps every night.

But there were also computers. *Free* computers. Aaron had complained once that typed pages were cold and impersonal, but Meg had insisted on using a computer, even though that meant she had to go out and find one. Longhand, she believed, was reserved for personal correspondence, like letters to Jen, not for charts and stuff.

Meg put the tape Lucie had given her into her ancient Walkman and turned up the volume.

"Good evening, everyone, hello," she heard. "I'm Aaron Spector." A smattering of applause. "And you're not." A couple of people booed, low and hollow. Meg hadn't heard that joke before; she would have to tell Aaron it didn't go over very well via a note in the side column: *2 boos, no applause.* She tried to be very honest in her comments. She had a feeling Aaron's memory wasn't as accurate as it should be.

Meg heard the *pluck, pluck* of acoustic guitar strings under Aaron's voice as it eased from spoken word to song. "So here we go, and if you know the words, why, feel free to join in at any time." A pause. Nothing from the audience. "But if you do sing along, try to keep your voice down." More laughter, one hand clap, and then another. And the song began.

It was one of Meg's favorites, a happy tune about walking down a road and finding love along the way and realizing that forks in the road were there for the taking and neither was bad or good, just different, and maybe if you find love, you don't want to take a path at all, you just want to settle down and make a home along the road and watch others travel along.

So okay, it wasn't very poetic and it didn't rhyme, but when Aaron did it with the music, it made much more sense.

The general idea, the quaint and old-fashioned notion of finding the person you love and making a home with them—that didn't seem so quaint and old-fashioned to Meg. That seemed right, like what you were supposed to do with your life when you were all grown up. Certainly that was what Meg expected she would do, even if Lucie never seemed to buy into the idea.

Meg recorded in the remarks column: *light applause, approximately 10 persons singing along—3 male, 7 (?) female—* gender being an important consideration for Aaron, who was worried about his sex appeal. Not bad, she thought, for the leadoff before everyone got sloshed and sang "American Pie" and other Don McLean songs over Aaron's originals.

Meg turned off her Walkman and stared at the computer screen. It would probably take her till library closing to finish.

"What was that you were listening to?"

A voice behind her. Male. Young. Past puberty.

She turned. "Excuse me?"

The boy was about fifteen, sixteen, hair dyed blond at the ends, a late-summer experiment running its course. "That song? On your Walkman?"

Had she been listening to it that loudly? "It was . . . a friend of mine."

He was nodding before she had finished, his eyes searching her face, her clothes, her books, looking for something else to say before she went back to work. "Sounds good." His face was soft and doughy, a zit at his temple, one below his chin, but he didn't pick at them, she could tell. A patient fella, content to let them pop on their own instead of forcing them to burst and form red hills and black craters on his skin.

"Is that on a CD?" he asked.

"Uh, yeah, Aaron's got a CD."

"Maybe I'd like to buy it." The boy shrugged, apparently not happy with the words coming out of his mouth but powerless to stop them. He stared vacantly at her.

Meg smiled. Teenage boys were so . . . dim. This one, like all the others, probably just wanted to get laid. *Please.* Jen had counseled Meg a long time ago on that subject: "You have to truly love the person you're going to have sex with," she wrote, "and he should love you back. Then you know it's right."

Right. Meg planned on following Jen's advice. After all, Jen spoke with the voice of wisdom and experience.

"Um . . ." The towheaded library boy was wiping his hands on his jeaned thighs. "My name's Marty." He stopped. Waited. Like Meg thought, patient fella.

While she hadn't been the recipient of many invitations for dates, Meg certainly had seen enough Hilary Duff movies to recognize the signs of someone getting ready to ask an important question. "I'm . . ." At that moment, she wanted a new name. "Peget," she finished.

Why not? It wasn't as if it were a lie. It *was* her name—or one of them. She just hadn't used it in a while. Besides, it wasn't like she was ever going to see this guy again.

"That's, um, unusual. Is it Dutch?"

"Yugoslavian, actually." She smiled, lips pressed together.

"Did I see you here last week or . . . ?"

Meg chuckled. Like it was a bar. "My computer at home is broken."

"Really?" His face brightened. "I know a lot about computers if you want me to take a look."

"Oh, um, thanks, but I've got it covered."

Marty's face fell. "Oh."

Sorry, Marty, Meg thought as the boy walked away, *but you are not the one. And it's better this way, really. If I led you on, Jen would not approve.*

It was nearly eleven and Meg was reading, ignoring her pre-calc as she lay on the brown plaid sofa in the darkened apartment, warmed by an old blanket and the blue glow of the television. She heard a jingle of keys outside the front door and then the click of the lock turning.

She looked up as her sister walked in. "You're home."

"Hey," Lucie said in a weary voice.

Meg reached for the remote on the floor and muted the set. "You're late."

"You eat?"

"Pizza. You?"

"Burger."

"Work keep you?"

"Yeah." Lucie smiled shyly. "And Aaron."

"That's cool. I have his thing."

"Excellent." Lucie collapsed onto the sofa, leaned her head back against the wall, and closed her eyes. "Man, I'm beat," she said.

"You want to ask me about my day?"

Lucie turned her head without opening her eyes. "How was your day?"

"I went to school."

"Uh-huh."

"And it sucked."

"Uh-huh."

Meg stared at her sister: thirty years old but dressed like she was fourteen. Her baby-fine hair was held back with half a dozen pink plastic clips. She had Band-Aids on her knees from when she'd scraped herself moving furniture. She would not ask whether Meg had finished her homework or if she liked her new teachers. She would not tell Meg to invite her new friends over so she could meet them, and she would not suggest Meg try out for band or track or the chess club. With Meg and Lucie, it just wasn't like that.

Lucie's eyes fluttered open. "What time is it?"

"Five to eleven."

"You gonna watch?"

Meg rolled her eyes. "Duh."

"Save me a seat. I'll be right back."

"*You* want to watch?"

"Yeah. Let me brush my teeth first," Lucie said, heaving her small frame off the couch and heading for the bathroom.

Meg felt a little thrill run up the back of her spine. There was a time when she and Lucie watched every episode of *Friends* together, snuggled wherever they were, always on the brown plaid sofa. They knew all the lines, especially

Rachel's, and where each episode fell on the Ross-Rachel timeline. They would play a game, a sort of *Friends* version of *Name That Tune*, where the sister who guessed the episode in the fewest number of lines in the opening scene would win. The other sister would then have to wait on her for the rest of the show, bringing drinks and snacks and cleaning up the remnants. It was a game they both played well for many years. Then Lucie sort of faded, watching less and less frequently.

This would be a rare treat.

Meg unmuted the television and adjusted the rabbit ears to clear the picture, then flopped back onto the couch.

Lucie returned just in time to hear the opening chords of the theme song.

The two sisters each took a corner of the worn and tattered sofa. They hummed along with the Rembrandts. "I'll be there for yooouuuuu!"

Lucie pulled the blanket off Meg and covered her legs with it, then Meg tugged it back, leaving a quarter of it on Lucie. Back and forth and back and forth until the blanket was evenly apportioned to each sister. This was another of their games. Unspoken between them was the absolute equality in sharing the blanket—a rule established so long ago, Meg could hardly remember who had suggested it. They giggled like they used to, like when they first discovered *Friends* together.

On the set, the young *Friends* actors cavorted in a fountain, opening and closing umbrellas, smiling, laughing, enjoying being young *Friends* actors. "I'll be there for yooouuu. . . ."

As the show unfolded in Monica's impossibly large New York City loft, Meg felt sleep descend upon her. A comforting, familiar sleep, because no matter where in the world she and Lucie moved, no matter what lame school she was attending, no matter what crap was going on in their lives, there was one thing she could always count on: there would always be *Friends* on—somewhere—at eleven o'clock.

Chapter
FOUR

Dear Jen,

How are you? I am fine.

One of my all-time favorite episodes was on last night, the one where Ross and Rachel do it for the first time in the museum where Ross works. I love it when you say you're sorry and he says it's a juice box. I never got that until Reggie explained it to me. I thought he had, like, ruined your dress or something. What did I know—I was only thirteen!

Guess what? Lucie's taking me shopping for new clothes! I think her generosity was influenced by the happy envelope she got the other day. She hasn't gotten one of those in a while.

So far, I gotta say I'm totally unimpressed with the student body at Hollywood High. I have yet to meet a Spielberg kid or a Hanks offspring or even a Stallone brat! I mean, where are they? Do you think they put

*all the famous kids in the same class with a private cafeteria and basket-
ball court? And do their bodyguards have to take freshman English and
earth science, too?*

All right, I gotta go.

Hugs,

m

With each letter that she carefully folded and stamped, Meg
liked to imagine Jen on the receiving end. She used to picture
her lying in her bed in a flouncy white nightgown, tucked
under a lacy bedspread, reading her letters while a maid
brought her lattes and English muffins with raspberry jam.
Of course, now that Meg was older, she knew better. These
days she imagined Jen returning from an early-morning yoga
or Pilates class, picking up her mail on her way into her stun-
ning yet earth-friendly mansion. She would shuffle through
the junk, toss aside the bills until she found Meg's letter.

"Meg! I wonder what she's up to," Jen might say when
she sat down on the patio with an iced tea. Her hair would
be tucked behind her ears, wet from her post-workout
shower. She would probably be wearing flip-flops, and her
sunglasses would be resting on top of her head.

"Oh!" she might gasp when she read about Meg's D in
history.

"Ha!" she might laugh when she read about Meg mis-
taking Lucie's shaving cream for antiperspirant.

"Ohhh . . ." she might sigh when she read about Meg

being left alone in the apartment for an entire weekend.

"I will definitely have to write her soon and catch her up on everything," Jen probably said to herself. "She sounds like she could use a friend."

But then her agent would call, or her manager, and she would have to go do something extremely important. Meg was certain, though, that each time Jen got one of her letters, she made a mental note to write to Meg very, very soon.

Truth? Okay, truth: Meg hadn't received a letter from Jen in a while. Practically three years.

And it was weird, too, how the letters had simply stopped. She had been writing and receiving notes from Jen since she was nine years old and then, one day, Jen's envelopes just didn't arrive. It couldn't have happened at a worse time. Lucie was moping and miserable and completely falling apart, dumped by the latest guy in her life. Could Meg even remember his name? It was all going so wrong, and Meg really needed a friend. So she continued to write and mail, week after week, but nothing came in return. They were moving a lot then, but even so, the post office managed to re-route Lucie's credit card bills and Gap catalogs to the new address.

Then finally, one day, Meg mentioned it to Lucie.

"She's busy," Lucie had said. "She doesn't have time for pen pals anymore."

"But I'm not a pen pal!" Meg had cried. "I'm her friend!"

"Don't be silly. How can she be your friend when you haven't even met her?"

"That doesn't matter! I tell her everything. And she helps me with all my problems and gives me awesome advice and crap."

"Don't say crap," Lucie had scolded.

Meg remembered holding up a letter from two years before. "This is when she told me all about how to give myself a manicure." And another. "And this one is when she helped me with long division." And a third. "And this one is when she explained how to French-kiss." She let the pages fall. "She can't be too busy—she can't!"

"Meg," Lucie said impatiently, "someone probably wrote those for her—"

"What?"

"Big stars have people who do those kinds of things for them. But you can tell *me* stuff if you want. I can give you advice."

"You?" Meg had scoffed. "No offense, Luce, but *no way*."

Lucie clammed up then, tossed back her hair, and nodded her head.

Meg had felt sort of bad about it and still kind of did, but honestly, how could she tell Lucie the advice she needed was *about her*? How could she complain to *Lucie* about moving and not having friends and living with a sister who couldn't care less about her?

The answer was simple: she couldn't.

Meg stopped writing completely for nine whole months, but it nearly killed her. Because there was stuff she *really,*

really wanted to tell Jen. But she was worried: had she said something wrong, written something insulting, criticized Jen in any way . . . was there a *reason* Jen had stopped answering her?

It couldn't be that what Lucie had said—although it made some logical sense—was true.

And then, weeks later, Meg saw Jen talking to Barbara Walters on TV. Jen told Barbara that she had been so busy and self-involved in recent months that she felt like she was ignoring her friends. But she treasured her girlfriends for their support and their words of wisdom, she insisted, and she hoped they could forgive her.

Meg stared at Jen then, Jen with her gorgeous Malibu tan and her yoga-perfect body, and said, *Yes, of course I forgive you.* And that very night, she composed a real doozy, a double-sided four pager, informing Jen of all that she'd missed and promising to keep writing for as long as Jen wanted to hear from her.

Which would probably be forever.

Meg's all-time favorite dinner was French toast.

The meal, despite its Gallic pedigree, was surprisingly easy for an American girl to make. Bread, eggs, milk, and cinnamon were all that was required, and if Meg wanted to get fancy, she used thick slices of sourdough bread or great big chunks of sweet Hawaiian loaf. She added gooey maple syrup and pats of butter and voila! Utter deliciousness.

"Mmm . . . what do I smell?" Meg heard Lucie ask when

she opened the door. Her face appeared next to the stove. "Awesome!"

Meg grinned and waved a spatula at her. "Put your stuff down. You're late."

"What did I do to deserve this culinary treat?"

Meg lowered her eyes coyly. "Nothing."

French toast was actually one of Lucie's favorites too, and okay, so maybe Meg was trying to be a little nicer to her sis, knowing they would soon be shopping for new clothes. But no matter what, they needed to eat, Meg reasoned. So it was kind of a win-win situation.

Meg reached into the bag of Ralphs Private Select Label Enriched White and withdrew a handful of bread. "Would you get me some more paper towels from the bottom shelf, please?"

Lucie bent down and opened the cabinet. "Sure. Where are the . . . ahhh!" She stumbled back and leapt onto a chair.

"Omigod!" Meg screamed, and jumped onto the chair beside her sister. There, on the linoleum floor, handily blending in with a brown burn hole, was a cockroach twice the size of a Kennedy dollar.

"Go on!" Meg shouted at the insect. "Take what you want and leave!" But the roach didn't budge. Its antennae twitched and its head moved from side to side.

He sat there, alone and still, and Meg found herself softening toward the ugly creature. "Maybe he's scared," she said.

"My ass. We have to kill it," Lucie insisted.

"Uh-uh. Killing animals is bad karma."

"I'll remember that the next time you order a cheese-burger."

"I'm a vegetarian," Meg declared, "starting now. Besides, you can't kill it if I name it. I'm calling him Gregor Samsa."

"What? Meg, come on. We'll do this together. You chase him into the corner and I'll step on him."

"Don't kill Gregor! Can't we take him outside instead? Please?"

Lucie made a face but gave in. "Fine."

Meg grabbed a *People* magazine and Lucie trapped the bug under a juice glass, then they ran down the stairs and let him out, watched him scurry into the bushes under the apartment building. "Go, Gregor! Be free!" Meg cried.

Lucie shook her head. "Who's Gregor Samsa, anyway?"

Meg shrugged. "It's from a Kafka novel."

"Good evening, ladies." The girls turned to see Aaron coming up the sidewalk.

"Yay! Aaron's here!" Lucie stood up and ran to her boyfriend. He was carrying a duffel bag, Meg noticed. She tried not to think too much about what that meant as the couple exchanged a flurry of kisses.

Aaron was cute, Meg supposed, for a forty-year-old. He smiled a lot, but there was an undeniable geekiness to him. He wore glasses when he drove, metal-framed John Lennons, but not when he performed. He said fuzzy shapes were easier to sing to.

"So, Meggie," Lucie said sweetly, her chin touching her chest. "Is it okay if Aaron stays for dinner?"

"Dinner? Uh, yeah, sure."

"Oh, goody. Aaron, sweetie, do you like French Toes?"

"French what?"

Meg whipped her head around to her sister. They had never talked about French Toes to anyone; it was their own little secret. "Lucie . . ."

Lucie ignored her, playing instead to Aaron's amusement. "When Meg was five, she thought it was 'French Toes,' but I kept telling her no, it was 'toast.'"

"Lucie, stop," Meg said in a low, warning voice. There was no need for Aaron to know this about them, about her.

"So one day she took a slice, dripping wet with eggs, and dropped it in the *toaster!*" Lucie roared with laughter. "She pushed the handle down and sparks went, like, everywhere!"

Meg, red-faced and annoyed, led the way upstairs. Everything had been going so nicely, she thought, and then Lucie had to go and do a thing like this. Using their lives—Meg's life—to make herself look good, or better, or smarter to a guy.

"Don't forget to tell him how you took the toaster back to Macy's the next day and pretended it never worked," Meg said as they arrived at the landing outside the apartment.

Lucie pursed her lips and looked up at Aaron. "It was brand new and she ruined it! What was I supposed to do?"

Aaron laughed. "Don't put me in the middle."

Good for you, Meg thought.

With that one sentence, Aaron scored just a little more of her respect—and maybe even an extra slice of toast. "Dinner will be ready in five minutes."

Two hours after her magnificent meal of French Toes had ended—along with Lucie's incessant mooning over Aaron during the cleanup—Meg lay on her stomach, head hanging over the side of her bed, staring at her history book on the floor. Tonight was two chapters on the Civil War and the assassination of Abe Lincoln.

President Lincoln went to the theater, she read. *He was shot by John Wilkes Booth. Booth did not like the president's politics.*

See Spot run. Run, Spot, run. Where the hell was she, in remedial history? Back in RC, she would have Mr. Petersen for history class, and she would get tested every week on the material she read, and there would be more than one book to detail all of American history from the Revolutionary War through the Gulf War. And there would be colonial maps and battle diagrams, and later Mr. Petersen would split the class into two groups and they would reenact the Inchon landing that Mr. Petersen was involved in during the Korean War that resulted in him losing the use of three fingers of his left hand because he was stabbed in the elbow by an enemy soldier whom he could have killed but instead brought back to camp to be kept as a POW.

But she wasn't in RC any longer, and she didn't have Mr. Petersen for history. She was in Hollywood now, and apparently Hollywood students were as dumb as a bag of rocks.

There was a knock at her door.

"Yeah?"

"It's Aaron."

A pause.

"Can I come in?"

"Uh, yeah."

Another pause.

"Are you sure? I can come back if you, you know, need some time. . . ."

"Dude, come in." Meg swung around on her bed and sat up.

Aaron stepped into the room and looked around. "Hey. Nice place you got. I take it you're a big fan of Green Day." He waved a hand at a poster Meg had tacked up on the wall above her bed.

"Yeah. I guess."

"I like them too."

"They're all right."

Aaron's gaze traveled to the nightstand. "Is that Jennifer Aniston?"

"Yeah."

"Framed picture and everything. Is that signed?"

Meg nodded. "Uh-huh."

"When I was a kid, I was a huge fan of the Fonz." He

stopped and looked at her. "You've heard of Fonzie, right? Arthur Fonzarelli?"

"*Happy Days*. Yeah." She discreetly rolled her eyes. Where did Aaron think she lived, with the Amish? "I've seen it on Nick at Reggie's."

"I wrote him this long letter about how cool I thought he was. I told him that if he was Richie's friend, he could totally be my friend." Aaron glanced down at the hands that wrote the letter, as if wondering how his fingers had managed to put such dorky yet heartfelt emotions to paper. "I told him it would be really neat if he was my brother and how much fun we could have." He laughed. "Back then, my older sisters alternated between beating me up and mothering me. I was desperate for a brother."

Meg raised an eyebrow. "Did he write you back?"

"Well, not Henry Winkler, but probably one of the studio publicists. I got a head shot back and a form letter that invited me to join the Fonz's fan club and told me to stay cool and stay in school. Aaay!" Aaron held up both thumbs and waggled them.

"Did you?"

"Stay in school?"

"No. Did you join his fan club?"

Aaron thought a moment. "Don't think I did. It was kind of a girly thing to do. How 'bout you? Are you a member of Miss Aniston's fan club?"

Meg was appalled at the suggestion. As if the two

situations were in any way comparable. "Uh, no. Jen is actually a really close friend of mine."

"She is?"

"We've been writing to each other for years."

"Oh . . . wow. That's cool." Aaron pushed his glasses up on his nose. "Does she answer you?"

She could tell Aaron thought she was delusional, possibly stalker material. That was okay; it wasn't like Meg hadn't encountered that reaction in the past. It wasn't other people's fault that they were closed-minded and couldn't accept the fact that a fantastic and beautiful star like Jennifer Aniston could be friends with someone like her.

Meg looked over at the photo. "She did answer for, like, four years. But lately, she's been busy, I guess. She's doing lots of movies now and probably traveling a lot. Going on location, they call it. So she doesn't have as much time. . . ."

Her voice trailed off. She so didn't feel like talking to Aaron about this. "Why did you come in here?" she asked bluntly.

Aaron blinked. "Oh, I was just wondering if you finished my last tape." He pulled two ten-dollar bills out of his pocket.

Meg held out the notes and tape and took the cash in exchange.

"Did you like it?" he asked.

Meg thought for a moment, then nodded once. "Yeah, it was all right."

Aaron turned the tape over in his hand. "Was I funny,

do you think? I was trying to be funnier this time. Did they seem to like me?"

"Sure." Meg shrugged. "Couldn't you tell? I mean, don't you ever pay attention when you're playing?" That was kind of mean, she knew, but Meg had to call 'em as she saw 'em. And she saw Aaron not seeing 'em. Or something like that.

"I'm always so focused on what I'm gonna say next that I can barely remember the last thing I said." He laughed and held up the notes. "So anyway, thanks."

Just as he was almost out the door, Meg called, "Hey. What time is it?"

"A little before eleven."

"Cool. Thanks."

She quickly scanned the rest of her history assignment, closed the book, and checked off *History* on her to-do list. Finally. Now the weekend could officially begin.

She ran into the living room and crawled under the blanket on the sofa. Lucie and Aaron were in Lucie's room, and the door was ajar. Meg heard Lucie's stereo click on and soft folk rock filled the air, but Meg didn't recognize the band. Lucie was big into the local music scene; Meg figured she'd really scored when she hooked up with Aaron.

"That's some imagination," Meg heard Aaron say.

The music was too loud for Meg to catch Lucie's mumbled response.

"I find that hard to believe."

Another low-toned answer from Lucie.

"It must be some kind soul at the studio or production company."

Curious, Meg got off the couch and took a few steps closer to Lucie's room. Through the crack in the door, she could see Lucie leaning against Aaron on the bed while Aaron dug into his duffel bag. "Did you ever tell her it probably wasn't Jennifer Aniston writing back to her?" He took a thin white joint out of a Baggie and lit it with the flick of a Bic lighter.

Lucie leaned over him and lifted the window so Aaron could blow the smoke out into the Hollywood winds. "When Meg was around nine," she said, "we were living in a crappy trailer park out in the desert, Palmdale or Joshua Tree? I don't even remember. Christ. Anyway, we didn't have a lot."

We had nothing, Meg thought.

"I couldn't afford to get her a lot of toys or books like other kids."

Because you couldn't hold a job.

"It was kind of a dark time in our lives. And one night we were watching *Friends,* which was Meg's favorite show. And she said, 'I wish I had friends like that.'"

So did you, Meg remembered.

"And I suggested that maybe she'd like to write a letter to one of them, and she picked Jennifer Aniston."

Aaron handed Lucie the joint. She brought it to her lips, using only the tips of her fingernails, and inhaled. She held the smoke for a long moment and then blew it out in a slow stream through the open window.

"A couple of weeks later," Lucie went on, "she got a

head shot back and a letter, and she was so excited. So she asked me if she could send another letter, and about a week after that, she got another one back. And that's how it started."

Aaron took the joint back from Lucie for a drag. He held his breath and spoke at the same time, and it sounded like one long sentence. "Wow-she's-really-famous-I-never-watched-her-show-and-even-I-know-how-famous-she-is." Meg heard a hollow exhale, *whooo,* and then Aaron's normal voice. "I just wonder how—"

"This one time? Meg wrote to Jennifer about how much she loved these Armani sunglasses she wore, so Jen sent her a pair!" Lucie shook her head, astonished. "Really fancy, with gold frames. Meg fell all over herself when they arrived. Wore them day and night. To school, to bed." Lucie snorted a laugh. "Then one day, she sat on them and broke them into a million pieces. She cried and cried. I tried to fix them but . . . you know."

Meg, hearing this, was furious. She waited for Aaron to shame Lucie for telling another secret story.

Instead Aaron said, "Wow." Meg could hear him smile, slightly stoned. "You're an amazing sister, you know that?"

"Really? Thank you, sweetie." Through the crack in the door, Meg saw Lucie press herself up against Aaron and kiss the side of his neck—Meg's cue to turn away.

She shook her head and walked back to the couch. She turned the volume up on the television and burrowed under the blanket—alone.

She should have known: even *this*, even Jen's letters, Lucie turned to her own advantage.

It wasn't surprising, really. But why? Meg wondered.

If Lucie's behavior was so predictable, then why did it still hurt?

The next morning when Meg woke up, she nearly jumped out of bed and into her clothes. Today was shopping day! She knew exactly what she wanted: a long straight denim skirt with a slit up the back, a black DKNY sweater vest, a matching long-sleeved tee, and black leggings. And some socks and underwear and maybe a new pair of Levi's.

It was quiet in the apartment. She sighed. Fine, *she* would make the coffee and breakfast. If she timed it right, maybe she could get Lucie to spring for lunch at the mall, maybe at the food court, or—no! There was a California Pizza Kitchen there. Excellent choice.

She poured the water into the coffeemaker and measured out the grounds from a can of Maxwell House.

Lucie loved CPK's five-cheese pizza. They could split that and a salad, or—no! An order of the spring rolls with the plum sauce. Lucie loved those, too.

The coffee gurgled and burbled as it dripped down into the carafe. Meg opened the cabinet and took down a box of cornflakes and two bowls. Then she stopped.

Oh, right. Aaron had spent the night. She hastily added some more coffee and water to the pot. Would Aaron also want cornflakes? She took down a third bowl and placed it on the kitchen table. A third bowl. A third spoon. A third napkin. It all looked so odd. Well, of course it was odd; three, after all, was an odd number.

But there was something even odder about the table: a piece of paper sat there with her name on it.

Meg, she read, *Aaron had an early rehearsal in NoHo and then we're going to Griffith Park for a picnic. See you tonight. Here's some cash in case you want to buy groceries. I think we need milk. Luv, L.*

Under the note was a twenty-dollar bill.

She read the letter again. Rehearsal. North Hollywood. Picnic. Cash. Milk.

No mention of shopping or clothes. No *we'll go later tonight or tomorrow or . . .*

Meg crumpled the note in her fist. Damn Lucie. Damn her and her stupid boyfriend. Meg hated them both.

No, no, it wasn't Aaron's fault; he didn't know any better. He didn't know Lucie had made plans, had made a promise. Lucie, on the other hand, should have known better.

Meg poured herself a mug of coffee. Fine, she would just go to the mall on her own, and she would let herself try on all the clothes she wanted without complaint.

She stirred in a tablespoon of sugar, then opened the fridge and reached inside for . . . aagh! No milk! Not one stinking drop. Meg slammed the mug on the counter and watched the sweetened brown liquid spill out over the lip and down the sides. She made no move to clean it up.

Why did her sister *always* do this? Men came first in Lucie's world; Meg, a distant second. Meg decided then and there that she never ever wanted to be like Lucie, a woman who was so obviously unhappy, so desperate for love that she lay down for anyone who bought her a drink.

Jen was different. Jen had respect for herself and for the people she loved. She would never have left Meg alone while she went to Burning Man with some random guy for four days. Lucie did that one year and then broke up with the guy when they got back.

Loser! Meg thought. She was so tired of getting the pointy end of the stick from Lucie, of being second choice, of being forgotten.

She stomped heavily through the living room, stopping to sweep Lucie's *People* magazines off the coffee table and onto the floor. She drop-kicked a sofa cushion against the wall and turned the television up loud to Telemundo.

Her hand tore at the doorknob to Lucie's room. Damn! Locked. She pushed her weight against the door. Not locked. Stuck. She wiggled the door open an inch, then two. No wonder it wouldn't open: the floor was covered in clothes and shoes. It looked like Lucie had merely dumped the contents of her moving boxes onto the carpet without bothering to sort through anything.

She picked her way through the sea of underwear, brushed aside jeans and tank tops, and found her sister's jewelry box. Meg fiddled with the child-size lock, used her nail to flip the button. She opened the box and a pink ballerina with a tulle tutu popped up on a spring, turning while a tinny version of "Sugar Plum Fairy" leaked out of the speaker.

Lucie had just one item of value: a ring that had belonged to their mother. It was a brushed metal band with a single pearl in the center, surrounded by a circle of diamonds. *Our mother's favorite ring,* Lucie had told her.

The rest of the box contained junk. Some dream-catcher earrings from Lucie's obsession with Stevie Nicks, piles of elastic-banded costume jewelry from early Madonna days, other odds and ends Lucie picked up along the way. Anything of value—like gifts from previous boyfriends—Lucie had pawned or outright sold.

Meg held the ring up to the window, watched the diamonds sparkle in the sunlight. Put it on her finger. Then, for good measure, she dumped the jewelry box upside down onto the bed, turned, and left for the mall.

Chapter
FIVE

Dear Jen,

How are you? I am fine.

I'm starting to think that Hollywood isn't all it's cracked up to be. No offense, since you live here and all, but the town is kind of dirty, and there are way more homeless people than I ever figured there'd be. I suppose I imagined it would be a little more classy. Like this guy down the street, right? There's a house, and there's this black stretch limo that sits in front of it every day, and I'm thinking, whose house is it? A movie star's or a rock singer's? Every day, I try to guess. Then Aaron tells me the guy in the house drives the limo for other people. Like, it's his job. He's not a celebrity or anything. That blows.

Aaron's a pretty okay guy. He can sing. He's got some potential. He asks me about school and if I do anything extracurricular, and I don't *think he does it just to be nice. I think he genuinely wants to know. But you know what happens when I get attached: things, people, places— they all go away. It's as if Lucie has some sixth sense that allows her to figure out the stuff I like and then make it disappear. I guess I should be glad she didn't make you disappear. Sometimes I think you're all I have.*

I gotta take off. It's almost twelve. Tonight's episode was the one where Chrissie Hynde sings "Smelly Cat" with Phoebe (classic!) and Phoebe's all like, that's not how you play it, like Chrissie isn't a total rocker chick. I love it, but then I get that stupid song stuck in my head for, like, days.

Love,

m

P.S. Aaron also told me that celebrities aren't actually buried under their stars on Hollywood Boulevard. I was disappointed, but maybe it's not too late. It's a good idea. I think I should suggest it to someone.

The Starbucks on Hollywood Boulevard was on the busiest section of the Hollywood and Highland strip, several blocks north of the high school. It was across the street from the old wax museum, east of the Guinness World Records Museum, and the closest coffee place to Meg's apartment. It was not in any way a quiet retreat for studying purposes, which was why everyone from school went there. That and to poke fun at all the tourists bumping into each other as they stared at the sparkly stars in the cement.

Meg and Reggie sat at a tiny table near the front window

with grande mocha lattes and a pair of blueberry scones.

"Look! There's Tom Cruise," Reggie said, pointing at a man walking by in a John Deere cap.

"Not even close," Meg said. "There . . .Tobey Maguire."

"The little guy? Nah, he's bigger than that."

They were playing Spot the Celebrity, a game they came up with the day Reggie swore she saw Julia Roberts eating a Krispy Kreme doughnut outside the Target in RC. Meg had to admit, the woman did look an awful lot like the actress: big hair, long limbs, wide mouth. She could easily have been a stand-in for the superstar—but under more careful inspection, she wasn't even close.

Since then, pretty much anyone was fair game. Any star could be "sighted" at any time. Points were awarded both for uncanny resemblance and outrageous lack of similarity.

"That's an Olsen twin," Reggie decided. "Look at the arms. They're like twigs. I could snap 'em just by breathing on 'em."

"Okay," Meg conceded, "but where's the other one? Don't they travel as a pair?"

"That *was* the pair. They're just really skinny."

Meg chuckled. "Really, really skinny." She drained the last of her latte and shook the cup at Reggie. "Would you get us more coffee? I've got three more chapters of this to get through."

"No problem," Reggie answered, leaping up from her seat.

Before meeting Reggie, Meg had never tried anything

more than a sip of Lucie's creamy, sugary java, which wasn't even close to a cap from the 'Bucks. Her first latte had been the result of New Friend autopilot, Meg's default mode whenever she met a potential New Friend. In New Friend autopilot, Meg would automatically answer in the affirmative to any question the New Friend asked. Like that girl out in Palmdale, the one with the Justin Timberlake fixation.

"Sure, I love JT," Meg had heard herself proclaim, "and I *adore* the JT chat room on AOL!" Even though she hadn't owned a computer.

Two years ago, when Reggie asked her if she liked Starbucks, she chirped, "Of course I do! Every day!"

Now she was practically addicted to the stuff.

"Thanks, dude," Meg said as Reggie placed a new latte in front of her. "There's a quiz on cell structure next Tuesday, so if we could focus on that . . ."

Reggie nodded but stared pointedly at her watch. "Meg, I, uh, I know I said I'd tutor you, but I can't stay too much longer."

"What? But we just got here," Meg started to protest. "We haven't even started the—" Then she paused. "Oh, right. Sure."

That certainly was fast, she thought. Reggie was moving on more quickly than the others had. Oh, well. So much for timing.

"I'd love to hang out," Reggie explained, "but it's such a bitch driving home during rush hour. It takes me, like, an hour and a half to get there."

"Oh, right, sorry about that."

"It's not a huge deal, but maybe you could come meet me instead."

"I can't drive," Meg said flatly.

"Well, maybe Lucie?"

They both knew Lucie was not a possibility.

"Yeah, sure," Meg said. She closed her biology textbook and slid it into her backpack. Then she grabbed her cup and stood up. "Can you drop me off first?"

"Well, wait." Reggie looked concerned. "I don't have to leave right this second."

"No, no." Meg frowned. "It's okay. Let's go." She wasn't mad. It was simply the nature of things, the circle of life, as it were. Perhaps she was hastening the end of her friendship with Reggie, Meg realized, but it was much better to finish it cleanly and decisively than to watch it slip through your grasp.

Reggie stood, not quite as reluctantly as Meg might have liked. They took their coffees and left.

Meg sighed as they walked to the parking lot. She would definitely miss their lattes and their games. *Don't get too close to anything or anyone,* she reminded herself. *It will always, always vanish in the end.*

They were silent in the Jetta until Reggie pulled up in front of Meg's apartment.

"Thanks for the ride," she said, then remembered Reggie's cell. "Here." She handed the Motorola to her friend. "Thanks for letting me use it."

Reggie's brow wrinkled. "It was a gift. You should keep it."

But Meg shook her head. "Free trial period's up. Can't afford it."

"Oh." Reggie stared down at her lap. "Okay."

"Well . . . take it easy." Meg got out of the Jetta.

"Yeah, you too." Reg frowned and put the car into gear. Meg waved to her former friend as she pulled away.

She wasn't sad, she told herself as tears pricked the corners of her eyes. Not really. In fact, as Reg made a left turn away from the building, Meg realized she was already thinking about her New Friend candidates at Hollywood High. Like that girl who had turned down the cigarette outside school. Maybe tomorrow Meg would find out who she was and ask her a question or two. If she responded well . . . hello, New Friend!

Meg turned toward her building and spotted a red-haired man leaning against the steps. His gaze alternated between a piece of paper in his hand and the Shanley girls' window.

As she watched, the man lit a cigarette and tossed the match to the ground, never taking his eyes off the apartment.

Oh, now who is this? Meg wondered, hesitating. Not the landlord. Meg had met him when they moved in. Could it be a bill collector already? Or one of Lucie's exes? He looked sort of familiar to Meg, but she couldn't place him.

She took a deep breath and sidled past the man, trying not to make eye contact.

"Excuse me," she heard the man say.

Meg had her hand on the door to her apartment and her keys in her fist. They might make a good weapon, just in case things turned ugly. "Yes?"

"I'm waiting for my sister, Lucie Shanley." The man pointed to Meg's apartment. "Are you . . . Margaret Anne?" His voice was low and soft.

Meg felt every muscle in her body go slack. "What did you say?"

"I'm Lonnie. Lonnie Shanley. I'm Lucie's twin brother." He took a step toward Meg, grinning wryly. "I take it she's never mentioned me."

The man's face swam in front of Meg. She struggled to bring it into shaper focus.

Did he say . . . *brother?* It wasn't possible. Wouldn't Lucie tell her if they had a sibling floating out in the world somewhere?

"I don't understand. How could you be . . . ?" She paused. "What did you say your name was?"

"Lonnie."

Lonnie . . . Meg rolled the name around in her brain. Had she *ever* in her life heard Lucie mention it before?

And even if she had, how could any of this be true?

Meg stared hard at the stranger before her.

Lonnie's hair was red . . . Lucie's was red.

Lonnie's eyes were blue . . . Meg's were blue.

Lonnie's chin was dimpled, sort of like Lucie's, and his ears stuck out like Meg's own when she tucked her hair behind them.

Was it—was it possible?

Lonnie, reading Meg's skeptical mind, removed a photo from his wallet and handed it to Meg. It was of Lucie. Definitely Lucie; Meg recognized the mischievous twinkle in her sister's eye. She was sitting on the edge of a pool in a one-piece bathing suit, no more than four years old. Beside her was a bony young boy, around the same age, who could very well have grown up to be the man standing before Meg today.

"It's my favorite picture of us," Lonnie said wistfully. "When we were both young and innocent." He laughed and took the photo back from Meg, carefully replacing it behind his driver's license.

"That could be a picture of anyone," Meg said, testing him. "Some other little girl."

Lonnie took a drag off his cigarette and blew the smoke up over Meg's head. "She's about yay high," he said, holding his hand to the level of his shoulder. "Short red hair."

"Long."

"Long now? Okay. Skinny arms. Wore a ring with a pearl thing in the center surrounded by diamonds."

Meg felt her jaw unhinge, but she recovered quickly. "Maybe."

Lonnie's gaze followed the trail of smoke from his cigarette. "Does she still like eating breakfast for dinner?"

Oh my God, Meg thought. There was no denying it. *It's true. He is our brother.* Her heart pounded once, twice—hard.

"So, um, what are you doing here?" she asked. But in

her head she was already racing through the possibilities. Maybe Lonnie lived in the area, maybe now he wanted them to be a real family; three siblings had to be better than two—and anything was better than just Lucie.

"Lucie and I need to talk," Lonnie said, rubbing the auburn stubble on his chin. "Do you know when she's coming back?"

"Soon." Meg pointed to her door. "Do—do you want to wait? You can come inside."

Lonnie cocked an eyebrow at her. "Should you be letting strange men into your home?"

"You're not strange," she insisted. "Like you said, you're our brother."

Meg turned and unlocked the door, her mind hyperaware of the apartment and its clutter. Which room was best to show off? Which room wouldn't embarrass the hell out of her? She led Lonnie into the living room and invited him to sit on the couch.

"Do you mind if I smoke?" he asked.

Meg bit her lip. Lucie would freak out if she smelled smoke, but even she had to recognize this was an exception to the rule—a really important exception.

"Sure, go ahead." Meg ran to the window and opened it wide, then turned back to her guest. "I have so many questions, I don't know where to begin. Why are you here? I mean, why now? How come I never heard of you before—never saw a picture?"

"My sister's not what you'd call family-oriented,

although fifteen years is a long time to stay so far away."

"Far away? From where?"

"New York," Lonnie said. "That's where we're from."

"Oh my God!" Meg gasped. "New York like New York *City*?"

"Yeah. Queens. You didn't know?"

Meg shook her head. "Lucie always said we were from California."

Lonnie fell silent. He shook out another cigarette and lit it with only one hand, using a match bent over the back of the matchbook. Meg thought it had to be the coolest move she had ever seen.

"So . . . she'll be home soon, right?" Lonnie finally asked.

"What? Oh yeah, real soon." Meg stared at Lonnie, drinking in every detail of him. As she watched him smoke, beads of sweat formed at his temples and rolled down into his sideburns. He wiped at his face with fingers that were chewed to bits, nails ragged and torn. Ten minutes ago, Meg was sipping a latte on Hollywood Boulevard and now here she was, inspecting her brother's hands. Was this for real?

She heard footsteps coming up the steps and then a mingling of masculine and feminine giggles.

Meg felt the corners of her mouth turn up in anticipation. "There she is! That's Lucie!"

Lonnie took a long drag off his cigarette and nodded his head slowly up and down.

"She is gonna be so psyched to see you!" Meg cheered. "Luce!"

"Oh my God, is that cigarette smoke? Meg, are you *smoking?*" Lucie called, her voice getting louder as she came through the kitchen. She stopped at the doorway to the living room. "What . . ."

Meg ran to her sister. "Look, Luce! Look! It's Lonnie! Our *brother!*"

Lucie's mouth closed to a tight line as she stared at Lonnie.

"Isn't this awesome? He's here, Luce, our brother is here! Why didn't you tell me about him before?"

"Hey, Lucie," Lonnie finally said. "Good to—"

"Get out of my house."

Meg glanced from one sibling to the other. That wasn't what Lucie was supposed to say. "Luce, no. Lonnie came to see us all the way from New York."

"I don't care where he came from. I do not want him here."

"What is your deal?" Meg asked. "Why are you being like this?"

"Lucie, we need to talk," Lonnie said, trying to take his sister by the arm. She shook him off.

"We have nothing to talk about. Ever. Now leave."

Aaron's head popped in the doorway behind Lucie. "Hi! Everything okay in here?"

Lucie and Lonnie stared at each other while Meg looked on helplessly.

"Who's this? Your husband?" Lonnie asked.

Lucie kept her mouth shut.

"Aaron Spector," Aaron said, holding out his hand. "Boyfriend."

"Lonnie Shanley. Brother."

Aaron took the man's hand, appeared to be holding his surprise in check. "Brother. Wow. Okay. Good to meet you, man."

"Isn't this awesome, Aaron? We have a brother!" Meg said.

Lucie glanced at her sharply. "He is *not* your brother." She turned back to Lonnie. "Get the fuck out of my house. Now."

"Lucie, please," Lonnie said again, this time with a hint of desperation in his voice. "She needs you–"

"She doesn't need me."

"I need you."

"I don't care." Lucie crossed her arms over her chest. "Get out."

"Luce, no!" Meg cried. "He came three thousand miles–"

"He wasted his time." Lucie took a seat on the sofa and fingered a rip in the fabric.

"What is *wrong* with you?" Meg couldn't believe the way her sister was acting. This was their own brother, their flesh and blood.

Lonnie stood firm. "I won't leave until we talk."

Lucie rolled her eyes. "You are *so* melodramatic. Write me an e-mail. Call Western Union."

"I've *tried* to call you. I've *tried* to write you. And now I have finally tracked you down to this crappy apartment in this godforsaken city. You may have an unlisted number, but you made damn sure a certain bank in Manhattan had your address, didn't you?"

Lucie looked away.

Lonnie pressed on. "You *have* been getting your money, haven't you?"

"Lucie," Meg said sharply, "answer him."

When Lucie still wouldn't reply, Meg stepped in. "You mean the happy envelopes? She got one last—"

"Shut up, Meg."

Lonnie chuckled. "A happy envelope? Is that what you call it? Why don't you tell her what it really is?" He didn't raise his voice but kept it low. The coldness of it sent a chill up the back of Meg's neck.

"Did it ever occur to you that I didn't want to be found?" Lucie asked. "That maybe I wanted a life of my own? Did you ever think of that?"

Lonnie reached for his cigarettes. "Um, yeah," he said with a sarcastic drawl. "I think we figured that out a long time ago."

"Go. Now."

"Lucie, please, let Lonnie tell us why he came," Meg said.

"Mother is dying, Lucie, and I can't take care of her anymore." Lonnie shook out a fresh cigarette and lit it against the butt of the first. "I need you to come back and take over."

Mother? Meg tried to gasp, but her throat clenched at Lonnie's words.

"It's not fair," he continued. "She and I took care of Dad, and now, with her . . . I need my life back, Lucie."

Meg took a calming breath and tried to understand. "Our mother—is alive?"

It wasn't possible, she wondered, was it? The incredible surprise she had felt on meeting her brother turned to profound shock. Was her mother alive, and not dead from giving birth to her? Her head felt light and woozy.

"Meg," Lonnie said, turning to her. "Not—"

"No!" Lucie snatched the cigarette out of his hand and threw it to the floor. "This is my house," she said, grinding her heel against the burning tobacco. "And there is no smoking in my house!" Then she stomped to the doorway and pointed. "Now get out of *my* house before I call the police!"

Lonnie looked forlornly at the crushed cigarette on the floor before he moved to the door. "Please. I need your help, Lucie."

"Out!"

Meg rushed after Lonnie. "No! Wait. Don't go!" She turned back and pleaded with her sister. "Don't make him go! Lucie, please! I have to know more!"

Lucie grabbed the doorknob, pulled it open for her brother.

Lonnie slowly turned back to Meg, his eyes full and sad.

In that moment, Meg saw her chance.

"Take me with you," she said, not entirely sure what she was saying, not entirely sure she was serious.

"Meg—"

She looked over at Lucie, stone-faced and cold, and knew that she *was* serious. "Take me with you," she said with more conviction. "Take me to see my mother."

Lonnie's shoulders sagged, and the corners of his mouth turned down. He lifted his blue eyes to his sister. "Luce? Tell her."

"Tell me what?" Meg asked. She stared hard at him, then at Lucie. "Tell me *what*, Lucie?"

Meg's sister simply crossed her arms over her chest.

Lonnie rubbed a fist against his forehead. "Meg, I'm not your brother. I'm Lucie's brother."

"Okay . . ."

"Lucie . . . Lucie is your mother."

"My . . ."

Meg felt her stomach lurch. It was as if the floor had suddenly dropped out from under her, plunging her down an immense black hole.

"Lucie?" she whispered.

But her sister's eyes would not meet hers.

"Lucie!" Meg cried out, and then the room became heavy with silence. The things Meg wanted to ask, all her questions, hung in the air—real, but unspeakable.

Lucie remained silent, then turned away and made for her bedroom, closing the door behind her.

Meg heard the lock click into place.

"I'm sorry." Lonnie suddenly spoke up next to her. "That's not what you wanted to hear." He grabbed a pen from the kitchen counter and scribbled something on a slip of paper. He pressed the paper into Meg's hand. "If you ever need me . . ." He left the sentence unfinished and walked out the door.

Meg stood there, dazed, unable to move or react. Outside, she heard Lonnie's car start up and pull away from the curb. It turned at the corner, probably toward Sunset, speeding away from the apartment complex.

A part of Meg thought it wasn't too late . . . she might still catch him if she ran. But it was no use. Her feet were rooted in place.

She didn't know how long she stayed there—a minute, an hour, a day? Long enough for the sun to set—for the night air to creep inside, bringing gooseflesh to her arms and a chill to her toes in their sandals.

Meg stared at the doorway, at the place where Lonnie had so recently stood, uttering words she never thought she'd hear.

Lucie, her sister, wasn't her sister. No, not her sister at all. And Lucie hadn't denied it.

Lucie is your mother.

Four words that turned her world upside down, that knocked the wind out of her. Four words that echoed in Meg's head. Lonnie's voice speaking them, louder and louder, until finally they brought her to her senses.

Meg blinked once, twice, and found she was standing in the dark.

She reached out to lock the apartment door; then she

retreated to her bedroom. She pulled off her clothes and burrowed deep under the covers.

The darkness enfolded her, providing a comforting nothingness. Meg savored the lack of sensation as she lay in her bed, but soon, muffled voices floated in from the next room.

Lucie's and Aaron's voices. His: deliberate, even, steady, like a metronome. Hers: overlapping, a stream of syllables, strained and disjointed.

Meg wanted no part of *them*. She mashed a pillow over her head in an effort to drown out the sound. But Lucie's voice crept through the protective layers—still found her. Like the truth. After all these years.

The truth, Meg thought. *What is the truth? The whole of it?*

More specifically, if Lucie was her mother, then just who the hell was *Meg*?

Chapter
SIX

Meg could have skipped school the next morning and headed into Starbucks for a double cap with a hefty dollop of cream and maybe a sprinkling of chocolate instead.

Or she could have partaken of a shopping spree at Abercrombie for a dozen pairs of low riders and a belt with long leather fringe on it.

Or she could have made a headlong run down the streets of Hollywood stark naked, screaming obscenities at the top of her lungs.

But instead, Meg showered and dressed, ignoring Lucie's still-closed bedroom door. She went to school and attended a full day's worth of classes. She even paid attention in French.

She was a *normal* girl, after all. A *normal* student. Weird people had mothers for sisters and brother-uncles. But not her. Not Meg Shanley. She was a girl who went to school on time and attended every class and raised her hand when she knew the answer and smiled at people she passed in the hall. She handed in her homework, neatly printed, and laughed appropriately when people made jokes. She ate lunch outside in the courtyard where all the other kids were eating, or playing Hacky Sack, or throwing around their footballs. Because Meg Shanley's life was just as unremarkable as anyone else's.

Over the course of the day, through this steadfast application of denial, Meg somehow managed to forget about the reality of her life.

But after the final bell, with every step she took back to her apartment, Meg knew she would have to face Lucie.

Sister? Mother? Roommate? What would they be to each other now? She dreaded knowing, yet she had to find out. She needed to hear more. It wasn't fair that Lucie had kept the truth from her for so long. It wasn't fair that she had kept Lonnie and a grandmother—good Lord, a *grand-mother!*—a whole, real, normal life, from her.

Aaron was in the kitchen when she arrived home. The whole apartment smelled like melted cheese.

"What are you doing here?" she asked, less than nicely. After all, Aaron was associated with *that woman.*

"And a pleasant hello to you too."

Meg let her backpack fall to the floor. "She here?"

Aaron jerked his thumb toward the bedroom door.

"Hasn't come out. Not that I can tell—not since last night."

"Oh."

"Thought you might like a little dinner when you got home." He held out a spoon with an orange sauce on it. "Try this."

Meg expected bland American cheese or that fake Velveeta crap, but this was something else entirely: sharp, tangy, smooth. "Pretty good. What's in it?"

Aaron shrugged. "A little of this, a little of that." He took the spoon back and dropped it in the sink. He was a clean sort of fellow. Meg liked that about him. "How was your day?"

"Fine."

Aaron smiled, and it wasn't one of those *poor Meg* smiles but a caring kind of smile, one that said, *I like you even if your life is painfully white-trash-like.* He took down a box of elbows and emptied the contents into a pot of boiling water.

"I remember when 'pasta' was called 'macaroni.' And it cost about a quarter a pound. Now they've got all these fancy-sounding names and a twelve-ounce bag costs two bucks." He rolled his eyes as if marveling at the phenomenon. "Isn't it funny how people make simple things more complicated?"

"Uh, yeah."

"It's like coffee." He stirred the elbows with a long wooden spoon and spoke to the cheese sauce. "A quarter for a cup of joe. Nothing fancy, no weird names. It was just, 'Gimme a cup of coffee,' and the guy behind the counter would pour it from a giant metal urn and he'd hand it to you in a Styrofoam cup. Now it costs ten times as much and takes ten times as long to order. I've got better things to do with my time than wait for coffee. How about you?"

Meg knew where he was going with this. "This is for your act, isn't it? You're going to do this in your show."

Aaron shrugged, grinning. "I'm trying to connect with my audience. What do you think?"

"You do know that Styrofoam is bad for the environment, don't you?"

He pushed his glasses up the bridge of his nose. "Really?"

"Well, yeah, it just sits in the landfills and doesn't decompose like natural fibers do. You can't melt it because it releases toxic fumes, and you can't bury it because it takes up too much space."

"Tell me more."

"Jeez, Aaron. What kind of hippie are you if you don't know about this stuff?"

Aaron smiled. "Hand me that pan, would you?"

Meg reached for the glass dish at the end of the counter and brought it over to the stove.

"Rub a little vegetable oil on the bottom. Here's a paper towel."

"This?" Meg held up the paper towel. "Not reusable. But this pastry brush"—she pulled a plastic-handled brush out of the utensil drawer—"is. And don't ask me why we have a pastry brush but no can opener. It's just the way things are around here."

Aaron continued to stir. "I wasn't going to say a word."

Meg poured a tablespoon of oil into the bottom of the dish and swished the pastry brush in it, making the sides glisten.

"Guess I'll have to go back to the Chevy Chase bit," Aaron ventured.

"The what?"

"I'm Chevy Chase and you're not."

Meg stared at him quizzically.

"From *Saturday Night Live*?"

Meg shook her head. "Dude, that was not funny."

Aaron rolled his eyes. *"Kids."* He sighed, but he did so with a lopsided smile.

Meg liked that he smiled, liked even that he rolled his eyes. Liked the way he understood that—compared to him—she *was* a kid.

"Turn the oven to three-fifty," he instructed. "I'll get the bread crumbs."

"I'll get drinks." Meg took out a couple of Cokes and filled glasses with ice. When she popped the top of a can, a long *fzzz!* filled the kitchen. Then there was silence.

"Meg, I tried to talk to her," Aaron said, staring into his glass. "But she refused to even let me in."

Meg sort of pursed her lips and nodded. "Yeah, okay."

"I even slipped a note under the door," Aaron said with a short laugh.

"What'd you write?" Meg wanted to know because

if *she'd* had a chance to compose a note, she would have scrawled sentences like, *You selfish bitch, get your ass out here and answer my questions!* But she doubted Aaron would have chosen those exact words.

"I just said . . ." Aaron cleared his throat. "I said that I was here for her and that if she needed to talk, well, I would have an open mind. You know, that sort of thing."

He seemed embarrassed by the sentiment; he really was a nice guy, Meg thought. She nodded and sipped her Coke. The silence between them then seemed a lot more comfortable.

Meg glanced down at her watch. "Uh . . . if you don't mind, it's time for my show."

"I thought it was on at eleven," Aaron said.

"It's also on at five, seven, and one in the morning," Meg explained. "Today, I'm feeling like I need an early fix. Is that okay?"

"Oh. Yeah, sure. Can I watch with you?"

Meg nearly choked on her soda. "You want to watch *Friends*?"

"I'm always up for a new experience."

"You've *never* seen it?"

"Just bits and pieces. You'll have to fill me in."

"Um, okay. Well, there's these six friends who live in New York, right? Three guys and three girls–"

"Hang on." He reached for a pot holder and grabbed at the pot of pasta. "Why don't you bring our drinks in and I'll finish this."

Meg allowed herself a small smile as she took the glasses into the living room.

Thirty minutes later, Meg silenced the TV set. She turned to Aaron, who was sitting next to her on the couch.

"So . . . what'd you think?"

Aaron placed his hands on his knees and leaned back against the pillows. "Was that supposed to be a good one?"

"Heck, yeah. One of my favorites."

"You told me Rachel dated Ross."

"Uh-huh."

"But he was getting married to that other girl."

"Emily."

"Right. What gives?"

"Ross liked Rachel, then she liked him, then they were together, then they broke up, then they got married and then divorced, and then they had sex and she got pregnant."

"So they're together now?"

"No." Meg sighed. "That's the problem with syndication. The episodes never run in the right order. The other night, I saw, like, the very first one. Oh my God, the guys were totally thin and the girls were all normal-looking."

"It's a good show. I can see why you'd write to Rachel. She's pretty cool."

Meg sneaked a peek at Aaron, tried to determine if he was making fun of her, but no, he seemed sincere. "Yeah. But it's not Rachel I write to. It's Jen. Jen is awesome."

"Do you . . . could you tell me what she wrote to you?" he asked. "I won't tell anyone. I'm just curious. You know, the only correspondence I've had with a celebrity was that one time with Henry Winkler—"

"The Fonz."

He smiled. "Yeah, the Fonz."

Meg considered the request, considered Aaron and whether he had earned the right to read her letters.

Macaroni and cheese and the Fonz, she thought, making her decision. "Sure. I'll show you."

She went to her room and retrieved one of the shoe boxes marked *JA.* She held it out to Aaron.

"Wow. Oh, wow. That's a lot of letters. May I?" Aaron's fingers were poised above the stack of envelopes.

"Yeah . . . go ahead."

Gingerly, he lifted the top letter. That one was . . . Meg thought for a second. Yes, that one was from four years ago. April. A good one, as she could recall.

Aaron unfolded it, held it up with the tips of his fingers. It was so weird seeing someone else open one of her Jennifer letters. Lucie, yes. Lucie used to read them, but Meg never showed them to anyone else, not even Reggie.

"It's not made of gold or anything," she told him. "You can touch it."

She watched as his eyes scanned the words on the single sheet of lavender-scented paper. She leaned forward and sniffed. Nope. Nothing. It used to smell wonderful—light and powdery—but now she could only smell it in her mind. To Meg, it was the smell of purple.

This was the letter about the boy in math class. Meg had written Jennifer, told her all about this kid who teased her mercilessly. When she raised her hand to answer the teacher's question, he would cough into his hand, "Bullshit." And then the whole class would start laughing. At lunch, he would bump into her and point and laugh as her tray fell crashing to the linoleum and he never once apologized. She hated that boy.

Jen's advice: talk to him. *Smile at Jeff. Be your charming self and he won't know what to do. He's obviously trying to get your attention because he has a crush on you. Boys don't know how to talk to girls at that age,* Jen had written.

So Meg did just that—and it worked! Jen was *so* smart. She knew *everything.* She was so perfect. And Jeff had never bugged her again.

Aaron stopped reading, nodded, and folded the paper. He handed it to her and said, "That's insightful advice."

"Isn't it?" Meg could feel herself glowing. Jennifer could do that to a person, make someone feel like he or she could be perfect too. She always chose just the right word, the right phrasing. She knew exactly what would work, as if she had been through it all herself, and in a way, she kind of had.

Meg glanced up then and blushed, thinking of Aaron reading the rest of the horrifying details of her life. She covered the box quickly and moved it out of his reach. "Um, thanks for dinner. It was really, really good."

"You're very welcome," he said. "Maybe Lucie will have some when she comes out."

Meg shrugged. "Whatever."

"Look, Meg," Aaron began. "I just want you to know, like I told Lucie, I'm here for you if you need to talk. You just call me, okay? And don't . . ." He closed his eyes. "Don't hate Lucie, okay? I don't know why she did what she did. It's all very confusing. But please try to talk to her—"

Meg scoffed, shook her head.

"You must have questions. Isn't there something you want to know?"

Something? Some thing? Meg thought. Like her head wasn't exploding with all the questions that should be asked? "I guess."

They were sitting very close on the couch, and all at once Meg could feel the air between them as if it was tangible—thick and spongy. Like if she just leaned into it, into Aaron, she would find a place to rest her head, to truly rest. So she did and it fit perfectly, her head on his chest under his chin. She didn't want to cry; it wasn't like she was *sad*. What had she lost? A crappy older sister?

"You know . . . I was thinking . . . it'd be really cool if you added some Phoebe songs to your set." She could feel his chin nod on the top of her head. "They're funny and smart and you know, people would like them and they'd sing along." She heard her voice crack on the last couple of words. She swallowed hard, tasted something metallic in the back of her throat. "There was this one episode when she sang these really wacky songs to these kids and the parents got all freaked out, but she was just being Phoebe, you know? That's who she was. You can only be who you are." She blinked and felt her eyelashes stick together. "That's what Jen says too."

Aaron sighed, and a puff of warm cheesy breath caressed Meg's skin. "She's very smart."

"Yeah, she is."

Meg thought she could stay here forever, with her head on Aaron's chest, wrapped in a cocoon, a safe harbor from the stupid life she had. Aaron really *did* have potential; he really seemed to care about what happened to her.

"Meg?" she heard Aaron ask quietly.

"Mmm?"

"I have to go do my show now." He gently lifted her head off his chest and politely ignored the tearstains on his T-shirt. "Are you gonna be okay?"

She nodded. What else could she do?

He stood from the couch. "Thank you."

"For what?" Meg asked.

"For *Friends*."

She cleared her throat and waved him off. "You should know these things, Aaron. They're a part of our shared cultural heritage. I even wrote a paper on *Friends* for my seventh-grade social studies class."

"You did?"

"Yeah. I got a B-plus. The teacher didn't buy into my argument that Rachel should have a baby with Ross because his love for her is pure and not based on superficial values. She said our current conservative sociological climate meant that a top-rated television show would never have another Murphy Brown." She paused. "I never understood that Murphy Brown comment, but who's right now? I should go back and get my A."

Aaron grinned, and in her mind's eye, Meg saw him reach out and tousle her hair.

But he didn't.

"Good night," he said. "Good luck."

"Yeah." Meg sighed. Aaron *had* potential; too bad Lucie had screwed that up, too.

Meg took a bobby pin from a drawer in the bathroom and bent the two ends back to form a tailed *V*—the kind you'd get if you were writing the letter in cursive. Then she pinched the center and placed it lengthwise in the lock in Lucie's door. Once in, she wiggled it back and forth and simultaneously turned the knob. A moment later, she heard it click. It was one of the few movie tricks that actually worked.

She opened the door and found Lucie sitting, fully dressed, on the edge of her bed. The room was still a mess; nothing had been picked up since the last time Meg was in here. She could even see the dream-catcher earrings among the dirty clothes on the bed. But one thing was different: the window was propped open with a book and Lucie was blowing smoke through the screen. Not the kind of smoke

Meg expected, but cigarette smoke, thick and slightly green.

Where did Lucie get cigarettes? Meg wondered. *And when? Did she slither out the window and down the wall?*

Perched so calmly, her hand moving to her mouth and then lowering, smoke escaping her lips and nose, Lucie looked like an entirely different person. Meg barely recognized her. Who was she?

And, more importantly, who was *Meg*?

Through all the years and all her first names, she had always called herself a Shanley. If she wasn't a Shanley, then . . .

"Lucie, who is my father?"

Meg had expected a fight, had expected tears or rage, some semblance of emotion, but Lucie wouldn't oblige. She remained on her bed, staring straight ahead, barely moving. "Nathaniel Holland. He was a senior when I was a freshman. He played football."

Lucie paused, and Meg waited for her to continue. The silence was excruciating.

"He was dating the student council president, and I was on the cheerleading squad when I met him. He was cool and popular, and I wanted to be cool and popular. We hooked up at a party, I promised him sex, and I became his girlfriend. I was fourteen. My mother wanted me to have an abortion, but it was too late. She sent me out west, to Glendale, to live with Dad's cousins." She took a drag on the cigarette and exhaled a long trail of smoke. "I never went back, and you know the rest."

Meg tried to digest the facts. "So your mom and Lonnie's mom is—"

"Your grandmother."

Oh God, she thought. *It's true.* A *grandmother.*

"Where is my father now?"

"I don't know," Lucie, not-her-sister, said. "Wall Street, maybe? He was one of those types."

"How can you not—"

"We didn't keep in touch, all right?" Lucie snapped, lighting a second cigarette off the butt of the first. "He doesn't know about you."

Meg blinked. "Doesn't know I like Green Day and the color pink or—"

"Doesn't know you exist."

"Or that. Right."

Meg was acutely aware of the cigarette smell clinging to the sheets and furniture and walls. It was as though she could *feel* the smoke, the tar residue. It clung to her skin and hair and clothes. She rubbed her eyes with her hands to get it out, get it away, stop it from attacking her, but it was too late. Her eyes felt sore and abraded, as if she had trudged through a sandstorm. This wasn't going at all how she expected, although, honestly, there were no guidelines for such an encounter. Rachel and the gang were pretty traditional when it came to the whole family unit thing.

"Who sends the happy envelopes?" she asked.

Lucie leaned closer to the window, her chest drawn

forward as if she were being pulled from outside the building. "His parents. To keep us away."

"Oh." She shuffled in the doorway. "Why, Lucie?"

"Because they didn't want us around. They didn't want Nate to know that—"

"No. Why didn't you tell me the truth?"

Lucie stared at the window screen and then tapped the ashes of her cigarette onto the sill. "You're going to leave now, aren't you?"

Meg thought about it: uncle, grandmother, father . . . never had 'em, now she did. And she needed them . . . she'd always needed them. "Yes," she answered.

Lucie shook her head slowly from side to side and smoke trailed out of her mouth as she did so. "They'll hurt you. *He'll* hurt you."

"How do you know?"

"Because they hurt *me*."

Meg felt emotion begin to rise up in her—but she couldn't put her finger on what it was: anger? Fear? Sadness?

No, it was disappointment, Meg realized. Profound and utter disappointment that, when given the chance, Lucie wouldn't do more. Meg always, always wished she would try harder, but Lucie never did.

"All right. I'm going now."

"You're sure you want to do this?"

"Yes."

Lucie blew a stream of smoke out through her nostrils,

kept her lips pressed tightly together. In profile, Meg couldn't tell if she was upset or merely bored.

Don't you even care? Meg wanted to shout, but it wasn't going to be that sort of ending for them. It would be a whimper, not a bang.

"If you go," Lucie said, "don't come back."

"Excuse me?"

"If you leave, I don't ever want to see you again."

That shouldn't have stung so much, but it did.

Meg forced herself to take a look around Lucie's room, at the disheveled blandness of it all. "Fine."

She backed up then, closed the door, felt the lock with the bobby pin. She was moving in reverse. Reversing action as if she could reverse course—reverse time.

But she couldn't. She had always wanted more than Lucie could give, and now she could actually have it.

She had to take the opportunity—had to keep moving—because there were more questions.

And the one question Lucie had never answered was why?

Chapter
SEVEN

Alma Shanley lived in a row house. Brick. Cream-colored curtains in the front windows. An empty planter on the front stoop. A black iron railing. And a mailbox attached to the side of the screen door that said *Shanley*.

Behind that steel gray door with its convex peephole and the number 104 in black, curved lettering was her grandmother, her *maternal* grandmother, the "maternal" being Lucie, as hard as it was for Meg to get her mind around that fact.

There was a doorbell, its ivory-colored button lit and golden. Over her shoulder the sun was high in the sky. It was afternoon here, but back in LA with Lucie, it was morning. She couldn't think about that now. That was the past. This was her future.

Meg put her bag down on the sidewalk and stared up at the row house. She was amazed she was able to focus at all, having not slept a wink on the plane or on the taxi ride from the airport. She took a deep breath and reached a finger out to the doorbell.

Pressed.

The crescent moon of her fingernail stuck in the side, and she heard a prolonged beat of the dull metallic echo of chimes. Before the bell's notes had faded completely, the door opened.

"Meg?" Lonnie came closer to the screen, his blue eyes squinting against the sunlight. He glanced over her shoulder to the street, past her. "Come on in." He held open the door, and when she didn't react, he grabbed her suitcase and pulled her inside. The foyer was cramped and warm, and there was a narrow staircase that led to the second floor. Lonnie was dressed in a pair of old jeans and a faded Stones concert shirt over a white long-sleeved tee that emphasized his skinny frame. She liked the look on him.

She must have been staring for a long time because Lonnie cleared his throat self-consciously and said, "Your flight was okay?"

Meg nodded, and her voice came out all strangulated as if she were holding her breath and speaking at the same time. "It was . . . great. I . . . should I call you . . ."

"Lonnie. Just Lonnie. Anything else would be weird, you know?" He put a finger to his lips and then pointed behind him. "Your grandmother's sleeping right now. We had lunch a little while ago, but she'll be up in an hour or so. She doesn't sleep very long these days."

"Oh, right. She's sick."

"Dying, actually." Meg must have had an odd look on her face because he added hastily, "She has cancer. The treatments take a lot out of her."

"Uh . . . what kind?"

"Chemo."

"No, I mean the cancer."

"Lung. She was a lifelong smoker."

"Oh." Meg eyed a pack of Camels on a small table next to the staircase.

Lonnie nodded quickly and guiltily. "I know, I know. I'm buying the patch next week, I swear." Then he surprised her with a grin. "Are you hungry? Let me get you something." He rushed off to the kitchen, but hungry as she was, tired as she was, Meg wanted to linger, wanted to drink in every detail, to imprint it on her brain.

This was her family's living room, with its checked sofa and leather Barcalounger and shaggy area rug.

This was her family's staircase, with its wooden rungs and its shag-carpeted steps.

This was her family's bathroom, with its globe-shaded lights and its speckled porcelain basin and its shag-carpeted toilet seat.

Shag carpeting. Very popular in the Shanley household, Meg noted.

"Meg? Did you get lost?" Lonnie popped his head

around the kitchen's swinging door and smiled. "Do you like pork chops? We had pork chops last night. I could heat some up if you want."

"Oh yeah, sure," Meg said. "Pork is awesome."

She took a seat at the table in a straight-backed chair with a flowered cushion on it, one of those tie thingies meant to soften a hard chair. All of the furniture here felt lived in, worn but cared for. Unlike the Wal-Mart crap she and Lucie had, *this* furniture didn't look like it was put together with an Allen wrench. Meg ran a stealthy hand along the table's surface: ah, yes. Real wood.

Lonnie took a foil-covered plate out of the fridge and stuck his nose in it. "Smells okay. I'll just put it in the microwave." He stabbed a fork through a chop and dropped it on a plate. "Mashed potatoes and applesauce?"

"Please."

While the microwave spun and whirred, Lonnie leaned awkwardly against the counter and folded his arms. "So . . ."

"So . . ."

"This is kind of crazy, huh?"

She nodded, relieved he had said it first. "Yeah, sort of."

"It's a lot to take in, I know," Lonnie said. "I promise I'll try to ease you into it. Whatever you can do to help me out with your grandmother is great." He sighed. "I've needed help for a long time, believe me. Can't really afford a nurse, you know."

Meg started at the mention of money. "I'll pay you back

for the plane ticket as soon as I can. I can probably get a job after school and—"

Lonnie waved her away. "No, no. Don't pay me back. Just lend a hand with Alma."

"Absolutely. I'll do whatever I can."

The microwave pinged then, and Lonnie removed the plate, using the edge of his shirt as a pot holder. He placed it in front of her.

"Thank you." She stared at the steam rising from the food. It was all gray: gray pork, gray potatoes, gray applesauce. She was fairly certain applesauce wasn't supposed to be gray. But it wasn't bad, this pork, and despite its grayness, the applesauce bore a faint flavor resemblance to apples. "It's good," she said.

"Yeah?"

"A little chewy but good."

Lonnie watched her eat for a moment and then looked away. "She told you everything?"

Meg nodded, still chewing. "Pretty much."

He rapped his fingers on the counter. "And you came anyway, so that's a good sign." Then he laughed. "Alma's not nearly as bad as Lucie probably made her out to be."

Just then, the phone rang and Lonnie stepped into the living room to pick it up. "Hello? Yeah, hang on." He came back into the kitchen and pulled on his jacket. "I'm gonna take this outside," he told Meg. "Keep an ear out for her, okay? She'll need help getting to her walker. She's terrified she'll fall and break her hip." And then he slipped out the back door.

"Uh, okay," Meg agreed, but inside her chest, her heart hammered. She hadn't even met Alma yet! Meg kept very still, chewed very quietly, and prayed that her grandmother wouldn't awaken.

She wondered what Alma might look like. Would she have Meg's strawberry blond locks? Would their eyes be the same? Their noses? Would people out on the street, seeing grandmother and granddaughter walking arm in arm, remark: "Why, look at your cheekbones! You both have the exact same cheekbones!" And then would grandmother and granddaughter look at each other and smile, happy to be standing so close to one another that perfect strangers could comment on their similarities?

Meg wondered about that and then laughed to herself, thrilled that she even had the chance to wonder at all. A year ago, a month ago, such a thought would never have crossed her mind.

She finished the chop and potatoes. The applesauce was simply too gray. Maybe she would offer to cook next, she thought. Maybe Lonnie and Alma would like French Toes.

"Lonnie?" she heard a voice call from beyond the kitchen.

Meg froze. That must be her grandmother. Should she go to her? Was it time?

"I'm up, Lonnie."

Without rising from the table, Meg lifted her head and scanned for signs that Lonnie had heard his mother and was making his way back inside. But no, he remained out of doors, talking on the phone, smoking a cigarette.

"Lonnie!" the voice called sharply. "I'm up now!"

Well, Meg considered, maybe she should just plunge in headfirst. She tiptoed to her grandmother's alcove just off the living room, the door slightly ajar. She pushed it open farther and was met with a warm old-woman aroma. It was gently perfumed and soft, inviting. The room itself was quite small, as if it had been something else in a previous life, an office, perhaps, or a laundry area. Now it contained only a twin bed, a nightstand with a lamp, a dresser, and a walker.

The old woman's eyes met Meg's and widened. "Who are you?"

Meg smiled her brightest, most granddaughterly smile. "I'm—"

"Lonnie!" the woman screamed.

Meg held up her hands. "No, it's okay. I'm Meg. Your granddaughter."

Alma's chin drew back into her neck and she pulled the thin coverlet up above her shoulders. She was not as old as she appeared, Meg knew, but the disease had aged her tremendously. She did not have Meg's cheekbones. "Lonnie!"

"I won't hurt you—"

A door closed and Lonnie's footsteps hurriedly approached. "Is everything all right?" He looked from Meg to his mother.

"Who is *she*?" The old woman pointed at Meg with a bony finger.

Lonnie pulled Meg into the room. "This is your grand-daughter. I told you she was coming."

"Is she yours?" The woman's eyes blinked rapidly beneath lashless lids.

"Good Lord, no. This is Lucie's daughter. Margaret Anne."

Meg grinned, tried to look harmless. "People call me Meg."

The old woman's knobby fingers lowered the blanket to her chest. She was wearing a pink nightgown, cotton, thinned from age and use and trimmed with yellowed lace. A cameo brooch sat at the base of her neck suspended by a delicate gold chain. *Pink,* Meg thought, *my grandmother is pink.* Pink blanket, pink dressing gown. All but her skin, which was an ashen shade of white, had a rosy glow. Her hair, though it was a wig, was also pinkish. Which made Meg wonder, if you could choose your hair, why would you choose old-lady hair?

"How do you do," Meg said softly. "It's nice to meet you."

The woman didn't respond, merely stared blankly in Meg's direction.

"She gets a little confused sometimes," Lonnie said apologetically. "Mother, say something, for God's sake."

"It's time for my stories," she announced, and allowed herself to be helped up to her walker. As Meg followed,

Lonnie guided his mother to a corduroy recliner at the far end of the living room.

Meg sort of stood there, not knowing whether to sit or stand, talk or keep her mouth shut, so she just stared at her grandmother, who stared at the TV. Finally, Lonnie rescued her. "Meg, why don't we take your stuff upstairs? You know, get you settled in," he said as he picked up her suitcase. "You two can visit later."

Upstairs, he led her to the far end of the hallway. "The bathroom is there." He pointed as they walked past. "And my room is that one, closest to the stairway." He paused at a closed door. "This will be your room." He opened the door and flipped a switch on the wall. The room was bathed in a golden glow that came from a lamp on the nightstand beside a canopied double bed. It was a very girly room, with white lace curtains that matched a white lace bedspread and dust ruffle. In one corner there was a vanity with an ornate mirror and a chair with its own lace cushion. Meg entered the room. Along one wall sat a toy store's worth of teddy bears and Barbies and stuffed animals and dolls with porcelain faces and a Raggedy Ann and Andy lying arm in arm.

"This was Lucie's room," Lonnie said. "Not a thing has been touched in here since she left."

Meg set her backpack down on the white shag carpet and frowned. *Her* room. *That woman's.* She hated the idea, but there was no other place for her here. It was Lucie's room or the couch, and she doubted Alma Shanley would want her soaps interrupted by a wayward visitor. She would simply have to grin and bear it.

It would only be temporary anyway, she thought, until she found her father.

"There's extra stuff in the linen closet next to the bathroom," Lonnie said. "And anything else you need, just let me know. I want you to be comfortable for as long as you're with us." He seemed to place a meaningful emphasis on the last two syllables.

"Lonnie, I really appreciate this. God, I can't even believe I'm here." Meg felt light-headed and giddy. She could blame some of it on jet lag, sure, but not all. "I can't believe I have a family now. You and Alma and, you know, my dad." She glanced up at him shyly. "Would you . . . do you think you could help me find him?"

"Of course," Lonnie said warmly. "I'll do whatever I can." He shoved his hands in the back pockets of his jeans. "Take your time up here. And come on down whenever you're ready. We can talk about getting you into school around here."

Meg nodded and smiled, suppressing the urge to squeal or jump up and down. "Thanks, Lonnie."

When he had left, Meg investigated the remnants of her mother. In a corner of the room were three plastic milk crates filled with CDs. Tucked behind them were several cardboard tubes; Meg pulled out posters of Nirvana and R.E.M. The closet was filled with about a mile of Lucie's old clothes: skirts, dresses, pants, blouses, sweaters, shoes, jeans, hats, jackets, belts. There were more clothes than Meg had ever dreamed of owning herself. On the vanity were barrettes and pins and boxes of costume jewelry.

She took a seat on the edge of the bed and regarded the room and its contents. She felt overwhelmed. The room was Lucie, yet not Lucie. It was intact, a shrine to the lost daughter.

If you go, don't come back, Lucie had told her.

She wouldn't. She'd make this place her own. She would never, *ever* go back.

Chapter
EIGHT

Astoria, Meg soon discovered, was utterly unlike anyplace she had ever seen. First of all, the streets were outrageously narrow. And they were all mono-directional. And then there were the houses—rows and rows of them, made of brick, attached one right after the other with pointy roofs and iron gates on the basement windows. All of this was set amid a backdrop of faded, empty warehouses.

Sitting at a coffee shop not far from her grandmother's home, Meg took out a map and attempted to look like a native—if a native had need of a subway map, which she totally wouldn't, of course.

Memorize, she told herself, *memorize.*

Astoria was so close to Manhattan, just a short train ride away. She could buy a MetroCard and ride the subway all

day, all night, from the Bronx to Wall Street and out to the
airport and Shea Stadium . . . if she was into that sort of
thing.

Maybe she would be, maybe she could be. Maybe she
would discover the joys of baseball games and walking in
the rain and throwing a Frisbee in Central Park, and maybe
she would transform herself into a New Yorker and become
one with the hustle and bustle from the Upper East Side to
Greenwich Village.

She tried to picture herself carelessly tossing out directions to anyone who asked. "You want to take Broadway to
Houston," she might say, "and it's not *Hyoo*-ston, it's *How*-
ston." And then she would hurry off to her next destina-
tion because *everyone* hurried in New York. In fact, in the
short time she had been sitting in this café, Meg had seen
no fewer than a dozen patrons buzz in and out, newspapers
stuffed under their arms, juggling waxed bags of doughnuts
and muffins with their cups of coffee. It seemed like only
she and the elderly bothered to sit and sip at the Formica
tables.

Meg folded her map over and located the corner in
Greenwich Village where Monica's building was. Across the
street would be Central Perk, the coffee shop where all the
Friends hung out.

Yes, she knew these locations weren't *real*, and no, she
wasn't a moron, for God's sake. She knew *Friends* was only
a show shot on a soundstage in Burbank. She just wanted
to see where they were *supposed* to be. Was that so wrong?

She sneaked another peek at the map, at the tangle of multicolored subway lines. Letters, numbers, uptown and down. Bridges and tunnels carrying passengers from borough to borough, city to suburb. Where in all of this was Nathaniel Holland? Like Waldo . . . was her father here in Times Square or there in Herald Square? Upper East Side or Upper West? Maybe he was right here in Astoria, right under her nose, and all she had to do was reach out and touch him.

Meg tried to picture her father. God, oh God! This was her new life starting *now*!

The waitress poured more coffee into Meg's cup without bothering to ask. This had an irritating effect on Meg, especially since she had gotten the coffee to just the right color and sweetness level and it had cooled to precisely the correct sipping temperature. Now she would have to start all over again.

She tried not to let that bother her, focusing instead on how nice it was to get the free refill.

This would not be her coffee shop, she told herself. Once she was settled, she would find the place that would be hers to hang out in, where everyone would know her name and the barista would prepare her cup exactly the way he knew she liked it.

"Do you have a ladies' room?" she asked the waitress.

The woman eyed her suspiciously. "What are you gonna do in there?" she barked in a heavy accent.

"I need to freshen up," Meg said brightly. "I'm meeting

my uncle, and we're going sightseeing all over Manhattan. I'm from California, you know, and—"

The waitress held up a hand. "Don't need your life story. Christ. It's behind the counter."

No, this would not be her coffee shop, Meg told herself again. Her place would have scented candles in the restrooms and plants hanging in the windows and nice people. There, everyone would be nice.

Dear Jen,

How are you? I am fine.

Here we go again. Another new school, but this time I am three thousand miles away. Lonnie has been really cool, taking me places and showing me things. We went to the Upper West Side, to the Natural History Museum, where Ross used to work. And there was this awesome fifties restaurant on 57th Street that could totally be where Monica roller-skated as a waitress. Remember that? And she wore the blond wig and her boobs caught on fire. Oh my God, that was totally hilarious.

We took the 4 train down to Battery Park and saw the Statue of Liberty out in the harbor. That was way cool. Lonnie says you can take a ferry out there and go inside, but they don't let you climb all the way up to the top anymore. He says when he was a kid, he went up to the crown and it was really cramped and claustrophobic and that was when he discovered he was afraid of heights.

Remember the very first episode (I've only seen it like a gazillion times!) when you walked into the coffee shop with that wedding dress on?

It was like a fresh start for Rachel. She was running away from what she knew wasn't right. That's just like me.

This is it. This is the start of my brand-new life! Everything is going to be different from now on.

Your friend,

m

"I remember our first day, lo these many years ago," Lonnie said as he and Meg walked the handful of blocks to the brick-and-concrete monstrosity that was RFK High School. To the rest of the world, the place was known as HS189. Meg kind of liked the idea of a number: it added to the orderliness of things.

"Lucie and I had been inseparable from kindergarten on," Lonnie continued. "That's one of the problems with being a twin: same schools, same classes, same clothes. Mercifully, my mother wasn't able to find too many outfits that matched, what with us being the opposite sex, and she couldn't sew or knit, so we had very few twin clothes."

"But you guys are fraternal, not identical," Meg said, remembering that fact from her biology class. "Two eggs, two sperm."

Lonnie grimaced. "I hadn't wanted to think about sperm at eight o'clock in the morning, but—so?"

She laughed. "I just meant you look similar but not identical."

"Twins are twins." He shrugged. "Everyone always says,

'Aren't they cute?'" His voice adopted a high, mocking tone. "Lonnie and Lucie, Lucie and Lonnie. Partners for life. So much for that, huh?"

They passed a produce stand that Lonnie called a bodega, a tiny grocery store with one of everything, he said. A man in a New York Mets baseball cap raised his arm and waved to her uncle, who waved back.

"Lucie and I stopped being twins when we went to high school," he said. "We agreed that we would go our separate ways, do our own thing."

"That's cool."

"Different friends, different classes, hell, different lunches, even." He stopped and looked up at the school. "Good old RFK High. If I could go back and do things over again, I think I'd start here."

Inside, the hallway was abuzz; they had arrived between classes. Meg tried to stick close to her uncle and not let the stream of students separate them as they looked for the principal's office. Already Lonnie was proving himself to be the opposite of his twin: he didn't just send Meg off on her own into the wilds of Queens.

"This school holds 1,257 students spread among four grades and 250 faculty members. Forty percent of each graduating class goes on to higher education, five percent do not graduate at all, and the average age of each graduate is eighteen years and seven months.

"And *that's* high because of people like Louis Vitale,

who was left back three times his freshman year and can barely write his name," said Nikki Hernandez, Meg's very own tour guide for her first week at RFK High. "*Pobrecito* Louis. They had a big party when he finally made it."

Nikki worked afternoons in the school administration office, she told Meg. She knew practically everything there was to know about the place and was the perfect person, according to Principal Betts, to show Meg around. Especially since the two of them had nearly identical schedules.

"They totally love me in there," Nikki had said shortly after meeting Meg. "They let me volunteer for whatever I want."

Meg had been startled by the admission and Nikki's enthusiasm; "showing the new girl around" didn't seem like something anyone would want to do.

"This is the language wing," Nikki went on. "French, Spanish, German, Japanese, and Latin. I know absolutely no one who takes Latin. I have no idea why we even have Latin. We should have Italian instead. That would be amazing and so much more useful. Then I could translate the Via Spiga web site on my own. How cool would that be?"

She pointed at the floor near Meg's feet. "I love those boots. Very retro."

It took Meg a moment to realize it was her turn to say something; Nikki had been talking nonstop since they met.

"Oh, thanks." She looked down at her shoes: a pair of black vinyl zip-ups with two-inch heels. She had found them in Lucie's closet and reluctantly forced her feet into them when she felt the cold concrete through the soles of her Steve Madden knockoffs.

"Come on, let's get to lunch, okay? Deidre and Tanya are going to meet us at the corner table where we usually sit, which is kind of close to the basketball team, but not so close that they think we *want* to sit near them, you know? And sometimes Jason, who's the team captain, he'll come over and sit, like, five *feet* from Tanya. She has *such* a crush. . . ."

Meg took a close look at Nikki as she regaled her with tales from the caf: she was a brunette with the longest, shiniest hair Meg had seen outside of a Pantene commercial, and she had perfect skin and emerald eyes. She wore a mini similar to Meg's, although it was plain black and unpleated, and her navy blue turtleneck was a little tighter around the bust. Her figure was shapely, perhaps a tad too shapely in the hip and thigh areas if she wanted to be on the cover of *InStyle*.

But evidently Nikki didn't care, and that made her all the more appealing to Meg. Besides, Meg thought, she looked kind of like Jen during season two when she had that great hair but before she got too skinny.

". . . and this is our trophy case."

Meg followed Nikki's pointing finger to a small case filled with gold- and silver-colored plaques and statues.

"We're kind of award-challenged around here, if you know what I mean. These are mostly second- and third-place trophies. . . ."

There were a few recent team photos—track and baseball and softball. Meg had never had much interest in sports. She'd rather curl up with a book than throw a ball. But her father, now, *that* added something extra into the gene pool. She searched among the pictures and plaques for his year.

Her father's class would have been 1992, the year Meg was born. He was a football player, Lucie had said. Meg looked past the trophies to the back of the case, where photos of teams from the previous century were located. Where, where . . . there! Off to the left, not in the exact center but definitely *there*, was the football team from the fall of 1991.

"First place," she heard herself whisper.

"What's that?" Nikki saw the photo too. "Oh yeah, that was the last time any football team at RFK got any sort of trophy and the only first-place award. This year's team is undefeated, though, so everyone's hoping we'll get something new in there soon."

A tall guy stood in the back row of the team photo. Dark brown, nearly black hair, cut in a Marine's buzz, just like the rest of the players. High cheekbones, a strong jaw, a thick neck accentuated by the padding he wore beneath his blue-and-white uniform.

N. Holland.

Meg's breath caught in her throat.

N for Nathaniel. Surely that was it.

Yes, but stop calling me Shirley, Meg thought.

That was her *father,* she wanted to shout. That good-looking guy in the back row, fourth from the left, with the carefree crooked smile. She searched the photo for clues, for a familial connection. Did his nose look like hers? His chin? His eyes! Nathaniel Holland's eyes, squinting against the sun, looked exactly like Meg's. Same tiny lines in the corners, same tangled lashes. Yes, that was him! That was her—

"Come on, let's get to the caf," Nikki said. She tucked her arm under Meg's elbow and propelled her away from the case.

N. Holland.

Nathaniel Holland. She was one step closer to finding him.

Chapter
NINE

Meg was eager to meet up with Lonnie after school at a bar under the elevated subway tracks. It had been nearly two weeks since she had arrived, and while they had been having fun and she had been settling in at school, uncle and niece had not had much time to talk about her father. This morning, Lonnie left her a note about making some phone calls from the bar. Unfortunately, every couple of minutes, the roar of the passing trains would rattle the liquor bottles behind the bartender and set Meg's nerves on edge. It reminded her of California's frequent tremors.

The waitress, who looked like a giant ear of corn to Meg, sort of pockmarked and yellow with long stringy hair, kept shooting Meg the evil eye until Lonnie introduced her as his niece. Then the woman practically fell all over herself getting Meg coffee and cream and bowls of pretzels.

"You know, they have all this on the Internet," Meg said, sliding onto a bar stool beside her uncle.

Lonnie had three phone books spread out on the table and was checking off names with a black felt-tip pen each time he called a listing from what looked like the bar's phone line. "Inter-what?" he joked. "I like doing things the old-fashioned way. Can't cross things off with a keyboard." He drew a line through a name. "No to Miss Nancy Holland in Sheepshead Bay." He glanced up. "I'm sorry, sweetheart, but this isn't as easy as you'd think."

Meg pointed to a name in the Manhattan book. "Well, then, how about this one? It just says 'Holland.'"

Lonnie nodded. "Let's give it a shot." He dialed. After a moment, the phone buzzed and he quickly pulled it away from his ear. "Not in service." He gave her an apologetic smile. "Sorry."

Meg wasn't about to give up that easily. There was a whole city out there to search. "Well, what about Wall Street? Lucie said something about how he was 'that type.' Maybe he's a stockbroker or something."

Lonnie shrugged. "Possibly."

"Is there some kind of listing of who's on Wall Street?"

"It's not an actual street."

"Sure, it is. We saw it when we went to Battery Park."

Lonnie shook his head. "No, not like that. When you

say someone works on Wall Street, it doesn't mean literally. It means they work in the business, the financial business, like stock brokerages and investment firms."

"Couldn't we at least *start* there?" Panic in her chest was making her voice rise; she swallowed hard to keep it low. "We have to start somewhere."

Her uncle sighed. "I'm sorry, Meg, I am. But Nate could be in London or Paris or Bangladesh. This is impossible."

"No." Meg leaned forward on the sticky counter and tried to get her brain to come up with something—a new approach to the situation. She was determined. "There has to be a way. How did *you* find *us*?"

Lonnie paused. "The bank—? Nate's *parents* take care of that. I think I heard they were in Florida, and Nate, well, Nate's not with them."

"Can't we find *them* in the phone book?" Meg asked. "Ask them where my father is?"

Nate pressed his lips into a thin line. "I'm sorry, honey, but the way I remember it, they didn't want Nate to know about Lucie. About . . ." He paused. "I just—I don't think they'd be very much help."

"Oh." Meg sighed. "Right."

They stared at the tissue-thin sheets of the White Pages in silence.

"Did you know him?" Meg asked.

"Honestly? No. I didn't know Nate very well. He was a few years older than me and Lucie, and Lucie and I kind of . . . separated around then."

"But didn't you see them together? Like when he came to pick her up for dates or the prom or—"

Lonnie frowned. "It wasn't like that. There were no dates or proms. It wasn't that sort of relationship."

Meg's chest felt heavy under the weight of this new information. "Oh," she said again.

Two trains crossed overhead, and the bar shuddered. Meg could feel the bones in her hands and feet and head shake.

Finally, Lonnie cleared his throat. "Nate was a good-looking guy, now that I think about it. I guess you could say he was handsome."

Meg thought of the picture in the trophy case. He *was* handsome.

"You kind of look like him," Lonnie said.

"You think?" Meg's fingers touched her face, traced its outline.

"From what I remember, yeah. The nose, the lips."

They were just crumbs, pieces of memories; Meg wanted more.

"Was he tall?"

Lonnie closed his eyes in thought. "Taller than me, definitely. Six feet, I think, maybe six-two."

Her genes were getting better and better. "Was he popular?"

"Absolutely. All the girls were in love with Nate Holland, and all the guys wanted to be his friend." Meg stared, waiting, but Lonnie had nothing more to add. "That's about all I can remember now."

"That's cool, really cool. Thanks." A consolation prize, Meg realized, was all Lonnie had to offer at this point. He was trying, though, and she appreciated that he wanted her to feel better. It would have to do for now.

"Lucie should have told you about him."

Meg looked into Lonnie's eyes, grateful. "She should have told me about you too."

Lonnie pulled a cigarette from his pack. "Listen, about your father . . . I don't want you to get hurt, Meg."

"I won't get hurt, Lonnie. I'm a big girl."

Lonnie stopped and held her gaze.

"What? What's wrong?"

He frowned slightly. "Nothing. It's just—you looked a lot like Lucie just then." And then he shook his head as if shaking loose a cobweb. "Let me check that Internet thing on my friend Tony's computer, see if I find anything there."

"Thanks, Lonnie," Meg said with an eager smile. "You're awesome."

Lonnie looked away, his cheeks suddenly flushing. "Yeah, yeah. Why don't you go find me an ashtray?"

Chapter
TEN

The first of December brought with it a frosty wind. What better way to combat the cold than to snuggle up with *Friends*? Meg had been in Queens for over a month, and she had yet to glimpse the fabulous *Friends* gang on her grandmother's set. Thankfully, Lonnie was taking Alma to her chemotherapy regularly; "lending a hand" for Meg meant babysitting her grandmother while she was glued to *Wheel of Fortune*. Night after night, they watched the letters turn; it was mesmerizing and monotonous. Meg had kept quiet and not demanded the channel be changed, but it was making her remote finger twitch, like a television junkie's: she was in desperate need of a *Friends* fix.

So one night, when her uncle was at work selling furniture at his friend Tony's store and Alma had her eyes on the

Wheel, Meg tiptoed up to Lonnie's room and pushed open the door. He had to have a TV of his own, right? He was a grown man and a good guy, and if he knew what dire straits she was in, he certainly wouldn't mind her trespassing.

Compared to the shrine that was Lucie's room, Lonnie's looked like no one had ever lived in it. Bare walls, monochromatic bed coverings, a simple frame, and a shag rug.

The room was devoid of any personal mementos, photographs, tchotchkes, or even stray lint, pens, loose change. Lonnie's desk, which faced a blank wall, was one of those pressed-board, faux-wood rectangular jobs with an armless office chair. Sadly, no TV. Maybe, it occurred to her, he was a monk or a wannabe priest. Maybe he practiced a strict form of Buddhism, denying himself earthly pleasures, answering to a higher power, achieving enlightenment through abstention.

She suddenly realized she knew virtually nothing about her uncle. She knew about his job at the store, yes, and she knew his family, sure, but what about his personal life? Lonnie had never mentioned whether he had gone to college or traveled to Europe, if he had a girlfriend or a boyfriend, if he was ever married or divorced.

Curious, Meg went to his desk. Again, she felt certain that Lonnie wouldn't mind—that he would want his only niece to know more about him.

She started with the bottom drawer of the desk and surprise! Out popped a stack of *Playboy* magazines. "Ah, jeez!" She jerked her head away.

Now, Meg had certainly seen her fair share of naked women in gym classes and movies and in her own mirror, so it wasn't as if these parts were *new* to her. But Miss December's parts were unlike any she had ever seen up close.

The rest of the desk drawers were locked, which made Meg wonder about a man who kept his *Playboy*s easily accessible but everything else locked tight. She returned Miss December to her place, but as she did so, a half-dozen Polaroids fell onto the floor. The woman in them was most decidedly nude, but in a far less artistic manner than the beautiful model. This woman was probably in her mid- to late twenties, her breasts not nearly as taut as the centerfold's, her thighs more dimpled and round. She wore a bright smile and nothing more, which made the photos seem far more lurid than the airbrushed art of the *Playboy* photographers. Meg turned one photo over but found no name, no date, as she would have written; it was as naked as its subject. Whoever the woman was, Lonnie must have believed she was Miss December's equal; why else would her photos be in such an honored place?

She slipped the Polaroids back into the magazine and closed the drawer. Was this all there was to her uncle, this one desk? Where were his clothes, his shoes, his dirty under-wear? Where was his *stuff*?

She made her way back down to the living room, where Pat Sajak was calling out letters to a plastic, sequin-gowned Vanna White.

"Is there a *P*?"

Bing!

"Two *P*s."

Light applause.

"Would you like to solve the puzzle or spin again?"

"I'll spin again, Pat."

"Moron," spat Alma.

Meg tucked herself into a corner of the couch and trained her eyes on the television. Click-click-click as the contestant spun the wheel. The other contestants clapped and cheered. "Big money, big money!"

"Three hundred." More applause.

"Is there an *M*?" The man, who looked like his name should be Schmedley McSchmendrick, with thick-lensed glasses and wearing a bow tie, clasped his hands as if he were praying to the game show gods.

"Oh, Vanna," called Pat flirtatiously. "Show us your *M*s."

"Oh, *you*," Vanna replied with a shake of her sequined butt.

Light audience laughter. Two whoops. Meg felt like she was transcribing one of Aaron's shows.

"Moron," Alma muttered again. "There's no *M*."

Buzz!

"Oh! Sorry. No *M*s."

The audience sympathized with a long "Awww."

"Answer the goddamn puzzle," Alma said.

Meg stared at the letters. *H*, blank, *P*, *P*, blank was the first word. The second began with another *H*. . . .

"Happy holidays," she said. Alma turned to look at her. "That's the puzzle. Happy–"

"I solved it already." Alma shook her remote at the set. "All these people are morons. Don't have the sense God gave a chicken."

The image of a bunch of chickens spinning the big wheel with their beaks popped into Meg's head, and she stifled an urge to giggle; she had a feeling her grandmother didn't care much for a hearty chuckle. What *did* her grandmother care for, aside from her soap operas and simple-minded game shows? Meg hadn't yet been asked about Lucie, about their life in California, which was okay for the most part, because Meg certainly didn't need to be reminded of *her*. But how about something like, "Do you like school?" Or, "Do you have a boyfriend?" Or, "Do you play sports?"

"Uh . . . Alma? Do you know if Lonnie's coming back tonight?"

"Coming back?" Alma turned sharply to Meg. "Of course he's coming back. He's working hard at the store with Tony. What do you mean, is he coming back? He's a *good boy*." Alma caught Meg's eye and held her gaze for a split second longer than was comfortable for Meg. Obviously "good" was something to aspire to. Meg broke her grandmother's stare and turned back to the television.

Mr. McSchmendrick had gained control of the board again and was scratching his head, mouth moving silently.

"Man, this guy is dumb," Meg said.

Alma scowled. "I can't watch this anymore. Here." She held out the remote. "Change it to your show."

Meg reached a hand out to take the channel changer

from her grandmother, but Alma wouldn't let go of the remote. "Where did you get that ring?" She pointed to Meg's hand. "That's Lucie's ring."

"I, um, borrowed it from her."

"That was mine."

Our mother's ring, that's what Lucie had said. Our mother. Really, it was Lucie's mother's. She started to slip the ring off her hand. "Do you want it back?"

"I gave it to Lucie for her First Communion."

"Her what?"

"Didn't your mother ever take you to church?" Meg shook her head, and so did Alma. "She was baptized and received her Holy Communion at St. Ambrose's, three blocks from here. Father Flammia performed the service."

The remote went limp in her grandmother's hand, so Meg took it and laid it in her own lap.

"A beautiful church, very comfortable pews. Padded kneelers." Alma's fingers played with the cameo brooch around her neck. "I haven't been in years, of course. Lonnie won't take me because of my sins. But I need to go back. When God calls me, I want to be able to face Him proudly and with no regrets." Her eyes sought out Meg's, then turned away. "Lucie's fingers were so small that she wore the ring on a chain around her neck for the communion service. When she got older, she wore it on her finger, that same one you're wearing it on. Never took it off."

Meg stared down at the ring on her hand. She had taken it because she liked it but also to spite Lucie, who hadn't even noticed it was missing. She might not have cared, but Meg and her grandmother did.

We care, Meg thought. *We appreciate what's valuable.*

"We'll go to church together, all right? To St. Ambrose's? And you'll take me to confession." Alma placed a bony hand on Meg's arm, and Meg felt the soft old-lady skin, thin and loose, against her firm flesh. There was a sparkle in her grandmother's eyes Meg hadn't seen since her arrival in Queens.

Having been raised without religion, Meg had only a vague sense of what confession was, based mostly on having seen it on TV and in the movies. But if it could make Alma happy, well, okay, then. She would try it.

"Sure," Meg said. "I'd be glad to take you." And then she aimed the remote at the set and found the last frames of *Friends* before the credits rolled.

Chapter
ELEVEN

Dear Jen,

How are you? I am fine.

Oh my God, so the episode tonight was the one where Rachel has to tell the father of her baby that he's, well, gonna be a father, and Phoebe's all like, Bam! You're a dad, and I thought, wow, how awesome would it be if that was, like, me and my dad, you know? Like, what if he lives around the corner and I run into him buying a coffee or something and he sees me and bam! He knows right away who I am. I think it would be awesome, you know, but what are the odds, huh? Do you think it could happen?

Meg paused and took a sip of Diet Coke. She wondered, not for the first time, if Jen would understand her plight. Who could, after all, except a guest on *Oprah*? She was hesitant to give voice to her tale because it sounded so damn weird, so made up, like a story on TV. But Jen was so amazing and so worldly, and she had heard so many strange things about Meg's bizarre life, that she had to understand this turn of events. As Meg had been there for Jen during her troubles, she knew Jen was there for her too. Somewhere, thousands of miles away, but she was there. She was reading and listening and caring for her.

Meg remembered when she was nine, and she and Lucie had just moved to El Monte, she had begged her sister to let her take gymnastics after school with all the other girls. At first, everything was just dandy. Meg learned to walk a balance beam and to do cartwheels and front handsprings. But somewhere in the middle of the year, she began to sprout while all the other girls remained tiny. She started to trip over her feet on the beam and to get stuck on the vault; she became awkward and graceless. When the other girls pointed and laughed at her, Meg poured her heart onto her stationery and hoped that Jen would tell her what to do. She did. Of course, she did. She was Jen, she was amazing and wonderful, generous and kind. In her very next letter, she taught Meg some Spanish swearwords.

Meg put aside her soda and reached into the back of Lucie's closet, into the cubbyhole where she hid her Jennifer letters. Here it was: *Try this,* Jen had written on a sheet of lavender paper. *Tell them,* "Come mierda." *It means,* "Eat shit." Meg smiled at the memory of the girls' mouths opened in little *o*'s when she let loose at the next practice. It was also her last practice. Oh, well. Gymnastics was lame, anyway.

"Whatcha giving your parents for Christmas?" Deidre asked the lunch table on the Wednesday before vacation. She was dressed in red and white—a *fromage* to the holiday, she kept telling the girls—until Meg finally and kindly informed her that *fromage* meant "cheese" in French.

"What do I mean, then?" On top of Deidre's blond head sat a Santa cap with a fuzzy pom-pom that she batted between her hands when she was bored. *Bat-bat-bat.*

"I think *homage.*"

"You're sure?"

"Pretty sure."

"Huh. What do you know about that." *Bat-bat-bat.*

Tanya sighed. "I've got three parents and six brothers and sisters to buy for. I'm getting them all gift certificates to Blockbuster."

"That's original," Deidre said. "You gave them that last year."

"I did?" Tanya cradled her head in her hands. "Why didn't you tell me sooner?"

Nikki and Meg shared a secret smile. It hadn't taken long for Meg to fit into this group; Deidre and Tanya accepted her as quickly as Nikki had, perhaps faster, because she came to them stamped "Nikki-approved." She wondered if the threesome had recently lost a fourth member, someone who had moved or been expelled, and whether she had simply come along at the right time to slip into the open slot. Whoever it was, Meg hoped she wasn't coming back.

"How 'bout you, Meg?" Nikki asked. "What's on your gift list?"

"Oh, well, I guess I don't have one."

"Everyone's got to have a list," Tanya said. "Even if you don't get anything on it, you have to have something to wish for."

"I know what *I'm* wishing for," Deidre sang. She leaned across Nikki and stared at the varsity basketball team's table.

"The *whole* team? That's a mighty big wish list," Nikki said.

"How will Santa get them down your chimney?" Tanya asked.

Deidre smiled. "He can bring *me* to *them*. I don't mind."

The girls roared with laughter, and Tanya swatted Deidre playfully on the arm. "You are a very bad girl. Santa won't bring you anything."

"Okay, okay," Nikki said, calming the table down. "You've got your wish list—"

"What about me?" Tanya asked. "I have one!"

Deidre and Nikki sighed and said together, "Jason."

Meg laughed. Even *she* knew that one.

Tanya smiled, suddenly shy. "Yeah, maybe."

"All right, let's do Meg," Nikki announced. "See anyone you want on your Christmas list?"

"Me? I, uh, I don't know anyone yet."

"You must have seen someone you like," Deidre insisted.
"I'll let you have one of mine."

"No, Meg needs her own," Nikki said. "Let's find her
one."

The girls began looking around the caf and murmuring
to themselves:

"How about him?"

"Too short."

"He's fine."

"He's got a girl."

While part of her was mortified beyond belief that the
girls were trying to score her a crush, another part of Meg
thought it was pretty cool having her friends—that's *friends*
plural—playing matchmaker. She hoped they picked someone good.

"How about Juny?" Deidre asked.

Tanya clapped. "Yes, Juny! They'd be *perfect*. What do
you think, Nikki?"

Nikki narrowed her eyes at Meg, as if seeing her for the
first time, and rested her chin on her fingertips. "An excellent choice," she said. "Good call, girls."

The bell rang then, signaling the end of lunch.

Deidre whispered in Meg's ear, "Nikki doesn't think we're
smart enough for Juny, but you've probably got a shot." Then
she and Tanya leapt up from the table and raced to the door.

Meg asked, "Who's Juny?"

"Juny is my brother, Oscar Junior," Nikki said as she
piled Deidre's and Tanya's trays onto her own.

"You have a brother?" Meg asked, searching the cafeteria for a male version of Nikki. "Is he here?"

Her friend shook her head. "Nope. He's a senior. Different lunch."

"A senior?" Meg felt her pulse begin to quicken. It was good to date someone a little bit older, she told herself. Jen always did.

"You want to see a picture of him?"

"Uh, sure."

The girls stopped at Nikki's locker, which was covered on the inside with photos of Nikki and her boyfriends and girlfriends and family and pets.

"Wow," Meg gasped, taking in the collage. Her own locker was bare of any personality.

Nikki caught her gaping and grinned. "Kind of a lot, huh? What's in yours?"

"Well, you know, the usual stuff," Meg stuttered. "I haven't had much of a chance to get things up." She made a mental note to bring some pictures from *People* tomorrow. "Is this all your family?"

"That's my *mami* and *papi* at *mami's* fortieth this year." Nikki gestured to a young-looking couple, posing in front of a restaurant. "That's my baby sister, Mariela." A six-year-old with big dark eyes and a shy smile. "You know Deidre and Tanya. That's my friend Gaby who moved away. This is Keesha and Scott and Lisa and David. You've seen them around. And this was our cat, Whitney J.Lo, 'cause she was such a diva. She got hit last summer."

Meg was, as usual with Nikki, overwhelmed. There was a sheer abundance about her: clothes, hair, body, friends, family. And yet she seemed perfectly capable of keeping track of it all. Like a Scout leader or an army commander, Nikki appeared to know where everyone and everything was at all times.

There was also a sense of permanence about the pictures in Nikki's locker. They were the sign of someone who'd been there for years and who was sticking around for a while, a luxury Meg never had.

"That's him." Nikki pointed to a photo of a guy in a football uniform.

"You're not serious," Meg said, her eyes locking onto the picture. Juny's blue-black hair was tousled and shiny, like his sister's, and his chin was dimpled. He reminded Meg of Keanu Reeves, except chiseled and built. *Whoa, dude.*

"He's gorgeous," she breathed.

"He's not bad, I guess. Wanna meet him?"

Meg searched her friend's face for a sign she was having a laugh. "Are you kidding? He could be an Abercrombie model."

"Um, no. He's way too smart for that."

Meg smirked. "Yeah, sure, fix me up," she said with a sarcastic drawl. "Get yourself a date with Leonardo DiCaprio while you're at it and we'll double."

Nikki closed her locker door and spun the dial with a practiced flip of her wrist. "Hey. Big party. My house. Friday after Christmas. He'll be there. You'll be there. See what happens."

Meg couldn't remember ever having been invited to a party that didn't involve a clown and Pin the Tail on the Donkey. "Okay, great. Thanks."

"Come on, we'll be late for study hall, and then we'll have to sit in the front with the Ramirez twins." Nikki stuck out her tongue and crossed one eye.

The two marched down the center of the hallway toward study hall. When Meg was alone in this sea of people, it was a desperate, breathless scramble to get to class. With Nikki, it felt like being with Moses. She raised a delicate hand and the masses parted before them.

"So tell me, seriously, what would you like for Christmas?" Nikki asked.

"I'm sort of not used to celebrating Christmas, really." Meg hoped that didn't sound too lame. Was she assuming her new friend was a New Friend too quickly?

"Oh, okay."

Meg hastened to explain. "Lucie and I never had much money, so we usually ended up making something for each other or having a special dinner or something."

"You made things? Like what?"

Had Meg told anyone—Reggie or even Jen—about this before? "Well, uh . . . this one year, Lucie was into scarves, you know, the silk ones you wear around your head, like to protect your hairdo? She saw Reese Witherspoon with one in this movie and . . . anyway, I couldn't afford to get her a brand-new one, so I went to a thrift store and I got a bunch of men's handkerchiefs, the little square ones? And I sewed them all together and made her one big scarf . . . for around her head."

Lord, how lame-sounding was *that*? While Lucie was able to come up with cool and original crafts, like the Scrabble-piece necklace she made for Meg one year (the wooden tiles were glued side by side, spelling out her name), that silk scarf was the best of the gifts Meg had concocted. There were also the macaroni angels that attracted roaches, the barrettes she pasted sequins and sparkles to that fell apart when clipped to actual hair, and, the cream of the crop, the string anklet that got caught on Lucie's heel the second day she wore it and sent her sprawling face-first onto the sidewalk. Compared to those gifts, the scarf was, hands down, the best thing Meg would ever create in her lifetime.

And that was seriously busted.

Meg stared at the tiled floor. "You know. Whatever."

"You *made* a scarf? That is so awesome."

"Huh? Really?"

"I am crazy impressed. I wish I could be less materialistic like you and your mom." Nikki laughed. "But I like *things*, you know? I can't help it."

No one ever said Meg didn't want things. She just never *had* them.

She was on the verge of explaining this when Nikki shook her head. "God, I can't believe I just told you that. I sound like a Hilton sister."

"Ew. Not a chance." Meg paused ever so slightly as they

passed the trophy case and her father's photo. "But I'll warn you if you're getting close."

"*Chica*, why do you keep stopping to look at that case?" Nikki asked, pulling Meg along. "Come on. If we're late, you're sitting next to the ugly Ramirez."

"They're identical," Meg said. "How can one be uglier than the other?"

The bell rang and the girls picked up the pace.

Nikki winked. "You'd be surprised."

It was just before Christmas when Alma announced her intention to be "cleansed." This meant attending confession with Father Flammia. Meg, wanting to be a dutiful granddaughter and a helpful niece, escorted Alma to St. Ambrose's Catholic Church a few blocks from home. This wasn't as bad as it sounded. She and her grandmother had, she believed, settled into a quiet—very quiet—groove.

Once her eyes adjusted to the maroon light of the church, Meg saw stretched out before her one long aisle leading up to the altar, separating two sets of pews, and a gigantic naked Jesus nailed to a cross. His privates were politely covered with a torn cloth, and there was plaster blood dripping from his head, hands, and side.

Kind of gross. Yet Meg had a hard time tearing her gaze from it.

She escorted her grandmother to the confessional and left her walker at the edge of a pew, then tiptoed to the back of the church. From there, she watched a couple of elderly ladies hobble together to the votive candles beneath a plaster statue of the Virgin Mary with a plaster baby Jesus in her arms, wrapped in plaster swaddling clothes.

One of the ladies stood beside the table while her friend deposited coins in the locked change box, lit a candle with a long thin stick, and then braced herself against the other woman to kneel and bend her head in prayer. In this way, they took turns praying as they moved from statue to statue.

Meg pulled the padded maroon vinyl kneeler down and took a place in one of the pews. She bent her head before the altar, before Jesus, before God. Lucie had never taught her to pray, had never taken her to church. All Meg knew about Mass or what was conventionally known as "services" she had gleaned from television, and even that was only the random flicker of an image as she passed by *Touched by an Angel* or *7th Heaven* on her way to Jen and the gang.

Dear Jesus, she thought as she stared hard at the plaster son of God at the head of the church. *Can you give me a father for Christmas?*

No, that was a letter to Santa, she realized, not the Lord.

Dear Jesus, she started again, *I didn't know I was supposed to be a Catholic, but I think I could be a good one. I think I'm pretty kind, and I'd give money to charities if I had money to give. And I don't discriminate against people, which means I'm tolerant, although I'm not sure that's a prerequisite for Catholicism.*

She shook her head; scratch all that.

Dear Jesus . . .

The Lord's palms, held open in sacrifice, had been pierced through the center with crude, jagged nails. Sacrifice. For others. That was a pretty solid message.

Dear Jen . . . I think I might try the Catholic Church. What do you think?

She heard a gentle, masculine cough and turned to see an elderly priest struggling to help Alma back to her walker. She hurried to help him out.

"Thank you, Father," Alma was saying. She pulled Meg closer to her. "This is my granddaughter," she said proudly. "Margaret Anne."

"Call me Meg."

The priest, a plump, pale-complected man with solemn eyes, held out his hand. "A pleasure to meet you, Meg. I'm Father Flammia."

Meg stared at the man's hand hanging in the holy air. Was she allowed to touch a priest? Would he be unclean afterward and have to wash his hands in Pope-blessed water?

"Margaret Anne," Alma whispered sharply. "Shake the man's hand."

"Oh, I'm sorry," Meg said. "I . . . you're . . . I mean, I'm not clean."

"I beg your pardon?" Father Flammia smiled.

"That's enough," Alma said. "We'll see you at Christmas Mass, Father."

Outside, Meg was surprised to see Alma buoyant, uplifted, as if confessing her sins had legitimately removed a weight from her shoulders. *You are absolved, my child,* Meg imagined the good Father Flammia saying. *Go out and sin again.*

"I don't imagine you have much to confess at your age," Alma said.

"No, not yet," Meg answered truthfully.

Alma fixed a hard gaze on her. "You do know what sins you must confess, don't you?"

"I've got the drift of it pretty much. Murder, adultery, theft, that sort of cr—stuff." Meg smiled. "Don't you worry. I haven't done any of those things."

They walked in silence for the next block. Meg started thinking again about joining the church. She was pretty sure Nikki and her family attended regularly, which might mean that if she went to Mass, she'd get to see Nikki's brother, Juny, all dressed up. Was that reason enough to join?

"There are other ways we disappoint our Lord," Alma said, continuing the line of conversation. "Smaller sins that may not appear to be as evil as murder and adultery but that are just as destructive. *Wanting* murder is a sin too. I was afraid the Lord would never forgive me for that, which is why I stayed away from Him for so many years. Your mother did some very evil things that destroyed many people's lives, Margaret Anne. She should have confessed her sins, but she didn't. Hell awaits the man who has not confessed before God." Alma stopped in the middle of the intersection, and Meg noticed her hands were barely touching the walker's rubber handles. "I am here to make sure you don't follow in your mother's path." Her eyes clouded over, and she looked beyond Meg, beyond the intersection.

One step ahead of you, Alma, Meg thought. "Don't worry. I am nothing, *nothing* like that woman."

Alma nodded, and then a car honked, reminding them where they were standing, and Meg guided her grandmother out of the street.

Chapter
TWELVE

If a person was ever in need of a ladies' room while roaming the Upper East Side of Manhattan, it was Meg's considered opinion that person should immediately take herself to Bloomingdale's, where the women's lounge looked like it was lifted from the queen's quarters in Buckingham Palace. She was fairly certain that, had *Friends* actually filmed in the store when Rachel was an employee there, they could have shot entire scenes in the ladies' room.

Meg really would have liked to purchase her Christmas gifts at Bloomingdale's, but everything in the store was so expensive. She could only afford to use the facilities, and barely that.

So after a quick stop to refresh—and to apply a liberal dollop of complimentary hand cream—she hightailed it to

Chinatown, where she bought her grandmother a pair of silk slippers, her uncle a lacquer pen set, and two pseudo-jade hair combs for Nikki, the green being the perfect complement to Nikki's eyes.

Meg could hardly believe she had a list of gifts to buy! She, who had never before had a list, now had one with three people on it. She could just imagine the reactions her gifts would get. Lonnie would smile appreciatively and place the handsome set of pens on his desk. Nikki would squeal, "*Querida*, you shouldn't have!" and immediately wear the combs in her hair. And her grandmother would silently acknowledge Meg's good taste and slip her sad old feet into the shoes. That would be so sweet.

She considered sending a little something to Aaron in LA, an acknowledgment of the Christmas card he had sent her the day before. It was one of those groovy hippie "Peace on Earth" cards that was perfectly suited to a guy like Aaron. On the inside, he had written a note: *Thinking of you and hoping you're happy. We miss you.*

"We" like they were still a couple, Meg had thought, although the card was signed by Aaron alone.

Meg finished her shopping and exited a crowded Chinese market onto Canal Street. She had been practicing her "street face" (not so different from her "subway face") whenever she went wandering. It seemed to her that New Yorkers inherently possessed an attitude of utter boredom, that they could walk at a brisk pace without ever seeing anyone—however noteworthy or outrageous they might be—in their paths. She was close to that. If not boredom, then at least Meg was able to project an air of detachment while inside she was thinking, *Oh my God, I'm doing this! I am actually walking in New York City on my own!*

That very thought was running through Meg's head when she felt something land on her faux-detached face. She looked up. Drifting from the sky were thousands upon thousands of snowflakes: fat ones, thin ones, wet, dry, square, round, all cold. Very cold. They tingled as they fell onto her skin, melted when they hit her jacket.

From somewhere deep in the recesses of her genetic memory—or maybe she had just seen it done so many times on TV—she held her face to the sky and stuck out her tongue. It took a couple of tries before she could get a flake to land, but oh, when it finally happened! Snow, glorious snow!

Standing at the mud-ugly corner of Canal and Broadway, being brushed aside by rush-hour pedestrians, she wondered about her fellow New Yorkers, jaded by years of nasty blizzards and heart-attack-high snowdrifts. Like the combs in her pocket, Meg knew that they were fake jaded, pretend jaded, and that they secretly longed for the childhood innocence of a snowflake on an upturned tongue.

In no time at all, a thin layer of white had blanketed the kebab cart near the bank and the counterfeit Prada bags on the corner. With the drop of every frosty flake, beauty gradually returned to Canal Street. Meg silently wondered if this was what it had looked like when the first pound of concrete was poured more than a century past. The area even smelled better, cleaner, newer as the snow fell. Meg wanted to hug every person she saw, from the woman hawking sticks of sandalwood incense to the stern-faced cop on the beat.

Snow meant winter and holidays and kids on their best behavior. It was the excuse for hot chocolate with gobs of marshmallow crème and thick stews with biscuits and loads of butter. It was why people wore mittens and fur-lined boots and neoprene socks, why they wrapped scarves around turtlenecks and tucked gloved hands inside muffs.

The main reason to go *into* the snow was to *come out* of the snow.

Meg, the former desert girl, rejoiced and clapped frozen un-mittened, un-gloved hands in the falling flakes. If she had been a different sort of person, she would have held her arms out and twirled. But as it was, this was enough. Just Meg and her presents for the people she loved.

And snow, glorious snow.

Chapter
THIRTEEN

'Twas the night before Christmas, and earlier in the day, Lonnie had brought home a fragrant Douglas fir, small but perfect in shape.

He set it up in its metal stand, then tried to sneak out right after dinner.

"Where are you going?" Meg asked, even though she already knew: her uncle spent so much time with his friend Tony, she wondered if she should start using quotation marks around the word "friend."

Then again, there were the *Playboy*s and Polaroids in the bottom drawer of his desk.

"Tony's store," he answered.

"It's open on Christmas Eve?"

"Last-minute gifts."

Somehow Meg doubted L-shaped sectionals and cherry-stained dinette sets were at the top of most people's wish lists. Lonnie paused at the door and pulled his jacket collar up above his ears. "When I get back, we'll decorate the tree together."

Meg smiled. *That would be perfect.*

Just then, an earsplitting shriek sounded from the kitchen, followed by the clatter of falling dishes and silverware. Meg and Lonnie rushed in to find Alma on the floor, on her side, with both hands clutching a soapy pan.

Meg reached Alma first and tried to help her up, but the woman shook her off.

"Lonnie," she beseeched her son. "Help me, please."

"Is anything broken?" Meg asked. Her grandmother ignored her.

"Lonnie, *please.*"

Lonnie pulled a chair from the table and moved it closer to Alma; then he helped her to a sitting position. "Come on, lean on my shoulder," he said, offering his mother his arm. Meg came around the other side and lifted Alma by the elbow. On three, they hefted her to the chair. Lonnie adjusted his mother's pink wig and wiped some soap off her hands.

"What were you doing?" he asked.

"I was just trying to help out," she whispered. "I don't want to be a burden."

"You're not a burden, Mother," Lonnie said with a wink to Meg. "But you are exasperating sometimes." He stood up and brushed his pants with his palms. "Okay, I'm off. I'll see you later."

"Where are you going?" his mother cried.

"I have to work."

"What? Wait! Lonnie, no, don't leave," Alma said.

Lonnie stopped and sighed. "I'm late."

"You have to take me to midnight Mass."

He quickly shot down her request. "Mother, how can you expect to attend Mass with all of those people? You can barely move around here. You just *fell* washing a dish."

"Tradition, Lonnie. Don't you have any respect for your heritage?"

"What's gotten into you? First you drag Meg to confession and now—"

"It's Christmas Mass."

"Good Lord, Mother. I'll take you tomorrow."

"Blasphemer!" Alma spat, then she began to cry.

"Meg," Lonnie said, ignoring his mother. "There's another box of ornaments in the basement. Go look for them, please."

"Can I get them later?" she asked, casting a worried look at her grandmother.

"Trust me," Lonnie said, "it's going to take a while. Try under the staircase in the blue trunk. Meg, please? Now?"

She glanced at Alma. A fall like that was probably frightening for an old woman. She looked back at Lonnie; his expression hadn't changed. "All right."

Meg felt their deliberate silence while she made her way

through the kitchen and downstairs. As soon as she was out of range, Lonnie's muffled voice sounded, deep and resonant, but with too much bass for her to hear clearly.

The basement, it turned out, was a sty, with everything from Costco-size packages of toilet paper to stacks of old newspapers and magazines. And it had an odd smell, like a combination of Lysol and mushrooms. And bleu cheese. And moldy cardboard. Lonnie was right: it took her a while just to get to the trunk under the staircase. She wondered if this errand was an excuse to get her out of the kitchen, if Lonnie thought he was protecting her from a family argument. Truth be told, she wanted to hear it all. This was her family, after all, and she wanted to be a part of it.

The trunk was painted a robin's egg blue, the color of a Southern California sky after a February rain. It had been a child's toy chest, as the teddy bears and drums stenciled on the sides attested. Meg sighed and lifted the lid. This must have been Lonnie's, for it contained typical boy-type items: a well-thumbed book of dirty jokes circa 1988, copies of *Die Hard* and *Die Hard 2* on VHS. A few old concert T-shirts.

A handmade card: *TO MY FAVORITE BROTHER*, it declared in giant capital letters in red ink on thick construction paper. On the inside: *Happy Birthday to Us!* And below that, *Love, your twin, Lucie Shanley*. There was no date on the card, but Lucie couldn't have been more than five or six when she wrote it, with assistance, Meg assumed, from Alma. Meg held the card by its edge as if it were an ancient artifact. Was there a corresponding one in

Lucie's collection, she wondered, from brother to sister?

Doubtful. Lucie didn't care about family. She'd probably thrown it away years ago.

Meg put the card back in the trunk and continued on.

A high school yearbook: 1995.

Another: 1994.

A third: 1993.

And . . . *The Guardian.* RFK High. Class of 1992. Embossed maroon pleather. Gold-stamped spine.

My father is in there, Meg thought. Nathaniel Holland. Class of 1992.

Her heart chug-chugged as she held the book in her hands. She gently lifted the cover with two fingers, revealing the glossy front sheet. There was a drawing of a Greek warrior, with one hand on his sheathed blade and the other on his muscled thigh. This was RFK's mascot, its Guardian.

There was the name of the principal in 1992, and the vice principal, and the editor of the yearbook, and the yearbook staff for that same year.

Uh-huh, uh-huh. Okay, good. See? Meg could turn the page gently, without ripping to the back, without losing her cool. Oh, there was page two and a photo of the school in 1992; look at how many more trees there were back then and fewer bars on the windows and—

Get on with it! Meg's brain screamed.

It was no use resisting that brain. Meg found the sports photos first, found the football team. It was the shot that was in the trophy case, only in black and white, and her father—her *father*!—looked paler, more washed out without color. There were a lot of names at the bottom, and Meg counted over . . . fourth from the left, top row . . . *N. Holland*. There it was. Right there in black and white, Helvetica typeface. Italics. Her father. And now, Meg had her own picture of him.

She flipped rapidly through the individual photos, found the *F*s—Forrester, Franco, Fuqua. The *G*s were next—Glassman, Girardi, Gutierrez. The *H*s—Hessel, Hill, Horshowitz . . . no, back, back . . . Holland.

Holland.

Nathaniel Holland.

Nate.

And there . . . his graduation photo. Dark wavy hair, longer than in the team photo. Dimples in both cheeks. A cleft in his chin and dark eyes. He looked smart and smooth-skinned and popular. He had a friendly look about him, too, like if you asked him where there was a gas station, he would tell you and not send you off on a wild-goose chase across town. And honest, too, like if you dropped something that was worth more than a couple of bucks, he'd pick it up and give it to you and not try to hook it. Meg knew that if he stepped out of this square and off the page, she would find him charming.

"Hello there," he would say in a wishing-well-deep voice. "My name is Nate, and it's my greatest pleasure to meet you."

"How do you do," she would say right back. "I'm Meg Shanley."

"What a lovely name."

"I'm glad you like it. I'm your daughter, although you never met me."

"But I knew you existed," he'd say, and brush a calloused hand through his waves. "I knew you were somewhere, and I've been waiting to meet you."

Meg would blush. "Well, here I am."

"You look exactly like I thought you would," he'd say with a smile. "You're beautiful."

"Just like you."

"You have my eyes."

"Your eyes."

"And my smile."

"Your smile."

"And you're tall and muscular and athletic—"

"Not really into sports."

"—just like me."

"Yes, just like you."

And he'd stare at her for a long time, drinking her in, imprinting her image on his frontal lobe, and then they would smile identical smiles, think identical thoughts: *We are now complete.*

"Meg?" Lonnie's voice came, calling her back to the real world. "Are you okay down there?"

"Fine." She hastily shoved the yearbook back in among the momentos from Lonnie's lost childhood.

A step on the stairs, then two, coming closer.

She met him at the base of the staircase. "Hey."

"I'm gonna stick around for a little while longer. Till your grandmother feels better." His eyes were searching the basement—looking for something? "So much crap down here. Sometimes I forget the things we have shoved into the nooks and crannies." His gaze caught hers and held it. Those blue eyes, open and sincere, reminding her of her first encounter with him in LA. He nodded, and then she nodded back, an understanding, unspoken. He knew. Had remembered the old yearbooks in the basement and sent her to the trunk on purpose.

Merry Christmas, Meg, his eyes said.

And what did hers say in return? Meg doubted that any expression could adequately convey her feelings at that moment.

Thank you, Lonnie. Thank you.

Chapter
FOURTEEN

Dear Jen,

How are you? I am fine.

It snowed last night, and the neighborhood looks like Disneyland in December, when they spray all this fake snow on the trees and junk and all the little kids pick it up and try to make snowballs with it but it just cracks in their hands and makes their skin smell like chemicals. Well, here it's real, and even if there isn't enough to make snowballs, at least you don't smell like plastic foam.

What a great Christmas! Lonnie and Alma gave me a ton of new clothes, which are perfect and which I love. Today we're going to Christmas Mass—my first time! I hope I don't mess up. I'll have to watch Lonnie for cues.

Do you think Lucie is spending Christmas alone, or is Aaron with *her? Sometimes I wonder if she got a new job, but she must have, because she always does, and if she's living in the same apartment. Then I wonder if she wonders about me, if she's thinking about what I'm doing.*

Like going to a big party! Lonnie said I could go to Nikki's house on Friday night. I don't know if he told Alma, but I can't imagine it'll be a big deal. Maybe I can wear one of my new outfits!

Xmas hugs!

m

"We sit on the inside aisle for Mass, Margaret Anne, sixth pew from the front," Alma said as Meg helped her up the handicapped entrance on the side of St. Ambrose's. "The Shanley family has always sat in the sixth pew from the front."

"That's not true, Mother," Lonnie said. "*You* always sat in the sixth pew."

"Your father did too."

"No, he didn't. He never went to church." Lonnie rolled his eyes. "Meg, your grandfather never went to Mass, regardless of what *she* says."

"We will sit in the sixth pew from the front, on the inside aisle," Alma stated. "Lonnie, adjust my hat. I can't attend Mass looking slovenly."

The old lady was actually the best-dressed of them all. She wore a wool suit with a chiffon blouse and, on her head, a squarish wool hat with a pearl-tipped pin stuck through the front flap.

Lonnie held the door open by its brass handle and ushered the ladies in. "Enjoy."

"Wait," Meg said. "Aren't you coming in?" Momentarily panicked, she sucked in a cold blast of air, freezing her lungs.

He shook his head and pulled a fresh cigarette out of his pack. "No thanks. I don't need to see the inside of that monstrosity until I'm lying in a coffin."

"But I don't know what I'm doing!" Meg protested.

"Just watch the old ladies in front," Lonnie said with a laugh. "That's what everyone else does."

And then he let go of the door and they were swallowed by darkness.

"The sixth pew from the front," Alma whispered loudly. "On the—"

"Inside aisle, yes, I know."

The church had been decorated for this day, ostensibly the Lord's birthday, with red and white potted poinsettias and green garlands and white candles burning everywhere. It was a veritable fire hazard, and Meg hoped this day wouldn't end in a crush of human destruction should someone accidentally tip over one of the displays.

Up at the podium, off to the right, was Father Flammia, in white robes and a white satin scarf around his neck. It looked like a scarf to her, although it was probably something religious and not a regular neck-warming scarf at all. From the back of the church, she could hear about every other word:

"And . . . Lord . . . Christ . . . unto . . . people . . . and . . ."

Someone coughed, and she missed the next couple of syllables.

She counted six rows from the front and found the pew Alma was attached to. There were already a dozen or so people sitting on each side, spread out comfortably.

"How about this row instead?" Meg suggested, pointing at one of the back rows. "It only has two people in it, and we could sit on the inside like you want."

"No. The sixth pew from the front."

The whole of the congregation was complacently smiling and nodding as the priest intoned from the altar. A few of the younger kids were staring off into space or at the stained glass windows or paging ahead through the hymnals. Generations of families surrounded her: parents with teens and toddlers and babies, and grandparents, and kids home from college for a holiday visit.

And behold, on the other side of the church, sitting in the fourth row from the front, was Nikki and her family. *Nuyorican*, Nikki had called herself once before, her father Puerto Rican and her mother Irish. Catholic, no matter how she sliced it. She was dressed in a subdued wool sweater set and a floor-length skirt, Meg noticed when they all stood up to recite something or other. Her silky hair was tied back in a ponytail, and she wore very little makeup. Beside her was a young girl, and they shared a hymnal as they sang.

That must be her sister, Mariela, Meg thought.

To Nikki's right were her parents, and on the far end—

oh! Juny, Nikki's older brother, even better-looking than the photo in Nikki's locker.

Meg's heart fluttered as she stared at Oscar Junior: like a male version of his sister, his hair shone in the sunlight and his perfect skin glowed. But unlike his sister's skin, his was darker, more olive, and his hair blacker. His shoulders were broad and muscular, filling out his Sunday suit like a mannequin in a shop window.

Damn.

The combination of incense and warm bodies was making Meg light-headed. She tried to think of something else. How about her favorite holiday *Friends* episode? The one where Ross and Monica danced at the New Year's Rockin' Eve party but it was, like, weeks in advance and they were the oldest ones there and completely lame? That was a good one.

Ross and Monica were Jewish, Meg remembered that, but it hardly ever came up. They never talked about going to temple or how they couldn't eat certain foods like pork, and Ross never wore one of those beanies. Meg used to think Rachel was Jewish, like the Gellers, but, like the other Friends, she never got religious at all.

The scene where Monica and Ross did the dance they had choreographed when they were teenagers, only now they were thirty and even dorkier, popped into Meg's head. Hilarious! She tried to hold her giggles until everyone was shaking hands. *Peace be with you and you and you.*

At Mass's end, the congregation boisterously filed out of

the church, liberated for another few days for some, another year for most. As they exited, Meg spotted the Hernandez family at the side door and tried to look pious when she saw Nikki wave to her.

"Hi, Nikki!" She kissed her friend on the cheek. "Are these your parents? Hello, Mr. and Mrs. Hernandez. I'm Meg Shanley."

"Hello, Meg," Nikki's mom said.

Nikki's dad nodded quickly and headed down the steps to meet Oscar Junior. Meg watched them go, disappointed.

"Hi, Mrs. Shanley. I'm Nikki Hernandez. This is my sister, Mariela, and my mom, Kathleen."

"That's not a spic name," Alma said.

Meg's heart just about stopped beating altogether, and she could feel her cheeks burn. "Oh my God . . ."

Mrs. Hernandez's smile slipped ever so slightly—as if she'd heard such a slur before, but not in a long, long time. "Hello, Mrs. Shanley." She smiled pleasantly. "Are you new to our parish? We're here every week, and I'm not sure I've ever seen you before."

Alma huffed and shuffled her walker toward Father Flammia.

"Isn't *she* charming?" Nikki's mother said when Alma was a few steps away.

"Oh my gosh, I'm so sorry—"

"It's okay, Meg. Can't teach an old dog, as they say. Why don't you go talk to Nikki while your grandmother and I have at it?"

"Are you—"

"I'm teasing. Go, go."

Nikki and Meg stepped off the main walkway to the side of the church. Mariela clung stubbornly to her sister's arm.

"Where'd your brother go?" Meg asked Nikki, trying to play it cool and casual.

"Juny? Why?" Nikki asked with a sly smile.

"I just wondered."

"Want to put him on your wish list?"

"Maybe . . ."

"The party. Don't forget."

"You like Juny," sang Mariela.

"Shhh!"

"You like Juny!" The little girl pointed at Meg. "You like Juny!"

"Mariela, *chulita*, quiet!" Nikki said harshly.

"You like Juny," Mariela whispered.

"*Mija!* Stop or else Santa will come back and take away all your toys."

The little girl gasped and was quiet.

"So, what'd you get for Christmas?" Nikki asked. "Anything good?"

"This," Meg said, holding out her velvet skirt. "And a couple of sweaters."

"Cool! I got a new cell, which I totally needed, and this amazing leather jacket—"

"Nik! Mari! Let's go!" Mrs. Hernandez called her girls.

"We've got to get home to make dinner." Mariela dropped Nikki's hand and ran to her mother.

"It was nice to meet you," Meg told Nikki's mother politely.

"My pleasure," Mrs. Hernandez said. "I hope we'll see you on Friday." Then she shot Alma a faceful of daggers and left with her daughters.

As Nikki and her family disappeared into the crowd, Meg could feel her temper rising. "What did you say?" She whipped around to the old lady. "She was my first friend here, and it's Christmas! Couldn't you be nice?"

"They shouldn't be in this neighborhood. This neighborhood used to be civilized," Alma said a little too loudly for Meg's taste. "Now there's spics and coloreds—"

"Please be quiet!" Meg maneuvered her grandmother around the congregation. "We have to meet Lonnie." She guided her grandmother down the handicap ramp, stopping halfway down to close her coat.

"Who . . . is *that*?" Alma froze.

Meg turned and followed her grandmother's gaze. There, down by the sidewalk, was Lonnie . . . and his girl. Meg recognized her from the pictures, Lonnie's own Miss December. She was in her early twenties, a little rough-edged, with brassy highlights in her shoulder-length blond hair. She would be pretty, Meg thought, model pretty, Jennifer Aniston pretty, if her skirt wasn't quite so snug around her ample behind, if her top didn't reveal quite so much cleavage, and maybe if she used a lighter touch with the Wet 'n' Wild products.

Two little boys raced across Meg's path and laughingly fell on top of each other at Lonnie's feet. Not missing a beat, he reached down and scooped one up in each hand and cradled them under his arms like footballs. They squealed with delight.

Alma was aghast. She grabbed onto Meg's hand, her rosary digging into Meg's skin. As if he sensed them watching, Lonnie's head turned and he stared back.

"I think that's Lonnie's girlfriend," Meg said.

"Nonsense," Alma said. "Lonnie doesn't have a girlfriend."

"Um . . . I think he does."

"Let's go, Margaret Anne, let's go."

"But Lonnie's expecting—"

"I'm not waiting for *him*."

Meg cast a glance over her shoulder as she and Alma walked away. She watched as Lonnie dropped to the ground and rolled in the snow while the boys pelted him with snowballs. He looked happy.

In the days following Christmas, leading up to the party, Meg received no fewer than a dozen calls from the girls to coordinate wardrobes. In one, Nikki announced her plan to wear a green cashmere-blend V-necked sweater with a matching knee-length skirt and black boots so the others could work around it. For Meg, Nikki liked the velvet skirt and sweater set that she said made Meg look like a holiday Gap ad. During a conference call, Deidre and Tanya said they intended to wear low riders and cropped turtle-neck sweaters, which Nikki vetoed as far too trashy. All the while, Meg just smiled at her phone, amazed and thrilled that these calls were coming for *her*. Would the Christmas gifts never end?

By the time Meg made her grand entrance at the party in the Nikki-approved velvet outfit, the Hernandezes' brick-face row house was packed from top to bottom, front door to back. Meg found her friend, the gracious hostess, in the kitchen.

"You do this every year?" Meg said, not once but twice to Nikki, the second time a little louder to make herself heard above the din.

"It's kind of what my parents are known for."

Deidre and Tanya popped up in front of them. Both were in tasteful longish skirts and flowered blouses from Anthropologie. Evidently, they had given in to their hostess's request for decorum, although they were wearing three-inch spike heels that, Meg thought, couldn't have been easy to walk in on icy concrete.

"We're going out to the patio," Tanya said. "I think Jason's out there."

"Don't do anything stupid," Nikki warned. "You know how those boys gossip." She turned to Meg. "You want something to drink?" A bowl of punch sat on the kitchen table along with pitchers of eggnog and cases of soda. "*Mami* makes the best nog." She handed Meg a cup of thick, creamy eggnog. It was yummy, like dessert.

"It looks like the whole school is here—with their parents," Meg said. "How do you manage that?"

"My parents are, like, really cool. People don't mind hanging with them." Nikki gestured with her cup. "You could have brought your uncle if you wanted."

"He's home with my grandmother."

"You could have brought her too." Nikki looked at Meg, and the two burst out laughing.

"Yeah, right," Meg said.

Nikki headed into the living room, where they didn't have to shout; Meg followed. "Is she your mom's mom or your dad's?"

"My . . . mother's." Meg nearly choked on the word.

"And she's the one in Hollywood, right?"

Meg nodded.

"Is she there for work or what?"

Meg almost spilled her nog on that question. The idea of Lucie being anywhere for work was crazy. "Uh, no. No, she's not."

"She's not an actress or anything?"

Okay, she really was going to have to put her glass down if she wanted to continue this conversation with Nikki. "She's not, no."

"Is your dad there too?"

"Wow," Meg marveled. "You ask a lot of questions."

Nikki covered her mouth with her hand. "I'm sorry. Juny tells me that too."

Meg laughed to show no harm was done. "It's fine. It's

just . . . my family is a really long and complicated story."

"Gotcha."

Meg remembered Nikki's present in her pocket and was glad for the diversion. "I have something for you." She pulled out the box and handed it to Nikki. "Merry Christmas."

"Yay!" Nikki said. "I have something for you too."

The two exchanged their gifts and carefully unwrapped them.

"Ooh!" Nikki exclaimed. "Pretty!" She held the combs up to the light. "I love them. Thank you, sweetie!"

Whew, Meg thought, relieved she had made a good choice. "I thought they'd look good with your eyes. Since they're green and all."

"Perfect! Now you open yours."

Meg opened her box and found a pair of brushed metal hoop earrings with tiny freshwater pearls dangling from them. "They're . . . beautiful."

"They match your ring! Right? Here, hold up your hand."

Save for the diamonds, it was an amazingly close match.

"You noticed," Meg said, a note of wonder in her voice. "Thank you."

"Well, jeez, you wear it every day," Nikki said. The two girls hugged, and then Nikki lowered her voice, although there was no one in the immediate vicinity. "I told Juny all about you, and he totally wants to meet you."

"He does?"

"You want to meet him now?" Nikki looked around the living room. "He's probably out on the patio with the guys. Come on."

Meg stood still. "Now?" *Whoa.*

"Sure. You look fantastic." Nikki grabbed her by the arm and pulled her through the kitchen. They were stopped by Mrs. Hernandez at the door to the patio.

"Nikki, sweetie, would you help me make more eggnog?" She touched Meg's cheek with hers. "Meg, welcome. Juny's on the patio."

Meg shot her friend a look. Did *everyone* know?

"Nik, please. The nog."

Nikki pushed Meg closer to the patio. "Go on," she whispered. "I'll be there in a second."

Meg stopped. Juny was at the center of a group of men and boys, holding court, telling jokes. His hair shone under the moonlight, and his eyes sparkled. As he raised a glass of soda to his lips, she could see, actually *see*, his muscles rippling beneath his shirt. *Oh God,* she thought. *Oh God, oh God, oh God.*

She spotted Deidre and Tanya hanging out in a corner of the patio. That would be her goal, she thought. She just had to get to those girls. She smoothed down her skirt, took the opportunity to wipe off her sweaty hands, and pasted on a smile.

Then she walked straight into the sliding glass door. Her forehead made a loud thud, and every person on the patio turned to look at the idiot girl who couldn't manage to see a door right in front of her.

Everyone looked, including Juny.

Meg hastily backtracked through the kitchen past Nikki and her mother.

"I'm just gonna step outside for a minute," she told them, rushing out before they could follow.

You moron, she told herself, *you're so clumsy.*

She drifted down the steps and felt the night air cool her flushed cheeks. The street was empty, and Meg was alone. Which only made sense—practically the whole neighborhood was inside the Hernandez home, drinking eggnog and ho-ho-ho-ing.

Dear Jen, Meg thought. *I really screwed up this time. I wish you were here. You would know what to do.*

Meg touched the spot on her forehead that had smacked into the glass. It was tender already, and the skin felt puffy beneath her fingers. *Please don't swell up,* she thought, *please don't show everyone what an idiot I was tonight.* She stared up at the house. What should she do now? Go back inside? Sneak home without her coat?

In the absence of Jen, Meg knew she'd have to find an answer on her own. She looked out past the front yard, squinted hard, and imagined Jennifer Aniston strolling toward her from the street.

In Meg's mind, Jen paused at the iron gate and leaned against it, her perfect figure framed in a moonlit silhouette. *What would Jen be wearing on a night like this?* Meg wondered. Probably low-rise jeans and a short-sleeve T-shirt layered over a long-sleeve one—because Jen looked awesome all casual like that—with her hands tucked into her back pockets.

And she'd smile. "Hey, Meg. Ask me anything you want. That's what I'm here for."

Yes, Meg thought, *if she were here, Jen would say something exactly like that.*

"God, I don't even want to tell you what I just did." Meg groaned, shaking her head. "Nikki is never going to ask me over again, and Juny . . . well, maybe it's a good thing he doesn't know who I am."

Jen's brow would furrow in concern. "Oh, honey, it can't be that bad. Tell me how I can help."

Meg took a deep breath. "Okay, see, I don't know what to do in there. I'm not . . . I'm just not used to these types of people. I've never been part of the cool clique."

Jen would nod then, cross her arms over her chest, and ask, "Why's that?"

"Well—because the people who want to be my friends are usually the outcast types, the ones without friends, and since I move around so much, I can't be choosy, you know? I take what I can get."

Jen would tilt her head to one side as she considered, the moonlight making the ends of her hair glow like an angel's. "I think you're shortchanging yourself. There's no reason you can't have what you want instead of taking only what you can get. This is a different situation from LA, don't you think?"

"What do you mean?"

"You *chose* to come here, to Queens. Maybe this time *you* get to choose your friends." Jen's smile would be brilliant.

Meg's spirit lifted at the thought. "You think?"

"Why wouldn't these girls want to be your friends? Why wouldn't they want you to have a boyfriend?"

"The question is, why *would* they?"

"Because you're amazing and smart and pretty," Jen would say. Then she would hold Meg by the shoulders, her voice growing serious. "Honey, Nikki likes you. They all like you, and they want you here. You're no different from any of them, no better or worse."

"But what will I talk about? What will I *say*? Especially after this." Meg pointed to the lump forming on her head.

"Relax," Jen would instruct. "Take a deep breath. And just . . . be yourself. Talk about what you know. You'll do fine."

"Really?"

"Don't I know you better than anyone?"

"Yeah."

"So trust me. Now go, enjoy the party. And don't forget to introduce yourself to Juny."

"Juny . . ." Meg sighed.

"Yes?"

Meg turned and saw Nikki's brother standing at the bottom of the steps. Was he a mirage too? Had she wished him into existence the way she had wished for Jen?

Meg stared. Puffs of warm air came out of Juny's mouth as he breathed. He smiled.

No, he wasn't imagined. He was real, very real.

"Hey there, Hollywood."

Meg returned his grin. "Hi. Most people call me Meg."

"Meg . . ." Juny said the name, then was silent, as if letting it sink in. "Are you cold? Here." He laid his jacket across her shoulders, a varsity jacket with a gigantic white *K* over the left breast with two smaller letters, *R* and *F*, stitched on top. It was warm and smelled like Polo cologne.

"Then *you'll* be cold," she said, although he'd have to rip that jacket off her now; she had grown instantly, irrationally attached to it in the five seconds she had been wearing it.

"Nah. I'm used to it." He stuck his hands in his jeans pockets. "So, what? You don't like our party? You'd rather freeze outside in our front yard?"

Meg started to object but quickly realized he was joking. She smiled. "No, I just needed a little fresh air. Lots of people in there."

"Yeah, lots of people," he agreed. "Lots of invisible doors."

"Oh, man," Meg moaned. "You saw me crack my head. I knew it." She shook her cracked head in dismay.

Juny laughed. "Do you have any idea how many times I've done that?"

"No, but *you* didn't do it in front of a million people."

Juny pursed his lips in thought. "True. Don't worry, though. Half those people are drinking the spiked eggnog. They won't remember a thing. Your reputation is safe."

Meg pointed to herself. "I have a reputation?"

"Sure. You're the smart girl from Hollywood."

This was news to Meg. "I'm . . . smart?"

"Smart's not good?"

She paused, thinking. "Smart's okay, but pretty's better."

Juny's cheeks flushed pink, as though he were embarrassed. *Oh my God*, Meg thought. *Where did that come from?*

"Pretty—got it," Juny said. "See? This is why my sister has to fix me up. I don't know how to talk to pretty girls."

Meg felt her own blush race from the ends of her hair down to her pinky toes. "Yeah, right," she said. "I don't believe *that* for a second."

Juny gave a coy grin—an expression that looked *so* cute on him, Meg thought. "So, you're new here?" he asked.

Meg nodded.

"Kinda rough coming in the middle of the year, huh?"

"Not really. This is my second new school in . . . three months? Yeah, three."

"What?" Juny squinted. "No way."

"Serious! I once did three schools in six months, back when I was in second grade."

Juny laughed. "Well, aren't you the badass."

"Yeah, I am." Meg grinned. "So don't mess me with me, *Oscar*."

Juny's eyebrows lifted in surprise. His brown eyes twinkled. "You know, not many people call me that and get away with it. But you're new, so I'll let it pass."

When Juny looked at her—with that killer smile and dimpled chin—she felt a jolt of electricity shoot through her. Did his gaze have this effect on all girls, she wondered, or was it just her? She struggled to regain her composure. To focus.

Talk about what you know, Jen had said.

"We, uh, we moved around a lot," Meg told him. "At least once a year. Except for Rancho Cucamonga. We were there for two whole years."

Juny chuckled. "Rancho Cucamonga? That is *not* a real place."

"It is!"

"Come on. You totally made that up."

Meg laughed too. It did *sound* made up, like a pretend town from a Bugs Bunny cartoon. "It's totally real," she insisted. "It has a Target and a baseball stadium and . . . strip malls. Okay, it's sort of lame. But it exists, I assure you."

"You going back?"

"Back where?"

"To LA."

Back to LA . . . back to Lucie, Meg thought. This was their first Christmas apart, their first everything apart, and Meg felt a twinge of sadness. She could afford to be kind: after all, she had so much here in Queens—a family and friends—while Lucie had nothing.

But then a picture, unbidden, popped into Meg's head. Lucie, in her bedroom, smoking a cigarette. Looking so cold—like stone.

"If you go, don't come back," she had said.

Am I going back? Meg wondered. She returned her attention to Juny. His expression was warm—and he was so considerate—the opposite of Lucie.

Meg's sadness left her. It was Lucie's own fault that she was alone.

She shook her head then and tried to be casual. "Nah. I'm here for good."

Juny nodded.

Was that nod a sign? she wondered. Was he happy she wasn't moving, or was it just, *Hey, that's cool?*

He sat down on one of the middle steps and stretched long legs in front of him. "You want to sit?"

Meg definitely wanted to sit next to Juny, to feel their arms casually touch and their legs brush against each other, but she also wanted to keep her brand-new velvet skirt ice- and dirt-free. She leaned against the metal railing instead. "I can stand."

"So what brought you to our magnificent city, Hollywood?"

"Oh, you know, family."

"That's cool. Family's cool." Juny slid his hands under his thighs to keep them warm. "Got any brothers or sisters?"

"Well . . ." Meg shook her head; Lucie didn't count—not anymore. "No."

"Oh, man, *lucky*," Juny said, but he said it with a smile. "Nikki and Mariela are all right, I guess. But they can be such a pain sometimes. At least I'm the only guy. I never had to share my room or my clothes or my dolls."

Meg did a double take. "Your *dolls*—"

"Just wanted to see if you were paying attention," Juny quipped.

"Oh." Meg smirked. "Is there gonna be a quiz later?"

"Maybe, Hollywood—"

"Hey, guys!" Nikki interrupted, calling from the top of the steps behind them. "Aren't you cold out here?"

Meg and Juny shared a glance and a shy smile.

"You have to come in, *mijo*, stat. Mom's getting out the videos from when we wanted to try out for *Idol*. We have to stop her."

Juny rolled his eyes. "A couple of eggnogs and my mother's ready to humiliate us all." He stood and walked beside Meg up the steps to the house.

"What's in the eggnog?" Meg asked.

"The spiked version has rum. Lots of rum." Juny made a face. "And by the way, *I* didn't want to audition for *Idol*. That was all Nikki's idea."

"I believe you," Meg replied, holding in a giggle. That video sounded to her about as embarrassing as someone walking into a patio door.

Juny held the wooden front door open for Meg and gestured for her to go inside. She stepped across the threshold and could hear the rest of the party in full swing, a marked contrast to the quiet time she and Juny had so recently shared. She hesitated, reluctant to enter and break the spell.

What if that was it for her and Juny? A one-time conversation that never happened again?

Beside her, she felt Juny pause too.

"Hey, Hollywood," he said. "Maybe I can give you a call sometime?"

Meg smiled. One thought flashed in her mind:

Merry Christmas, Meg!

Love, Jen

The trite phrase "walking on air" was something Meg never anticipated would enter her mind, land somewhere along her medulla oblongata and reside there for a good half hour or so, but reside it did as she floated home after the party at Nikki's.

She caught a glimpse of her reflection in a car mirror and was startled to see that she didn't look half bad this evening. In fact, one could say she was downright pretty. The pink in her sweater brought out the strawberry accents of her blond hair and the long velvet skirt clung gently to her curvy hips. Nothing wrong with curvy, she thought. Nothing wrong with her sweater, or her skirt, or life, the universe and everything in it, and . . .

Oh my God, what if Juny *didn't* call?

No, no. He said he would call, but there was no one around to witness it, was there? Nikki was already in the kitchen by that point, and all the guests were on the patio or in the living room, so there were no *witnesses*. His exact words were, "Maybe I can give you a call sometime."

Maybe . . . sometime. Did those words cancel out the good part of the sentence? She decided to write Jen and ask her.

Meg unlocked the front door of Alma's row house and heeled off her shoes. The light in the kitchen was on, and Meg could hear the sounds of utensils. She sniffed smoke. Her uncle must be home.

"Hey, Lonnie," she started to say. "I had the best time at—what the . . . ?" Her jaw opened in surprise. For there—*standing* at the kitchen stove—was Alma.

On the table was a tuna sandwich. At the back door was the walker.

And on the counter was a cigarette burning in an ashtray.

"Oh my God. What are you doing?"

Alma's head turned, and for a split second, Meg saw a look of guilt cross her grandmother's face. It disappeared quickly as the usual Alma face—cold and blank—returned.

"You can walk!" Meg shouted.

"Nonsense. I can't walk." Alma was leaning one hip against the counter, yet otherwise seemed to have no trouble balancing on her own. As she turned around to face Meg, one knee suddenly gave way. She buckled briefly, then steadied herself by gripping the edge of the countertop with her fingers.

Meg pointed at her grandmother's legs. "You're doing it. You're doing it right now! This is unbelievable!"

Alma responded by taking a drag off her cigarette.

"And you're *smoking*?" In that moment, Meg contemplated the incomprehensible: a woman with lung cancer, who had lost her hair from chemotherapy and was reduced to wearing a pink wig was smoking.

Alma's eyes bored into Meg's. "*You* were supposed to be here with me," she said accusingly, as if that were enough of an excuse.

Meg shook her head. "I went to a party. Lonnie said it was okay."

Alma made her voice high and mocking. "Lonnie said it was okay," she mimicked. And then, "Where were you? Where's Lonnie?"

She was trying to change the subject, Meg realized, trying to throw her off track, but Meg fought to get back to the topic at hand.

"You—you can take care of yourself just fine. You've been lying to me . . . to Lonnie," she said. "Why would you do that?"

"Don't you call me a liar. I am your grandmother, and you will respect me."

"But I don't understand," Meg said, bewildered. "You make Lonnie feel bad whenever he goes out, but the truth is, you can do everything on your own."

Alma tapped her cigarette into the sink and slowly shook her head. "I need Lonnie here. With *me*."

"But you don't. And you don't need me either."

"How do you know what I need?" Alma spat. "You're just a child who shouldn't be here anyway."

Meg pulled back in surprise. She wasn't sure exactly what her grandmother meant by "shouldn't be here," and she didn't want to think about it.

"But Lonnie," she continued. "You keep him here when

he could be doing other things, when he could be making himself happy. Don't you want your son to live his own life? Don't you want him to be happy?"

Alma stared back at Meg and calmly smoked her cigarette.

"He needs to know the truth," Meg said. "I have to tell him."

The old lady laughed without humor. "He would never believe you."

"Maybe he would," Meg challenged. "Maybe he doesn't want to live here anymore."

"Of course he does. He loves his mother more than anything," Alma declared, though Meg could hear a fraction of doubt in her grandmother's voice.

The front door creaked open then, and Lonnie could be heard stamping his boots against the threshold. "Hello? I'm home!"

Meg turned toward the sound of her uncle's voice. *Everyone deserves the truth,* she decided. It hadn't been fair when Lucie kept it from her, and she wouldn't consent to keeping it from Lonnie.

She stared hard at her grandmother. "I'm telling him."

Meg would have sworn she saw panic on Alma's face, but the old woman hid this emotion well too. "Wait. Maybe—maybe I know something about your father."

Meg froze. "Excuse me?"

"I know something about your father," the old woman repeated. "In fact, I might know how to find him."

Alma had never once said anything to Meg about her father, never even acknowledged he existed, so why should she believe Alma knew anything at all that could help her?

Out in the hallway, Lonnie was hanging up his jacket and tossing his cigarettes onto the corner table.

"Well, Margaret Anne," Alma prodded, "do we have a deal?"

Meg folded her arms across her chest. "Prove it."

"He went to Columbia," Alma said.

"Where?"

"Columbia University. On a football scholarship. That's all I'll say for now."

"Mother?" Lonnie called. "Meg? Are you home?" Lonnie's hand hit the swinging kitchen door.

"Deal," Meg said.

In one swift movement Alma doused her cigarette in the sink and flipped the butt into the garbage. She slid into a chair and smiled up at her son just as he walked in.

"Hello, Lonnie," she greeted him sweetly. "Tea?"

Chapter
FIFTEEN

Meg stood under the hot water, letting the steady stream sting her hair, nose, and stomach. She tilted her chin, felt the warmth flow over her neck and chest. She had a date tonight and wanted every centimeter of her body to be clean.

A date!

Juny did indeed call. He called to request her presence at some New Year's Eve gatherings. And she had said yes, as calmly as you please. Why, yes, I'd be happy to attend a party or two, I certainly will clear my calendar, ha ha. Shall we meet at the subway, say, at seven o'clock? That would be lovely.

As she hung up the phone, gooseflesh ran up her arms and thousands of tiny blond hairs stood straight up, ready to take on the world.

Life was a magical thing, was it not?

Now, with her hair wrapped in a thick white towel, Meg stood at her closet door and fingered the clothes hanging there, a mix of old Lucie and new Meg. Old shoes here, a new blouse there, old skirt, new sweater. Every other minute, it would occur to her why she was standing at the closet, why she was choosing an outfit, and she would do a little dance of joy.

A date!

Calm down, she told herself as she took a seat at Lucie's vanity. Maybe it would be easier to start with makeup and jewelry. She opened the center drawer and rummaged around inside. The mess of beads and chains was not unlike Lucie's old jewelry box at home.

Not home, Meg corrected herself. *This is home.*

She held up a fat bracelet in hot pink plastic. Mmm, no.

What about this gold circle pin? Mmm, too conservative.

And this—

Meg pulled out a necklace with wooden Scrabble letters that spelled *Lucie*. The tiles were glued side by side and suspended on a thin plastic wire, just like the one Lucie had made for her so many Christmases ago. The letters were heavy and solid in Meg's hand. Seven points, she counted, and her heart softened the littlest bit.

Naturally, Meg had assumed Lucie would be around for all the big events in her life: her first day of school, her first period, and now, her first real date. She had hoped her sister would be there to help select an outfit, to fix Meg's hair, to tell her she looked beautiful.

But in reality, Lucie hadn't ever been there, had she? She hadn't ever offered advice on how to accept a good-night kiss or the proper way to flirt.

It had been Jen, Meg realized, not Lucie, who had done that.

Meg reached for the Princess phone on the bedside table, pressed its shiny gold-toned buttons, and listened for the *click, ring, ring* across the line.

"*Bueno?*" came Nikki's voice on her cell phone.

"Hi, it's Meg."

"*Querida!* Are you dressed?"

"No, not yet. How fancy are these parties?"

"Let's see, let's see." Meg heard Nikki exit her bedroom and start down the stairs. "He's wearing . . . what are you wearing? That? No, no." Back to Meg. "He's not dressed. He'll wear his khakis."

"Nikki!" Juny's voice protested. "Jeans, Meg! I'm wearing *jeans!*"

"No, he's not. Khakis and an oxford–*BEEP!*–and his brown–*BEEP!*"

"Nik? That's the other line," Meg apologized. "Can I call you back?"

"Of course," Nikki answered. "See you tonight, *chica.*"

Meg clicked over to call waiting. "Hello?"

"Lonnie?" It was a woman's voice–a stranger's.

"No, this is his niece, Meg. He's still working."

"Work—? Oh, okay, thanks."

"I can give him a message." A long pause. "Hello? Are you there?"

"Um . . . Antonia. This is Antonia."

"Antoni . . ." Deep inside Meg's brain, something crucial clicked into place. "Tony? Does he call you . . . Toni?"

"Yes, he does," the caller admitted. "Has he . . . mentioned me?"

Meg thought about all the times her uncle had said he was "just going to Toni's."

"He's definitely talked about you."

"Really?" Meg could hear the smile of relief across the line. "I know he doesn't want me to call the house, but he left his cell here, and I had to ask him something. . . ."

Meg tuned out at some point as the woman droned on about Lonnie. She was the girl at the church, Meg realized, the brassy one with the too-tight skirt and the rambunctious sons, the one who was looking at Lonnie as more than a friend. Meg had seen the wink, the touch of hand to elbow.

And she was the woman in the Polaroids, wearing only a smile.

Meg chuckled to herself. It seemed that, in spite of Alma, Lonnie was building his own life after all.

"Meg? Hello?"

"I, uh, I have to go now, Toni. I'll tell Lonnie you called."

After exchanging goodbyes, she hung up the phone and returned to the closet, determined to follow her uncle's example.

Time to get herself a life—and time to get ready for her date.

Juny was a very popular dude, Meg discovered later that evening. And by extension, so was she. At each of the parties the couple attended, Juny was hailed as the hometown hero, the local boy done good who would carry the mantle of RFK High to whatever college's scholarship was largest and most prestigious. Everyone wanted to be around him. This would have been completely and totally cool in and of itself, but at each opportune moment, Juny would take Meg by the hand and draw her into his group and ask, "Have you guys met Meg?" And there you had it: instantly, like in a dream, she became one of them.

Their final stop was back at the Hernandez homestead. A smaller, more intimate group than the Christmas party, it nevertheless grew in size as the clock inched closer to midnight.

Juny and Meg sat on the floor in the den, just the two of them, where a fire was burning cozily.

"Wow," Meg said, holding the palms of her hands up to the fireplace screen. "This is so cool."

Juny laughed. "The fire? It's the opposite of cool. Here, let me explain it to you. . . ."

"Stop," she said, playfully swatting him on the arm.

"You know what I mean." Her hair fell across her face and she brushed it aside in a way that she hoped looked flirtatious.

"Did you have a good time tonight? Parties can suck when you don't know anyone."

"No, no, it was . . . cool."

Meg wondered, had the English language completely abandoned her? Did she have no adjective in her vocabulary more sophisticated than "cool"?

"Yeah?" He took her hand in his.

"Yeah," she answered. "It was . . . awesome."

Awesome, Meg thought. *Oh yeah, that was a much better word choice.*

"You sure know a lot of people," she said.

"More like, a lot of people know *me.* Or they think they do."

"Because of football?" Meg could barely concentrate on what she was saying as Juny's fingers began playing with the ring on her hand. It was just a piece of metal he was touching, only an object, but it felt so intimate, so familiar. She liked it.

"Yeah. I mean, it's not like I'm comparing myself to a rock star or anything, but I don't know. It's weird. I get people coming up to me and telling me what I should do, where I should go to college. Stuff like that."

Meg looked at him, openmouthed, and laughed. "Am I supposed to feel sorry for you because you're popular?"

Juny grinned. "Shut it, Hollywood."

Meg felt her face flush, and it wasn't from her proximity to the fireplace. "Well, tell them to leave you alone. Tell them you already know what you're going to do."

"But I *don't* know."

"Can't you just lie?"

"*Dio*, no!" Juny said with mock horror. "Are you suggesting I be dishonest?"

"*Dio*, no," Meg repeated, teasing.

Juny's face grew serious. "Yeah, I guess I could pretend— to everyone except my parents. They're paying for it all, you know? And they're pressuring me. They want to know that I'm going to do something with myself. That it's going to be worth all the sacrifice." He turned and leaned sideways against the couch, facing Meg. "I think maybe—*maybe* I might like to write."

The revelation, and Juny's willingness to share it, warmed Meg's heart. "Really? That's so cool. What do you want to write about?"

Juny laughed. "I have no idea. All I know right now is, I like words. I like telling stories. That's okay, isn't it?"

"What? That you don't have every single minute of your life planned out until you die? Yeah, I think that's okay. Besides, the rest of your life would be kind of boring if you knew exactly how it would turn out." She smiled. "Can I read something you've written?"

"No," he said quickly.

"Why not?"

"Just—no." He looked down at the floor, smiling but

obviously embarrassed. "Anyway, I'm tired of talking about me. Tell me about yourself, Hollywood."

"Not much to tell." She shrugged. "You know I'm from LA. And I'm a sophomore."

"Tell me something I don't know."

Meg thought about everything that Juny didn't know. It was enough to fill days, *weeks* of discussion. But she could *not* go down that path—the path of secrets and lies. He would run away for sure.

"I'm a natural blonde," she said.

"That's something," Juny admitted. "Something really *lame*."

"Well, why don't you make something up, then? Something more interesting?" Meg asked. "What would you write about me if you were putting me into one of your stories?"

"Hmmm." Juny cocked his head, appraising her. "Let's see. I'd make you an undercover agent."

"Like Sydney in *Alias*?"

"No, like Julia in *1984*."

Meg gasped. "You do *not* read George Orwell. He's one of my favorite authors!"

"Why not?" Juny asked. "Because I'm a dumb jock?"

"No. It's just—"

"I've read a lot of classics," he bragged. "You name 'em, I've read 'em."

"Oh yeah?" Meg straightened up, rising to the challenge. "How about Faulkner? Steinbeck? Gabriel García Márquez?"

Juny didn't hesitate. "Yes, yes, and yes—in the original Spanish."

"I don't believe it!" Meg said. *But I love it!* she thought.

"Hey, you're interrupting my story," Juny scolded.

"Sorry. Go on."

"Okay. So you're a spy and you're at our high school, pretending to be a normal student, but in reality, you're here to . . ." He twisted his lips in thought. Then his voice grew dramatic, like the announcer's in a movie trailer. "You're here to foil an evildoer's plan to take over the world through rampant consumerism!"

"It's Nikki," Meg whispered. "She's the evildoer. Don't blow my cover."

Juny grinned. "How's that? I think I'll call it *Hollywood Spy Girl.*"

"Not bad," she said. "I'd read it."

"Is that 'not bad' for an amateur or 'not bad' for a football player?"

Meg was genuinely surprised by his self-effacement. Could the great Juny Hernandez suffer from an inferiority complex?

"You know, I have the utmost respect for football players," she said.

"Well, thank you," Juny replied. "Speaking for football players everywhere, we appreciate your support."

Meg stared into Juny's chocolate brown eyes, felt the warmth from the fireplace envelop them, and before she knew it, she said, "My father played football too. At our school."

Juny glanced up, interested. "Oh, really? What position?"

Meg felt her breath leave her in a whoosh. Oh . . . my . . . God. How did she let *that* escape her lips? "Never mind," she said. She scooted closer to the fireplace, felt the flames burn her cheeks.

"Did he like playing for RFK?"

"I don't know."

"Did he play in college?"

"I don't know."

"Didn't he tell you?"

Meg swallowed. "I don't know . . . him. I only know *about* him. Kind of. His name and where he went to school." She held her hands out to the fire, could see through the webbing between thumb and forefinger, between forefinger and middle finger, between . . .

"Did something happen?" Juny asked in a soft voice.

And then she told him. She just . . . told him.

"My parents . . ." Meg started, and then stopped. She felt her palms burning—forgot she was holding them up still—and pulled her hands back from the fire. "They were never married. My mother was really young, and she had to leave school, so she went to California and had me there. I didn't even know my father was alive. I thought he was . . . well, I thought he was someone else. And I thought my mother was someone else too." She paused. This was the tough part. "My mother—she told me she was my sister. I found out the truth a few months ago. I came here to find my dad. And that's my story."

Juny stared at her. Meg felt the seconds tick by. *You can run away now,* she thought. But then, Juny cracked a smile.

"You *are* a badass, Hollywood."

Meg watched, waited to see if Juny was teasing her, but he appeared to be serious.

"You won't tell anyone, will you?" she asked.

He shook his head. "Our secret."

"Do you think it was stupid of me to come here?" she whispered.

"Nah. You're pretty smart. I'd say really smart except, so far, you haven't named one book I haven't read."

Meg smiled. "I'll find one. Don't worry."

"I don't know about that. I have an awful lot of books. Come up to my room and I'll show you."

Meg regarded him with a modest smile. "What's that? Your line?"

Juny laughed. "No, but maybe I should use it. I might get the interesting girls that way."

And then he moved closer to the fire, closer to her. He leaned in, and his lips brushed her hoop earring, her present from Nikki; the vibration of metal through skin trembled along her lobe and down her neck.

"There you are!" Nikki called out, her voice in the den right beside them. "It's nearly twelve—come on!" She pulled them into the kitchen, which was crowded with Hernandez family and friends. On a tiny television on the counter, a crystal ball of light was slowly descending in Times Square.

"Five! Four!" the group shouted. "Three! Two!"

Meg looked up at Juny; their eyes met . . .

"One!"

And she felt Juny's lips against hers, warm and soft, and they kissed, and the people around them, their family and friends and Times Square, disappeared, leaving only the two of them in this kitchen, in this house, in this world. Meg wished it could be like this forever, the two of them locked in a never-ending kiss.

"Happy new year!"

Meg awoke early the next day—the next year!—unable to sleep another minute as Juny's new girlfriend. The kiss at midnight might not have signaled a shift in status, but the walk home and a second kiss at the door sure did. She felt goose bumps on her arms just thinking about it. What a way to start the new year!

At the bottom of the steps, on her way to make coffee, Meg felt cold air blow through her pj's, and she cinched her robe tighter. She followed the breeze to the kitchen, where she found the coffeepot on but empty and the back door open a good three inches. She flipped the switch on the coffeemaker, surprised the glass carafe hadn't cracked overnight from the heat. As she began to close the door, a hand stopped her. She jumped back.

"Morning," Lonnie mumbled as he brushed past her. He closed the door behind him.

"You're up early."

"So are you." He caught sight of the coffeepot. "Did you shut that off?"

"It was empty."

"Oh, well . . . let's make some more." As Lonnie bustled about the kitchen, rinsing the pot and adding the coffee grounds to the filter, Meg noticed he still wore his jacket. The cellar door was open, and the light was on.

"Lonnie, are you coming or going?"

Her uncle kept his back to her as he continued making coffee. "That's a funny question. Some days, I don't know."

Meg folded her arms over her chest, guarding against the cold. "Do you actually live here anymore?"

He chuckled once, like a hiccup. "Well . . . it's not that I *don't* live here. I just . . . also live somewhere else."

"With Toni," Meg guessed.

He turned. "How did you know?"

"Lonnie, please," she said. "You're not exactly stealthy. Besides, Toni's called here before, and your room is completely empty." She glanced up at him with a furrowed brow. "Well, not *totally* empty."

Lonnie colored. "It's been a gradual process."

"But why? Why not just leave and live with your girlfriend?"

"Now, *that* is funny. My mother would kill me."

Meg stood at the counter, hoping her presence would hasten the dripping coffee. She took down two mugs from the cupboard. "So what? She can live on her own, you know. She can walk. I've seen her."

Lonnie shook his head. "I know, and it doesn't matter.

I can't abandon her. She's already been abandoned twice. She'd be all alone."

"Abandoned?"

"Well, Dad died."

"Yeah."

"And before that, Lucie left and never came back."

Meg frowned. "I can't believe I'm about to say this, but it doesn't seem like Lucie had much of a choice. She was sent away."

"She wasn't supposed to be gone forever," Lonnie said, a hint of petulance creeping into his voice. "She was supposed to come back. She left me here, with them. It wasn't fair."

Meg wrapped her hands around an empty mug, warming it with her palms while she listened to her uncle.

"I never went anywhere. I never did anything. After Dad died, it was just me and her. And then she got sick and I figured, this is it. This is my lot in life. But then I met Toni. And that's when I went to find Lucie." He leaned back against the counter and let out a long sigh.

"I needed Lucie," he continued. "But God, am I glad *you* came instead. With your help, I'll be able to spend a lot more time with Toni and her boys. And you know, you've inspired me."

"Me?" Meg blinked. "I have?"

"Sure," he said agreeably. "You're an amazing kid. Left your home and traveled all the way across the country for what? No promises, no guarantees. But you did it. You've got some balls on you."

Meg wrinkled her nose. "Um, gross," she said.

Lonnie laughed. "Today I'm moving my baseball card collection. Think I'll sell it on eBay." He started toward the cellar door, then paused. "You're going to find your dad, kid. I know it. And then we'll both have exactly what we always wanted."

Meg smiled at her uncle's words. Although it saddened her that Lonnie wouldn't be around as often, it was actually a blessing in disguise. If she got her grandmother alone, maybe she would finally be able to ask her for the information she had promised.

Information about her father.

On the first day back after Christmas vacation, Meg was so nervous walking up the front steps of the high school that she could actually feel her temperature rise. She opened her coat and the lapels flopped over, the fresh air wicking sweat away from the thick wool. She felt like everyone she passed *knew* she and Juny had kissed, but were they officially boyfriend-girlfriend now? Did one date count? One date and two amazing, life-altering kisses?

She tried to take tiny steps so she wouldn't trip like some goofy, smiling idiot on her way to class.

Where was he now? she wondered. Was his dad dropping him off with Nikki? Was he driving himself? She was pretty sure he didn't have his own car, but she wasn't so certain he had first-period class. Should she know that if she was his girlfriend? She probably should.

She stopped at her locker and focused all of her attention on her books. This was school, after all, and she had to be able to stop thinking about Juny for just five minutes.

She stared at the inside of her locker door—at the two pictures of Jen and the cast of *Friends* she had taped there. *Jen,* she thought, casting a fond smile upon the magazine photos, *if only you were here to share this with me. I know you'd be just as happy as I am.*

"Meg! Hey, Meg!" She turned toward the sound. Nikki was standing at her locker a few feet down the hall. "Come here," she said, waving Meg over.

Meg clicked her lock into place, then hurried toward Nik, who held open her locker. "Pick one."

"Pick one what?"

"Pick a picture. Of *Juny.* Which one do you want?"

Meg stared at the photos. She had seen them before, but that was, well, *before.* Before the party, before the date . . . "I don't know what you mean."

"You two are dating, so you have to have a picture in your locker now. Which one do you like?"

"I, uh, I—"

Nikki tapped one of the pictures. "I like this one with Mariela at her birthday party. He's got a real natural smile there, and that shirt's a good color on him. There's this, in his football uniform, but it's kind of stiff, ya know? Like a portrait or something." She turned to Meg. "So . . . pick one!"

"They're all good, I guess. But you don't have to give me one of your pictures."

Nikki sighed. "You *have* to have one, Meg. I mean, until you get one of the two of you, which I can totally take next time you're at the house. I got this fantastic digital camera with, like, a billion pixels or something." She stood with her hands on her hips, apparently waiting for Meg to make a move. "Take this one," Nikki said finally. She carefully removed a photo of Juny, Nikki, and Mariela at the little girl's party and handed it to Meg. "Now every time you open your locker, you'll see Juny staring back at you."

"And you," Meg said with a smile.

Nikki laughed. "Yeah, you can't get rid of me, can you? I'm like a bad fungus."

"Who's a fungus?" Deidre asked, appearing at Nikki's locker with Tanya by her side. "It's Tanya, isn't it?" She made a big show of pinching her nose closed with her fingers.

"Shut it," Tanya scolded. Then she smiled sweetly at Meg. "Meg, dearest, I have a—"

"Nice work snagging the most eligible bachelor in school," Deidre interrupted. "And you, sis, good work."

"Thanks," Nikki said as she closed her locker door and spun the lock. "It's a gift." She and the two girls started down the hallway together. Nikki threaded an arm through Meg's, gently pulling her along beside them.

"Meg," Tanya tried a second time. "There's a favor I—"

"Now that you're Juny's girlfriend," Deidre interrupted again, "will you please tell Juny to tell Jason to ask *her* out?" She jabbed her thumb at Tanya. "She's crushing on him so bad she's driving me crazy!"

"Didn't I just tell you to shut it?" Tanya linked arms with Meg on her other side as the girls sauntered down the hall. "However, if you could *suggest* to Juny that Jason might want to ask me out, that would be great. . . ."

Meg let Tanya's rolling discourse about Jason wash over her. Deidre would probably comment next on the unlikelihood of that coupling occurring in her lifetime. Then Nikki would gently point out that Tanya really should consider a new, more demure wardrobe if she wanted a guy like that.

So this was what it was like to be part of a clique, Meg thought. To be popular and to have a boyfriend . . .

To be like Jen.

Cool.

Everything about her life in Queens was falling into place. Except the one thing she came for—her father.

She smiled to herself. That would happen too. She just knew it.

"Sure, Tanya," Meg said assuredly. "I'd be happy to talk to Juny for you. You and Jason will be dating before you know it."

Chapter
SIXTEEN

"I'm going to make you one of my favorite meals ever," Meg called to her grandmother as she flitted about the kitchen, getting out silverware and taking down plates and glasses. It was just the two of them this weekend: Lonnie was off with Toni and her sons. Meg hoped this would be an opportunity to have a heart-to-heart with Alma about her dad. Ever since the night of Nikki's Christmas party, it seemed like her grandmother was deliberately avoiding being alone with her.

Well, that would end tonight.

Ahhh, French Toes. Meg hadn't had such deliciousness since she left LA. She wondered if Juny might like this dish. Maybe one day she could make it for him. One evening—when it was just the two of them. She could set out candles and flowers, and then afterward—

Meg felt her skin blush all over just thinking about it. She really needed to learn to control that better. She fanned a napkin in front of her face.

It's dinnertime, she told herself. *Concentrate on dinner now.*

"Alma? Hello? Dinner's almost done." She waited a moment for her grandmother to respond.

Nothing.

"Hello?" Maybe she was still watching the Wheel, Meg thought. She went into the living room, where she found—

"Alma!"

Her grandmother was slumped forward in her recliner, a cigarette dangling between her fingers, perilously close to the shag. Meg ran to take it out of her hand, using just her fingertips to pick it up. She shook Alma awake.

Alma opened her eyes and scowled. "What are you waking me for?"

"You fell asleep with this." Meg held up the burning cigarette, and her grandmother snatched it back.

"Give me that."

"It's a really dangerous habit, Alma."

Her grandmother grumbled, but Meg couldn't make out the words.

"Fine. Finish that and come in. Dinner's ready."

"Maybe I'm not hungry," Alma snapped. "Maybe I don't want to eat without Lonnie."

Meg thought, *Whatever.* She wasn't going to let a cranky old woman stop her from having a nice meal. Besides, Alma hadn't eaten since eleven thirty. Her stomach was guaranteed to get the better of her eventually.

Meg patted the toast slices with a paper towel to remove the excess grease, then placed a pair on each of the plates.

Behind her, Alma sat down and arranged herself at the kitchen table. She spoke not a word but had both hands wrapped around the cordless phone, which was directly in front of her on the place mat. Meg set a glass, knife, and fork around the phone, then poured Coke into both of their glasses. "Do you like butter or margarine?" she asked. "I softened the butter up in the microwave for a few seconds."

Alma said nothing.

"Okay, I'll put both out and you can pick whichever. How about syrup? I found a bottle of real maple at the back of the fridge. I don't think it was ever opened, so it should still be good, right? I don't think it goes bad if it's refrigerated."

Again, her grandmother didn't respond.

"Okay, well, I guess we'll find out." She moved to place a dish in front of Alma, but the phone remained in her hands. "Um, can we move this while we eat?" Meg asked. She stood there for what felt like an eternity, waiting for her grandmother to do something. The plate started to tremble in her hand as the weight of it strained her wrist. Finally, the old woman took the phone off the table and put it in her lap.

"He's going to call me tonight," Alma said.

Meg let out an involuntary chuckle. Lonnie hadn't

promised he would call while he was away—he'd only said to ring him on his cell phone in case of emergency.

"Don't laugh at me!" Alma snapped. "I prayed for him to call me. I know it will be tonight."

The more often Lonnie was gone, the more Meg's grandmother would carry that phone around with her. She was sort of a sad figure, Meg thought, with her threadbare housecoat and her pink wig askew. Alma had been putting her wig on by herself, and she wasn't particularly adept at it.

She never asked Meg for assistance.

"Do you like the dinner, Alma?"

The old woman picked at the bread with her fork, mushed it down on the plate, then took a dry bite—no butter, no syrup, just egg-soaked bread.

"Lonnie never made breakfast food for dinner."

"Well, I thought it would be a nice change." Meg took a bite from her own fork. *Mmm.* In her estimation, this was a pretty damn good meal. The Shanleys had real maple syrup, not the fake crap she and Lucie always used, making this some of the best-tasting French Toes she'd had in a long while.

It was all about perspective, she thought.

"You have to put the butter and syrup on it." She demonstrated.

Alma made a face. "Too sweet."

"It's supposed to be sweet."

"It's dessert." She pushed her plate away. "Lonnie would

never make dessert for dinner. Get me something else."

Meg let her fork clang loudly on her plate as she rose from the table. "What do you want, then?"

Alma shrugged her bony shoulders. "Something else."

Meg stood at the fridge and tried to find another meal for her grandmother. Her own food was growing cold. She sighed heavily.

Perspective, she thought again. No need to get upset; she could heat her plate up again in the microwave.

"How about a sandwich? Ham and cheese? With a slice of pickle?" Meg took her grandmother's silence as agreement, so she pulled out the sandwich fixings and began to concoct a second meal.

"You know, Alma, we're going to be spending a lot more time together, just you and me," Meg said over her shoulder. "I thought, while we had the chance, we could talk some more about my father."

Nothing from Alma, so Meg continued. "You told me he went to Columbia, which is good to know, but it hasn't really helped me find him." Meg slathered mayo on the white bread and layered cheese and ham on top. "I need more information." She put the sandwich on a fresh plate, cut it diagonally down the middle, and gave it to her grandmother.

"Why are you looking at me like that?" Alma asked. "What do you want?"

Meg blinked. "You said you would tell me more about my father."

Alma shook her head. "When Lonnie gets back." She picked up her sandwich with one hand and kept the other on the phone.

Meg clenched her fists in frustration. "I wouldn't count on Lonnie being around much," she said. "He wants to live somewhere else."

"He'll be back," Alma argued. "I prayed for him to come back, and he will."

"I, uh, I really don't think so, Alma. He loves this woman."

Alma stared at the phone. "He loves *me*."

Meg took another bite of her now-cold French Toes. The butter sat in a perfect unmelted pat under an ooze of syrup. Was her grandmother for real? she wondered. Had she turned into Miss Havisham, the bitter, demented Dickens character who lived in her own world, determined to ruin the lives of those around her?

Alma Shanley had lived so many lies, had spent so many years manipulating her son. Was it possible she had succumbed to her own untruths—or was this just another scam for Meg's benefit?

"Look, Alma," Meg began. "I really need you to tell me what you know about my father. I think it's unfair of you to promise me something and then not follow through."

Alma finally took her eyes off the phone and gazed at Meg dispassionately. "He didn't love her."

"Who? My father?"

"He didn't love her, and she didn't love him. You were a mistake."

Meg felt like she had been slapped in the face. Her eyes stung, and she lost her breath.

"There," her grandmother said smugly. "Now you know something." Then she stood and returned to the living room with the phone.

Meg's head dropped to her chest as tears clouded her eyes. She stared at her lap and watched two fat drops of salty water land on her hands. She squeezed her eyes shut against further tears; she would *not* cry.

Her grandmother had to be wrong. She had to be.

Thank God for Juny and his family, Meg thought as she stood outside the Hernandez home, waiting for someone to come to the door. They were her refuge from her grandmother, her connection to a sane and loving household.

Mr. Hernandez and his daughter Mariela answered the doorbell almost as soon as Meg pressed the button, as if they had been watching her approach.

Juny's father smiled broadly as he held open the door. "Juny," he called. "You have a visitor."

The little girl did the same. "Juny, you have a visitor."

The Christmas tree and garlands of green were gone from the house, but there was still a festive air. By contrast, when Meg had packed away all the Shanley decorations, the air had all but disappeared. The people who lived here, she figured, made their own joy.

Mariela grabbed Meg's hand. "I can make hot cocoa with mini-marshmelons," she said. "Want some?"

"No, thank you," Meg declined politely.

"Are you two going to the basketball game tonight?" Mr. Hernandez asked.

"Yeah. They need the support," Meg said. "They're in last place."

"Then you should get good seats." Mr. Hernandez chuckled.

Father and daughter led Meg to the dining room, where Juny and his mother sat, the table covered with papers.

Juny smiled when she entered. "Hey! Sorry I'm not ready. We're working on college applications." He rolled his eyes so only Meg could see.

Mrs. Hernandez looked at her husband. "Did you bring home the one for SUNY Purchase? I didn't see it with the others."

"Let me check my briefcase."

"Which ones are these?" Meg asked. There must have been six or eight applications on the table, each one marked with Post-its and colored flags.

Juny shuffled some papers around. "Ithaca, NYU, Rutgers. Mom wants me to go to a local school," he said. "Dad just wants me to go somewhere. Anywhere."

"That's not exactly correct," Mr. Hernandez said with a grin. "I want you to get a *scholarship* anywhere."

"Can I get Meg some hot cocoa?" Mariela asked her mother. "With lots of marshmelons?"

"I think she said no, sweetie," Mrs. Hernandez said. "But maybe if you ask her again, very nicely, she'll say yes." Juny's mother winked at Meg.

Mariela strolled over to Meg and stood with her hands folded in front of her. "Meg, can I *please* get you some hot cocoa with marshmelons?"

"This might take a while," Juny said, gesturing to the applications. "And the hot chocolate is pretty good."

"Okay, then. Yes, please, Mariela, I'd love some."

The little girl's face broke into a wide smile. "Be right back!" she said. She skipped happily out of the room.

"She's very sweet," Meg remarked.

"She just wants an excuse to eat the marshmallows." Juny sighed. "Seriously, though, I'm gonna need a few more minutes."

"Meg!" Nikki called from the den. "In here!"

"I'll just go hang with Nikki," Meg offered. She found her friend sitting in front of the family desktop computer in the den.

"Mariela!" Nikki said. "Bring Meg's cocoa into the den, okay?" She turned to Meg. "She's gonna eat all the marsh-mallows out of your cup. Just so you know."

"Fine with me," Meg said. She took a seat in the chair next to the desk and peered around the monitor. A goose-neck lamp curled over the top, splashing a pool of light on the keyboard. "Whatcha doing?"

"I'm bidding on this amazing jacket," Nikki said. "Check it out."

On the monitor was an eBay screen and a photograph of a beautiful waist-length sheepskin jacket. "Is that real?" Meg asked.

Nikki shook her head. "Totally faux. But look at the pseudo-suede. You can practically feel how velvety soft it is right through the computer." And she ran a finger gently over the screen, as if she could indeed feel the fabric through it. "I like the light brown. What do you think?"

"Sweet."

Nikki sighed. "I know. Less than twenty minutes to go, and if no one bids higher than me . . ." She held up crossed fingers. "I can go about ten bucks more, but that's it. So, you guys going to the game tonight?"

"Yeah. Want to come?" Meg asked, hoping her friend would say no. It was fun doing things as a threesome or fivesome or eightsome with Juny and Nikki and their friends, but it felt like group dating sometimes. She liked being alone with her boyfriend so they could make out whenever they wanted.

Nikki must have read her mind. "Nah. It's always the same old, you know? You guys go. You'll have fun." Nikki's cell rang then, and she checked the number before answering.

"It's Tanya," she told Meg. "Should I let it go to voice mail?"

"Because I'm here? No, no. Answer her."

"She's probably just going to moan about Jason and try to drag me to the game so she can stare at him." Nikki moaned to herself as the phone continued to ring. "Ergh. All right."

She snapped open her cell. "Tanya? I am *not* going tonight, so don't ask . . . what? No . . . no, no, no. Hang on. Let me get my notebook." She covered the receiver with her hand and rolled her eyes. "Math drama. Meg, watch my jacket, okay? Let me know if someone bids on it." She took her phone upstairs, leaving Meg alone at the computer.

Meg stared at the screen, waiting for something to happen. She wasn't particularly interested in shopping online. She supposed it was the visceral thrill she liked about clothing, the feeling of fabric against her skin, of seeing herself in a new outfit—a new self, a new identity. She could be a debutante in a puffy skirt and white gloves. Or a biker chick in a leather jacket and chunky-heeled boots. A goth girl in black, a virgin in white. Actually, she was always a virgin, she thought with a chuckle, no matter what she wore.

But buying online was just *shopping.*

She moved the mouse on its jelly-filled pad and clicked on the Google link Nikki had in her Favorites. A new window opened with the search engine's web site. The cursor blinked in the empty box, a box just waiting to be filled with . . . a name? Her fingers twitched, poised above the keyboard. It was like the Internet was inviting her—no, *insisting* that she search for her father. Would she be able to find something Lonnie couldn't? At the school's computer lab and in the library, Meg had tried to do a search of her own. But each time, something had stopped her, something like fear gripping her heart. But here, in Juny's house, where she felt safe, maybe she would finally have the courage.

She peeked back at eBay: fifteen minutes to go. She was sure Nikki wouldn't mind.

All right . . . She typed the *N* and the *a* . . . all the way through to the *d* and then added *Queens*. She pressed enter and got over twenty-five thousand hits. The first few on the page looked like cemetery listings for colonial America. Maybe this Nate Holland was a distant relative or something. She paged through the listings, but the matches degenerated to web sites for tulip bulbs and Edam cheese. She refined her search by adding *Columbia University football*. No cemetery listings this time. Instead she got: *Nathaniel Holland, running back, out for the season with an injury to his . . .*

She gasped. Her heart hiccuped in her chest. She had found something!

She rolled the mouse over the hyperlink and was whisked away to an archived 1993 article from the *Spectator*, the Columbia University student newspaper. She skimmed from the beginning: in a game against Cornell, offensive running back Nathaniel Holland was tackled on the thirty-yard line and suffered a torn hamstring. He was expected to be out for the rest of the season.

Meg scanned the screen for more of the article, but that was it, a tiny blurb and no more. It was only a pdf file with no graphics or HTML links, and there was no further mention of Nathaniel Holland. She wondered about her father's football career: after his injury, did he ever go back? And what of his days at Columbia before that fateful game against Cornell?

This was *it*? This tantalizing tidbit? Meg wanted to scream. She clicked on every word in the article, hoping for a connection to something—but it was a dead end. This tiny morsel of information was both everything and nothing. It was more than she'd hoped for, yet nothing concrete she could use to find her father.

She clicked back to eBay and stared at Nikki's jacket.

Everything and nothing.

"Hey, did I get the jacket?" Nikki asked as she hopped onto the chair beside Meg.

"Hmmm?" Meg slowly turned to her friend.

"Are you okay?"

I found him! she wanted to shout. But she hadn't, not yet. When she did, she would tell Nikki everything and they could all celebrate. But not yet.

"I'm fine," she said. "The auction is mesmerizing."

"Two minutes to go and it's mine, mine, mine."

Meg felt her head nod, heard Nikki say something to her, even heard her own responses. But she had no idea what they were talking about.

The thing about looking for a father, she thought, *is that it's terribly, terribly distracting.*

Chapter
SEVENTEEN

Dear Jen,

How are you? I am fine.

Okay, so I've been doing something that is totally lame, and I can't tell anyone but you. Did you ever pretend you were married and practice signing your name with your boyfriend's name? Like Mrs. Meg Hernandez?

Anyway, I haven't been doing that, but I've been practicing . . . okay, this is queer . . . using my dad's name. Meg Holland. Margaret Anne Holland. Maggie Holland. Margie Holland. Which sounds best? I can't decide.

Technically, I am a Holland. I never should have been a Shanley. I was a Shanley under false pretenses. Lucie made me believe it, but it was never true.

I wonder what it will be like to be a Holland. I already know my father is smart because Columbia is a really good school. And he's athletic. And Lonnie said he was tall. And I've seen the pictures, so I know he's handsome.

But what's his personality like? Is he funny? Does he have a sense of humor? I think he must. Lots of smart people like jokes. They like clever jokes, not jokes about boobs and farts. They like Letterman and Conan. I wonder if he liked Friends. *He must have.*

So I think maybe in the not-too-distant future, I will sign my letters Margie Holland *or* M. A. Holland. *Yeah, that's pretty classy. I wonder if Lucie will feel it when I make the switch . If she'll somehow know that I've found my way to a new life—the life I've always wanted—without her.*

I'm so close to it, Jen! So close, I can feel it!

Love,

m

Meg didn't know what it was to be a Holland, but she had a pretty good impression of what it meant to be a Shanley. Irresponsibility—both physical and mental—seemed to be a key characteristic. There also appeared to be a cold, cruel streak that ran through the female side. Not a lot of hugs and kisses and definitely no "I love yous."

Manipulation was another skill the Shanleys possessed as a group, and Meg did not exempt Lonnie from that. And if a Shanley valued anything, it seemed to be distance.

A Holland, on the other hand, would be (could be, should be) the opposite of a Shanley. Kind and forgiving—perhaps affectionate and gentle. Just from the sound of their name, the Hollands seemed like a close-knit clan, one that kept in touch regularly and maybe sent a family newsletter every Christmas, proudly sharing all of the events in everyone's lives with friends and neighbors.

It would be good—no, *fantastic*—to be a part of the Holland family, Meg thought.

She heard the phone ring as she placed a stamp on her letter to Jen. Meg didn't move to answer. Alma was still keeping the cordless in her hand at all times so she could stab at the button the moment it sounded.

"Hello?" Meg heard in the living room. "Hello?"

She crept to the top of the stairs and looked down at her grandmother shouting into the phone. "Who is this? Is anyone there? Lonnie? Are you there, Lonnie?"

They had gotten about three or four of these hang-ups in the past week or so. Meg wondered who it could be.

Telemarketers, she supposed. The machine kind that didn't always start up at the sound of a human voice. Alma was convinced it was her son, checking in with her while he was with his girlfriend.

It might have been Nikki or Juny, Meg thought, but neither of them ever said anything to her about it like, "Ugh, your stupid grandmother keeps answering the phone." Besides, they were both very polite people, and Meg doubted they would be so rude as to hang up on Alma, even if she *was* an old bat who swore at them.

Alma didn't have caller ID, and the one time Meg

showed her how to use *69, there was no answer on the return call. If not Lonnie or Nikki or Juny, who could it have been?

Without warning, one name whispered in Meg's brain—*Lucie*.

But would Lucie have called the one person she told never to return? And did Meg want to be called?

Meg quickly dismissed both scenarios as extremely unlikely.

It wasn't long before Meg was invited to movie night at the Hernandez home, a quirky, semi-regular event that was education disguised as entertainment. Juny called it "edutainment." If the film chosen by one of the family members wasn't a documentary, then it had to be based on a book or novel that they could all read and discuss afterward.

"It's not all Jane Austen and the Brontë sisters," Mrs. Hernandez said with a laugh. "We alternate picking titles. Mariela likes horse movies, so she's picked *Black Beauty* on a number of occasions. Fortunately, it's been remade so many times we've had several versions to watch."

"How is that 'fortunate'?" Mr. Hernandez wanted to know. "I vote for *Blade Runner*." His wife shot him a look. "It's a Philip K. Dick story. Sci-fi counts."

Meg loved his logic, loved that he tried, loved that his girls ran roughshod over him and he let them, happily. She wondered if her father would be like that.

"Meg, you pick!" Mariela shouted. Then she sidled up

and whispered in Meg's ear, "Pick *National Velvet*."

Meg smiled, but Juny shook his head. "Meg's not picking anything. *We're* going out tonight."

"First Nikki, now you two." Mrs. Hernandez sighed. "Okay, Mari, looks like it's just you, me, Daddy, and *National Velvet*."

Mr. Hernandez groaned. "What about *Lord of the Rings*? There's plenty of horses in that."

Actually, *Lord of the Rings* would have been fine and dandy with Meg. And so would *National Velvet* or any of the *Black Beauty*s. She loved the idea of family movie night. And she loved that the Hernandez family wanted to include her.

When they arrived at the Astoria multiplex on 38th Street and 35th Avenue, the Vin Diesel movie they had planned to see was sold out, as were the Lindsay Lohan comedy and the Ashton Kutcher romance.

"I don't understand," Meg complained. "There's five showings of each one. How can they all be sold out?"

"Two for . . ." Juny said. He closed his eyes and pointed his finger at the marquee above a harried-looking cashier. When he opened his eyes, he said the name of the movie he'd randomly selected.

A cartoon—about a rat.

Meg laughed. "That's rated G. *No one's* going to see that."

The cashier agreed. "Only three people bought tickets."

"Good," Juny said, winking at Meg. "I need a lot of elbow room."

They took seats in the absolute last row of the postage-stamp-size theater. The other three people in attendance were a young couple like themselves sitting in the front and a single man who had the seat in the exact center of the room.

Juny took off his jacket and threw it over the seat in front of them. "You want any popcorn or Junior Mints?"

Meg shook her head. Then the lights went down and the trailers came up.

Anime crap.

Sci-fi crap.

Brad Pitt crap.

"Hey, another *Black Beauty* movie," Meg said. "Maybe we can take Mariela to see it."

"You're welcome to do that on your own. I've seen enough horse movies to last the rest of my life." Juny laid an arm across the back of Meg's seat, and his hand stroked her hair. She had worn it down tonight for precisely this reason.

"What do you think they're watching at your house?" Meg asked. "Did your dad get his way?"

"My dad *never* gets his way. They're probably watching *Shrek*."

"No horses in that one."

"There *is* a donkey. Close enough."

Meg was just about to mention the book connection

when Juny added, "William Steig. I know. You're not going to get one past me, Hollywood."

"Oh, I will," she replied with a smile. "Just you wait."

The movie started then, with a flash of brightly colored animation under the opening credits. There were no humans in this picture, only animals who sang and danced and philosophized about being good and true. In this cartoon world, life's complexities would be reduced to a single morality: bad guys would be punished and good guys would be rewarded.

No wonder the theater was empty, Meg thought.

"Hey," she whispered. "Next time, could we do the movie night with your family?"

Juny sort of cocked his head and looked at her. "Sure. We could do that. You have to read, though."

"I read."

"And you have to be prepared to discuss things."

"I discuss."

"And you have to have patience with Mariela when she asks for the fifty-millionth time, how come there was no horse in that movie?"

Meg laughed. "I can do that too."

"Okay. But listen, family dates do not count as real dates. Got it?"

"Got it."

"I mean, I love my parents as much as the next guy, but I don't want to share you *all* the time."

They watched the screen for a few excruciating moments longer.

"This is boring," Juny whispered in Meg's ear as he slid his arm from the back of her seat to her shoulders. As he settled in closer to her, shivers ran up and down her spine. She knew he was going to kiss her, but the anticipation—the not knowing *when* it would happen—was delicious. She hoped she never got over this feeling, no matter how many times they kissed. She leaned her head back against his arm as he curled his body over hers. His face came closer, closer, closer until their lips met and Meg felt Juny's skin melt into hers.

When they came up for air twenty minutes later, Meg felt her face tingle from the short stubble of Juny's beard. It didn't matter in the least. Tomorrow's redness would be a badge of courage, a mark of tonight's make-out battlefield.

"Hey . . ." Juny whispered. "Don't you like my kisses?"

"What . . . of course. Why?"

He ran his thumb below her eye and then pulled it away. "You're crying."

Meg quickly wiped her eyes. "I am? That's weird." She looked at her finger: it was wet, like Juny's thumb, which was so odd because she really didn't think she was upset. They were having a wonderful time, and they were talking about movies.

And family.

"I guess I'm a little jealous," Meg admitted. "You have

this great family. You have parents and sisters, and your sisters are real sisters, not fake ones that you find out are . . . I don't know, something else entirely."

Juny silently caressed the back of her head but said nothing.

"Every time I see your folks or I talk to Nikki, I think, Why can't they be mine? Why can't I have *that*?" She felt another tear wash down her cheek, and she grabbed at it before it fell any farther. "Pretty lame, huh? Feeling sorry for myself?"

"Meg," Juny said. "You're independent, and that's great. I love that about you. But sometimes, you have to let other people help you." He pointed to his chest.

"You?" Meg gave her boyfriend a wan smile. "You're sweet to offer, but what can you do? I've already done the phone book thing and the Google thing, and I even looked into one of those companies that find people for you, but they wanted way too much money. No offense, because I know you're a smart guy and all, but I don't think you can do much more than I can." She kissed Juny tenderly on the cheek.

Juny sat quietly for a moment, which allowed Meg to hear the bouncy kiddie music coming from the surround-sound speakers in the theater. Man, this *was* a bad movie.

"I like you a lot," Juny said slowly.

"I like you too."

"So I want to be nice and not tell you that's crap. But . . . I'm sorry, that's crap."

Meg blinked. "Excuse me?"

"I may not be able to help you myself, but I know some-one who can."

"Really? Who?"

"Nikki."

"Which Nikki?"

"The Nikki who likes to dress people up like they're giant Barbie dolls. My sister, duh."

Meg frowned in confusion. "How can she help?"

"She works in the principal's office. They totally love her there, and she can access files you and I can't."

Meg tried to follow his train of thought. "So?"

"You said your dad went to our school."

"Yeah, fifteen years ago."

"So there's probably something in a file somewhere with his name on it. Alumni stuff for when they're looking for donations or something like that."

Meg's heart quickened in her chest. "Oh my God. Juny, that's—that's a *great* idea!" She stood and began shrugging on her coat.

"Where are you going?"

Meg wound her scarf around her neck. "To find Nikki and ask her."

"Now?" Juny remained in his seat. "Aren't we going to finish the movie?"

"We're not even watching the movie."

"Yeah, I know," he said with a grin.

Meg hesitated. She sank back into her seat and let Juny help her off with her coat.

Okay, she thought, she could wait. After all this time, what was another hour or two? The anticipation certainly wouldn't kill her.

At least, she hoped it wouldn't.

The clock in Meg's chemistry class was stuck at two minutes to three.

The final moments of her day—before she could rush out to meet Juny and Nikki—were ticking by at a snail's pace.

She wondered, *Could time actually have stopped?*

Finally, the bell rang. Meg ran out the door and down to the administration office, where Juny was waiting.

"Hey," Juny said as he kissed her and wrapped an arm around her waist. "Ready?"

Meg steeled herself. "Absolutely."

He tapped on a door marked *Principal Arnold Betts.* They waited until they heard Nikki's voice respond, "Come in."

Juny's sister sat at a small cluttered desk outside the principal's inner office. Meg noticed she was wearing panty hose and pumps and a skirt that demurely covered her knees. She looked so grown-up, so sophisticated, like she belonged in an office. Meg could picture her running a company or being a buyer at a big department store, like Rachel, someday.

"Sit down, sit down." Nikki swiveled her chair so she faced Meg. Meg sniffed; was that perfume her friend was wearing? She felt like an awkward child in comparison. Then Nikki snapped her gum, giggled, and broke the spell of sophistication. "I don't have a lot of time until Principal Betts gets back, so let's get started."

"I'm so nervous," Meg admitted, as much to herself as to Juny and Nikki.

Juny stood behind Meg and placed strong, supportive hands on her shoulders. She relaxed almost instantly. This boyfriend thing was pretty awesome, she thought.

"Okay, give me his full name."

"Nathaniel Holland," Meg said. "Not sure if he has a middle name."

"Class?"

"1992."

"Juny said he got a scholarship to Columbia?"

"Right. He was a football player."

Nikki caught Meg's eye and grinned. "Oh yeah. The trophy case. Well, if he got a scholarship or a grant, we probably have a record of that too." She moved the mouse around its pad, tapped a few keys with the tips of her nails. "Okay. These folders are all arranged by year. Ah, you're lucky. We only go back to 1992. Looks like we're about to purge, too. Okay. Holland with two *l*'s?"

Meg saw the name in her head: *N. Holland* floating under her father's black-and-white snapshot. "Yes, two *l*'s."

"Okay . . ." Nikki stared hard at the screen. "Here we go . . . Your father went to Columbia University on a football scholarship. He was RFK's captain that year. Voted MVP. Lettered four years. *And* he was on the newspaper staff."

"A writer?"

Nikki nodded. "Just says *staff* here. Probably a writer."

Meg couldn't help but smile. Maybe her father worked for the *New York Times* now or the *New Yorker*. Maybe he was a novelist—like Juny aspired to be.

"Cool," she breathed. With each tiny tidbit she was given—the trophy case, the yearbook, the Columbia student paper, and now this—her father was becoming more real to her, more alive. For so many years, he didn't exist. For her entire life, he simply never was. Now that was all changing.

"Maybe your father wanted to be Jack Kerouac," Juny said.

"What do you mean?"

"Kerouac went to Columbia on a football scholarship too. And we know how that turned out."

Nikki shook her head. "No—*we* don't."

"Try reading something that's not in a magazine for once, *mija*," Juny teased.

"Too bad there isn't a magic button on that computer," Meg said with a rueful laugh. "One that would give us an address for him."

"Maybe there is," Nikki said coyly.

"What?"

"Maybe I *can* find out more." She glared up at Juny. "It's not a *book*, I know, but—"

Juny tugged on his sister's ponytail, but she shook him off and smiled sweetly at Meg. "Last year would have been your dad's fifteenth high school reunion. We might have his address if the alumni committee sent him an announcement."

"Are you serious?" Meg breathed.

Nikki held her hand up like a Scout. "May someone outbid me on eBay if I'm lying."

"Oh my God," Meg cried. "Look it up! Look it up!"

Juny placed a hand on her shoulder. "Are you sure you're ready to do this?"

"Of course," Meg sputtered, ignoring the echo of her mother's warning in her head. She gazed into Juny's eyes. "I have to know." Then she turned back to Nikki. "Please check."

Nikki began clacking away on the keyboard, navigating her way through folders and passwords, paging through sheets of names and numbers until finally, there it was: Nathaniel Holland. An invitation was indeed mailed to him for the reunion, but there was no checkmark in the column marked *RSVP*.

"Could be he was busy," Nikki said, catching Meg staring at the blank box. "Maybe he didn't have time to respond."

Or maybe the address was old and out-of-date and Nate Holland never received it.

Nikki pulled a Post-it off a pad and jotted down the address. She placed the paper in Meg's hand. "Even if he isn't here, we'll find him."

"Thank you," Meg said, and hugged her friend.

Juny pecked his sister on the top of her head. "I will never again give you grief about spending too much time on the computer."

"Promise?" Nikki looked up sharply at the clock on the

wall. "Go, go," she said, shooing them out the door. "Principal Betts is coming."

Meg sat in the front passenger seat of Mr. Hernandez's Ford SUV. The seats were plush leather, the stereo held an eight-CD changer and an iPod adapter, and there were about a million cup holders in the thing. Normally, Meg would have been impressed, but under the circumstances, it barely registered. Instead, she was fixated on the house in front of her.

"My dad says Brooklyn Heights shouldn't be a part of Brooklyn," Juny said, fiddling with the stereo's buttons from his place behind the steering wheel. "It's got these beautiful historic brownstones and really amazing views of the harbor and the whole skyline. It's not like anyplace else in the city."

Meg glanced up and down the street they were parked on and had to agree. Nathaniel Holland lived in one of those big, beautiful brownstones at the end of a quiet street, steps from the promenade. The house was gorgeous and gigantic, easily four times the size of Alma's row house in Astoria. How many bedrooms were there? Meg wondered. Five, six?

The drive from Astoria to Brooklyn Heights, to this street, this *house*, had taken no more than half an hour. After exiting the BQE, they had crawled along the neighborhood roads at five miles per hour, searching for the number on Meg's Post-it. Number 47.

And there it was. Seeing it nearly made Meg flip her decaf cappuccino into her lap.

"I think it might snow," Juny said, peering through the windshield and up at the blank sky. "Sort of feels like snow."

He was jittery, Meg knew, and not from the triple espresso he'd drunk twenty minutes ago. She was anxious too, although her anxiety manifested itself much more quietly; she had spoken not a word since their arrival in the neighborhood. When they had found the house, they hadn't rushed to judgment. They couldn't, after all, presume the house belonged to Meg's father. He hadn't returned his reunion invitation. He might have moved. Anything could have happened. So Juny crept past the house—so slowly, a turtle could have lapped him—right along the curb.

A sign on the front gate said *Holland.*

Meg inhaled sharply.

"There it is," Juny said. "Should we knock or—"

"No." Meg didn't hesitate.

"Why not?" Juny asked.

"Just—not yet," she had said. That was fifteen minutes ago. Fifteen minutes in which Meg merely stared at the house, willing it to reveal its secrets.

It was four in the afternoon, a weekday, yet no one was in the street. No child played in a yard, no neighbors gossiped over a fence.

Where *is* everybody? Meg worried. A panicky feeling rose in her chest. Juny must have sensed her anxiety. He took her hand gently in his own and rested it in his lap. Meg was thankful for his strong presence. They would wait.

Someone would be home soon. In an hour or two, after the workday had concluded.

"So, this is a nice car your father has," Meg remarked.

"Uh, yeah, yeah, it is," Juny said, perhaps surprised to hear Meg's voice. "We didn't have a car when I was a kid. My dad said they were impractical in New York, and we always took the subway. This is sort of a new thing for him."

"What made him change his mind?"

"Mariela. When she came along, the world shifted for my dad." He laughed self-consciously. "I guess it shifted for all of us."

"What do you mean?"

"Mari was born right after 9/11. I think at first, Nikki and I were a little jealous of her. I was just starting football in junior high, and Nikki was big into science then—"

"Nikki?" Meg had to interrupt. "Your sister, Nikki, was into science?"

Juny shrugged, smiled. "Nik's got a lot of sides to her, and they're not all covered in brand names."

Meg giggled, picturing Nikki in chemistry lab safety goggles with a little Dolce & Gabbana logo on the frames. "I'm sorry. You were saying?"

"There's not much more, really. Then 9/11 happened, and Mari arrived, and Dad decided we needed a car, something that would transport us all out of here if the Apocalypse came." He tapped the steering wheel with his hands. "So here she is. The vehicle that will save us from nuclear fallout, pestilence, and a rain of frogs."

"It's a magical car," Meg agreed. "So . . . Mariela . . . you're not still jealous of her?"

Juny turned in his seat and stared at Meg. "She's the best thing that ever happened to us. To me, my dad, all of us. She was unexpected, but not unwelcome."

Meg reached out, took Juny's face in both hands, and kissed him gently on the lips. "Thank you for driving me here."

"Anytime." Juny's jacket began buzzing. "Excuse me." He took his cell phone from his pocket, glanced at it, and turned the display toward Meg to show her the number. "My mother."

Meg nodded, and Juny flipped open the phone. *"Mami, qué pasa?"*

As Juny's conversation buzzed in her ear, Meg's brain whirred. *This is not the right time to meet my father,* she thought. Maybe it was the impending snow, maybe it was the time of day, maybe it was the unease she felt at what she was doing—sitting in a car, like a stalker, lying in wait.

No, she thought. She must be forthright and enter her father's life in an honest manner.

"Meg? I've got to get the car back," Juny apologized, snapping his phone shut.

"No problem. This is good. I'm glad we came, but . . ." She shook her head. "Not today."

"You sure?" Juny asked as he started the car.

"Yes." She cast a long, lingering glance at the house as they pulled away. "Definitely."

Chapter
EIGHTEEN

Dear Jen,

How are you? I am fine.
I'm going to meet my father.

Meg stared at the sentence, unable to continue. Never in her wildest imaginings would she have believed she would ever write those words.

I'm going to meet my father. I'm on the G train now, and it only goes between Brooklyn and Queens, which is pretty weird. All of the other subway lines go through Manhattan and—
My father lives in Brooklyn Heights.

She paused and stared at the last sentence.

> *My father lives in Brooklyn Heights. Right on the water, the East River, across from the Statue of Liberty, a stone's throw from Battery Park, south of the famous Brooklyn Bridge. (Why do you suppose people think they could buy that bridge?) I am nervous and a little scared, and I have no idea what will happen when I get there. I didn't tell Juny this time because I think . . . I have to do this on my own.*
>
> *Remember that episode, the one where Rachel goes to the airport to meet Ross to tell him she loves him and she doesn't know what will happen but she thinks it's going to be great because she knows he loves her? It's kind of like that, except it sort of ended badly for Rachel when Ross came back with Julie.*
>
> *Although you knew that—you knew the script and what was coming next.*
>
> *Too bad I don't have a script, huh?*

After leaving a long-winded note for Lonnie and Alma about an early-morning meeting at school, Meg arrived at 6:30 a.m. via the G train, which was not nearly worth the exception to the rule. Other than the very retro lime green background on all of the signage, the train was no more or less a subway: practical, efficient, and empty at six in the morning.

And it took her to her father's neighborhood.

His 'hood. She chuckled to herself. *Where he hangs with his homies.* As she walked down Bergen Street from the train station, she paused to drink in the surroundings.

This is the subway station he uses, she thought, *the 'Bucks where he buys his coffee, the newsstand where he gets his papers. I'm his daughter, and I'm seeing what he sees.*

She strolled down the block and stood next to a discreet brown-lettered sign declaring the neighborhood "historical." She stared at her father's house.

Historical. Worth preserving. Not to be destroyed or forgotten simply because something newer, shinier, prettier came along.

Meg wondered if Nathaniel Holland felt the same way about people.

She had brought with her a small knapsack filled with schoolbooks, and she had dressed as if she were going to school. Black mini, black tights, brown turtle. Her wool coat and thick-soled shoes. If anyone were to wonder, she would look like a Brooklyn Heights schoolgirl. If anyone were to ask, she was waiting for a ride.

No, thanks, my friend is giving me a lift.

No, really, I don't need directions.

Thank you, but I can wait.

She tried to keep her head aloft and not let it sink into her neck and shoulders and chest. Part of her had worried that the brownstone would belong to someone else this morning, that the lettering on the gate had been a mirage she and Juny had willed into existence. But no, it was still there, and it was still his.

Her father probably had a great big beautiful living room in that gigantic house, plus a den and a study where he kept his desk and books. And the kitchen was probably separate from the dining room, and maybe there was a cozy breakfast nook. Meg pictured a deck off the family room through sliding glass doors that led directly into a flower-filled garden and a yard just right for a medium-size dog—like a beagle or a spaniel. Her father likely didn't have this dog yet. After all, it would be all alone during the day.

But he would get one. Soon.

And at night, they would sit on a swing in the yard, Meg and her father would, and look at the Manhattan skyline and remark on how lucky they were to have found each other, at long last, in this place, this enviable place, where families were whole and children and dogs roamed joyfully.

Unexpected, Meg heard Juny's voice in her head, *but not unwelcome.* As it was with Mariela and her father, so it would be with Meg and hers.

She had been imagining all of this so vividly, staring off into the middle distance, that she nearly gasped when the brownstone's front door opened and a man stepped out onto the landing.

He was dressed in a dark suit with an overcoat and leather gloves. He was carrying an attaché case in one hand and was swinging the other back and forth as he walked briskly and efficiently down the front steps. His breath came out in short white puffs, which made Meg suddenly aware of her own breath. She exhaled, and a long white warm stream filled the air in front of her.

He placed his gloved hand on the front gate and flipped

a latch that opened it from the inside. The gate swung open with nary a groan or a creak, as if someone had been taking very good care of it. Judging by the quality of Nathaniel Holland's cashmere overcoat and his sharply creased suit pants, she thought he probably wasn't the one taking care of it.

He was almost to her now, about three feet away. Not close enough to touch, but she could see his brown eyes, his almost-black wavy hair, and the dimple in his still-chiseled chin.

The yearbook photo come to life; she half expected to see his name written in the air across his neck.

His hand pushed the gate closed. He turned, and in that split second, she took a step closer, closing the gap. He caught her eye, nodded.

"Morning," he said.

"Morning," she responded.

And he walked past her, took a path around her on the sidewalk, obviously careful not to brush against her. She was just a random schoolgirl to him, after all, a Brooklyn Heights schoolgirl who was waiting for a ride from a friend, and maybe he hadn't seen her in the neighborhood before, but that was okay because she looked harmless—*was* harmless—and she was merely waiting for a ride to school.

And all she had said was . . .

"Nate!"

Meg frowned. That's not what she'd said.

"Nate, honey!"

Half a dozen feet past her, Nathaniel Holland, her father, stopped in his tracks and turned around.

At the door to his brownstone, the home that Meg imagined sharing with him, stood a woman. She was pretty but plain, with short spiky blond hair, a heart-shaped face, and a petite figure wrapped in a yellow silk bathrobe. "Didn't you forget something?"

Nathaniel Holland, Meg's father, hurriedly moved to the gate. "What's that?" He reached a hand over the gate and maneuvered the latch on the inside, his face a question mark as he considered what he had forgotten.

At the door, the pretty-plain woman stepped aside and a little girl, no more than four years old, emerged. She put her hands on her hips and said, "Daddy, I have ballet class today. Don't forget."

Meg felt gooseflesh rise on her arms, as if a sudden wind had kicked up.

Another daughter, she thought. *Another girl.*

Nathaniel Holland, Meg's father, slapped a gloved palm against his forehead in dramatic fashion. "I'm sorry, Bunny. Of course I won't forget. I'll come pick you up the minute your class is over."

The pretty, plain, petite woman put her hands around her mouth in imitation of a megaphone. "Get there a little early so you can see her do her dance."

"They're doing a dance?"

"She keeps saying you never see her dance in her class."

Nathaniel Holland sighed. "Robin, I'll have to close up my accounts before four thirty."

"Nate." She put her hands on her hips exactly like the little girl named Bunny. "Five o'clock. And use the entrance on Lafayette. The Fourth Street side is closed this week."

"Lafayette. Got it. See you later, Bunnykins!" He turned to go, waving at the little girl as he did so.

"Daddy! You didn't kiss me goodbye!"

Nathaniel Holland, Meg's father, glanced down at his watch. His brow furrowed.

Robin, the pretty woman who was both plain and petite, gently guided her daughter back into the house. "Come on, Bunny. Daddy has to go to work."

"Okay. Bye-bye, Daddy."

"Bye-bye, Bunny."

Nathaniel Holland waved as the door closed. Then, with a grin on his face, he hurried down the walk, through the gate, and past Meg.

This time, without a nod.

Meg squeezed up against the back of the subway train near the door. As passengers passed from one car to another, a whoosh of stale air that might have been trapped in the tunnels for decades assaulted her. But Meg didn't care.

How could she have been so stupid? Why hadn't she thought of another family?

At the Metropolitan Avenue stop, most of Meg's car emptied and a handful of newcomers hustled aboard. A woman, lithe and graceful, wearing an expensive-looking, tailored-to-her-figure suit and carrying a stiff leather briefcase, walked straight toward Meg and took a seat facing her. She looked like Jen when Rachel was working at Ralph Lauren. Meg closed her eyes and wished that the woman *was* Jen and that she was here for Meg and Meg alone. . . .

"What's up, kiddo?" Jen would ask.

In her mind, Meg could see Jennifer Aniston's butterscotch-colored hair wound up in a shiny French twist at the back of her head; two tendrils would hang loosely along her cheekbones, perfectly softening the updo. She'd stare up at Meg, and even under the horrific fluorescent lighting of the subway car, Jen's blue eyes would sparkle.

"Something's wrong. Talk to me," she'd say.

"He has a family," Meg would tell Jen sadly. "I never imagined another family."

Jen's mouth, sober and stern at first, would turn up into a smile. "Unexpected. But not unwelcome."

"That's what Juny said."

"Smart guy," Jen would point out.

"Yeah."

"And cute."

"Yeah," Meg would agree.

Then Jen would uncross her legs and stand up, holding on to the metal pole as the subway car swayed and rumbled on the track. "Sweetie, you have to do what's in your heart. You've come so far. Don't turn back now. You deserve this."

"I deserve this," Meg would repeat doubtfully.

"You deserve to have a family that loves you. And they *will* love you. I just know it." Jen would smile then, and the car would seem to glow a little bit brighter.

"I deserve this," Meg would say again—this time with more conviction.

"That's my girl!" Jen would cheer. Then she would glance out the window as the train slowed into the Steinway Street station. "This is your stop."

"Steinway Street!" came the announcement over the subway speaker, startling Meg from her reverie.

"Oh!" She blinked a couple of times and grabbed her backpack. "Thanks . . ." she started to say.

The woman in the seat opposite her, who was not Jennifer Aniston, gave a quizzical smile.

"H-have a nice day," Meg said, and hurried through the doors before they closed.

At four twenty, Meg arrived at the Lafayette School of Dance, near Astor Place, which was, for most people living south of 14th Street, a nexus of activity. She had prepped herself for this trip all day while she sat through English and history and chem. She knew exactly how long it would take her to walk from school to the subway, take the R train into Manhattan, and walk from the station to the dance studio. She had it all figured out.

I deserve this, she told herself. *I deserve a family that loves me. Jen said so.*

The dance school was up a cramped and dark staircase on the third floor of a nondescript brick building. The smell of sweat and mentholated creams filled the hallway. Meg wandered past studios filled with jazz and modern dancers, young and old, and then . . .

. . . there they were: a dozen tiny girls dressed in black and pink with their hair tied back in braids or pigtails. A woman at the front of the mirror-walled room was holding her arms out and her heels together, toes splayed. All of her charges were trying desperately to imitate her. Well, several were trying. A few had wandered off to one corner to do some tumbling, and a couple of others were making faces in the mirror.

Bunny, Nathaniel's Bunny, was paying attention. The teacher reached one arm over her head and stuck one pink foot out to the side, and Bunny repeated the gesture perfectly.

Very nice, Bunny, Meg read on the teacher's lips.

Thank you. Bunny smiled back.

Meg stepped closer to the window, where a number of moms were stationed, their eyes on their preschool daughters. The young teacher came to the window and knocked. "You're welcome to come in now," she said, her voice muffled by the thick plastic. The women began filing in.

Meg looked around but couldn't find Nathaniel Holland anywhere. Bunny was inside, looking too. Her hands twisted nervously in front of her.

Late again. Meg could read the disappointment on the little girl's face.

"Are you coming?" Meg heard. She turned and found the dance instructor holding the door open. "We're going to do our dance now if you'd like to join us."

"Oh, I . . ." As Meg watched, Bunny dropped her head and shuffled back to her friends. "Um, okay," she said. She slipped past the teacher and took a seat on the floor at the front of the room—right next to the parents.

"Ladies." The instructor raised her hands and began counting out the music. "Five and six and seven and eight." The tune, a waltz, sounded vaguely familiar to Meg, as if it was a Muzak version of a classical piece.

The girls pulled themselves up tall and kept their hands by their sides as they ran to the middle of the room, toe-heel, toe-heel, directly in line behind Bunny. She, being the most prepossessed of the class, stood center stage and waited for everyone to join in two lines behind her. Then she began leading the class in a series of coordinated arm and leg movements.

They looked a little like those guys at the airport waving the planes in with fluorescent orange tubes, Meg thought. Like those guys, but way cuter.

The dance continued, and she couldn't take her eyes off Bunny. Her sister was so poised, she thought.

A chill ran up her arms at the thought—*her* sister.

As the music wound to a close and the girls sashayed off to the side, Meg saw Bunny sneak a glance out the window. Just a quick one and no, Nathaniel Holland still wasn't there, watching from the sidelines. Meg knew, because *she* had been looking too.

The class broke up, and all the children rushed to their mothers, who thanked the young instructor for turning their hyperactive daughters into adorable princesses.

And there was Bunny, alone, packing up her dance bag—pink, of course, with tutu-ed little girls on it—quietly heading out the door. She didn't look at all bothered by the fact that her father hadn't arrived. Instead, she carried herself as though this was just another part of the routine.

Meg smiled at the notion of a four-year-old having a routine. Like an assembly-line worker or an accountant.

"Bunny?" she called.

The girl stopped and peered at Meg warily.

"You danced beautifully today."

Bunny looked Meg up and down, and apparently decided she looked mostly harmless. "Thank you." She stepped outside to the carpeted waiting area and began taking off her pink slippers. Part of Meg had wanted to be jealous of the little girl, of her place in her father's house and life, but another part—the greater part—wouldn't let her.

"Do you need some help tying your shoes?" Meg asked. Then she winced. Did that sound like a line from *The Kidnapper's Handbook*? Just a step up from, "Want some candy, little girl?"

"No, thank you," Bunny said politely.

"Okay." Meg looked around again, saw no sign of Nathaniel. Where the hell was he?

"My name is Meg. What's yours?"

The girl looked up at her beneath dramatically heavy

lids. "You know. You called me by my name already."

Meg laughed. The kid was smart; she liked that. "You're Bunny." She smiled.

"That's not my real name. My real name is Beatrice," Bunny elaborated, fumbling a bit on her given name. "I have a hamster, but I hardly ever feed him because I really wanted a dog, but Daddy wouldn't let me, and in my room, I have my own telephone so I can talk to Grandma when she calls from Florida. Once I went on a plane to visit her." She narrowed her gaze. "All by myself," she concluded, as if daring Meg to contradict her.

"Wow." Meg responded with the proper amount of awe. "All by yourself? You are *so* grown up."

"I'm going to school all day next year," Bunny bragged. "Mommy says I can."

"Wow," Meg said again. "That's awesome."

"I'm waiting for my daddy," Bunny said. "He's probably running late."

Did a four-year-old understand the concept of "running late"? Or had she simply heard it so many times that it had become part of her vocabulary? Meg pointed to Bunny's untied boots. "You sure you don't want me to tie those for you?"

The little girl rolled her eyes. "I *know* how to tie them. I just don't want to."

"You'll trip and fall," Meg warned.

Bunny shrugged. "Maybe."

"You'll break your leg."

"Maybe."

"And you'll never dance again."

The girl's eyes widened. "Really?"

Meg smirked. "Maybe."

Slowly, Bunny extended her foot toward Meg. "You can tie that one."

Meg bent down on one knee, so close to the small child. "You know, Bunny . . . I'm . . . that is, I'm actually . . . from California. Do you know where California is?"

Bunny shook her head.

"It's on the other side of the country! And I took a plane all the way from California to New York."

Bunny's mouth formed a perfect little *o.* "All by yourself, like me?"

"Yes, exactly like you! I came here to see . . . to see your—" Meg looked down at the size-four shoe in her hand, at the blond preschooler standing in front of her.

No, this was not the right time, not the right place for Bunny to learn the truth. "I came here to see your dance school, actually, because I heard it had really terrific dancers. I enjoyed watching you dance very, very much."

A cloud passed across Bunny's eyes and Meg knew, she knew, the girl was thinking about her father. "I'm sure your daddy's just running late, sweetheart, like this morning."

"That happens a lot to daddies," Bunny agreed sagely.

"Yes, it does."

"Does your daddy run late too?"

"Well . . ." Meg hesitated.

From around the corner came a bustle of activity and then a relieved voice. "Bunny!"

"Daddy!" Bunny ran headfirst at her father and grabbed at his legs.

Nathaniel Holland, Meg and Bunny's father, scooped up his littlest girl and held her aloft. "I'm so sorry I'm late, Bunnykins."

"You missed my dance, Daddy."

"I know, honey, I know. Will you forgive a silly daddy?"

Bunny crossed her arms and shook her head, no.

"What if I . . . tickle you?" His fingers squeezed her middle, and she erupted in giggles.

"Stop it, Daddy! Stop it!"

"What do you say?"

"I forgive silly Daddy." Her cheeks were red with laughter.

"Okay, that's better." He pulled her up to his shoulder level and let her rest her hands on his head. "Oh, hello," he said, finally acknowledging Meg.

She took a deep breath and prepared to talk, for the very first time, to her father. "Bunny looked great today in class, Mr. Holland," she said.

"Thank you. Do I . . ." His eyes searched her face, and she thought she saw a flicker of recognition there.

"Meg. I'm Meg . . . *Shanley*." She tried to emphasize her last name without sounding like too much of a moron.

"Nate Holland. Bunny's dad." He rolled his eyes. "Obviously."

"Obviously."

"You look familiar to me," he said slowly, trying to place her. "Have we met?"

"You look familiar to me too." Meg crossed her fingers in her mind. "I'm from Queens, if that helps. Astoria?"

"My family used to live in Astoria—"

Please remember, Meg thought.

"But that was years ago, before you were born, I'm sure." He shook his head. "Oh, well. I must have seen you around here sometime when I came to pick up Bunny. She really loves her classes. She's always practicing in the house. Sometimes we can't get her to go to bed unless we've played some Chopin for her to dance to." He laughed. "I don't know how you do it, getting kids interested in classical music, but my wife and I definitely thank you."

"You're . . . welcome." Meg felt her chest cave in a little.

"She's not my teacher," Bunny said.

"What's that, honey Bunny?"

"She doesn't teach my class," the little girl clarified.

Nathaniel Holland blinked twice, and Meg would have sworn she had seen him pull his daughter—not Meg—tighter to him. "I thought you—"

"She helped me tie my shoes," Bunny said.

"I . . . yes, I did."

"But you're not her teacher?"

"No, Mr. Holland—"

"You called me by my name. Before I told you, you called me by my name. How did you know my name?"

Meg's heart thumped in her chest. This wasn't going at all the way she had intended. She had to think fast.

"I'm . . . I'm not Bunny's teacher, but I . . . help out here when I can, when parents need assistance or if they're, you know, running late. Like you were. So the girls aren't alone where someone could . . . harm them. I talk to them, help them tie their shoes or fix their hair so they don't worry about their parents forgetting about them. Like Bunny did today. With you."

There was a moment of silence when Meg stopped talking, which gave her ample time to wonder what jail cells were like in Manhattan.

"Well, thank you so much." Meg heard a note of relief in her father's voice. "I get so caught up at work, and it's hard to pull away. I know that's not much of an excuse." He sighed. "I'm glad she has someone here she can trust to take care of her until I arrive." He nuzzled the little girl's neck with his nose. "Right, Bunnykins?"

Bunny smiled. "I like Meg."

Nathaniel Holland lowered his daughter to the floor. "Get your stuff together and let's go home." He reached into his jacket pocket and handed Meg a card. "This is my office number."

Meg swallowed. "Your . . ."

"In case anything happens, if you need me. Like class gets out early or she gets hurt or something. Would you please give me a call?" His broad face was apologetic, asking *her* forgiveness.

Meg fingered the card's thick stock. "Of course," she whispered.

"I'm ready, Daddy." Bunny pulled a pink wool hat down over her ears and held her dance bag up to her father. "You can carry it."

Meg walked with father and daughter down the stairs and out to the street. Nathaniel stopped and turned to look at Meg. "You didn't have to walk us all the way out."

"Oh, I'm . . . finished for the day."

"Really? Too bad you don't live in Brooklyn Heights," he said. "I might have asked you to help Bunny get home." He stopped and then added hastily, "I would have paid you, of course."

Meg's heart beat harder. An invitation to her father's home. "I could do that," she heard herself say.

"You could?"

"Obviously not today, but next week, sure, and the week after, yeah." She saw him looking at her skeptically.

"But you're in Astoria."

"My—my boyfriend lives in Brooklyn Heights," she quickly covered. "What a pain, huh?" She rolled her eyes. "So if you want, I could, you know, take care of Bunny."

Nate Holland looked from one daughter to the other, not completely aware he was doing so, and then nodded. "Okay, sure. Give me a call and we'll talk about it."

"That would be amazing. Thanks."

"Bye, Meg." Little Bunny waved her pink-mittened hand.

"Bye, Bunny." Meg waved back as her half sister dragged her father down the street. After a moment, they disappeared in the falling snow.

Nathaniel's business card felt like it was burning a hole in Meg's pocket. She took it out and stared at it: *Nathaniel Holland, Vice President, International Sales*. And then the name of his company and the address.

Downtown, near Wall Street.

She brought the card to her mouth and gently pressed her lips against the raised lettering. "Hi, Dad," she whispered.

She would see him again, and Bunny too. And maybe in the not-too-distant future she would meet his wife. She was reluctant to put the card away, but the snow was falling faster and thicker, and soon the paper would melt in her hand. She slipped it inside her jacket pocket and felt its warmth radiate through her hand.

"Bye, Dad," she said quietly.

Chapter
NINETEEN

Meg and her grandmother sat in the sixth row from the front of the church on the inside aisle. No one sat near them, behind or beside, because they were an hour early for Sunday Mass. Unlike Lonnie, Meg wasn't bothered by church attendance. It was a small thing that would keep Alma relatively pleasant for a day.

Plus, Juny would be there.

Meg sighed. Life could not be better than it was right at that very second.

She had met her father. Her *father*. For years and years and years and in all of the places she lived and the schools she attended, she didn't even know she had one. There was only Lucie. And sometimes, there was barely that.

"Let me call my dad and see if he'll let me," she practiced

saying in her head. A slight roll of the eyes would be good directly following a line like that, she thought. Or how about, "My dad says I can stay out after the prom, but I have to be back by one."

Definitely. An eye roll was *definitely* called for there.

"My dad gave me a lift."

"My dad loaned me his car."

"My dad said the funniest thing yesterday."

Yeah. It was good. *All good.*

"What are you smiling for?" Alma asked in a sharp whisper. "Christ died for your sins and you're laughing in His house?"

"I wasn't laughing," Meg whispered back. "I was just . . . feeling His love, okay?"

The rest of the congregation began trickling in; Meg kept her eyes peeled for the Hernandez family. They typically arrived five minutes before Mass began. Of course, *they* didn't care where they sat, because *they* didn't have a crazy woman with them. Meg hoped Juny was wearing the sweater she liked, a maroon-and-navy cotton-wool blend with a black stripe around the collar. They were especially good colors on him with his dark hair and skin.

My father would probably look good in those colors too, she thought. She had only seen him twice, and both times he was wearing a suit. *But he must dress down occasionally, like when he takes Bunny to the park or skating.*

Meg decided then and there she wouldn't be one of those kids who always gave her father a tie for his birthday. She would only give him things that they could use together—like DVDs to watch or CDs to listen to, games to play, and tickets to shows. Bunny could come too, and Robin, the mother, because they would all be *The Hollands*—one happy family.

"Wipe that smile off your face," Alma said. She smacked her hymnal against the back of Meg's hand.

Meg calmly shifted her butt over a few inches, leaving a blank space between herself and her grandmother.

Nate and his girls, Meg thought. *That's what people will say when we pass by. There go the Hollands.*

As Meg stood with Bunny on the 6 platform in the Astor Place subway station, she felt like she was in possession of a giant egg—an easily damaged, thin-shelled object that could crack at any moment if she were to look aside, even for a fraction of a second, distracted by a shiny object on the tracks. She was petrified she would lose the little girl, misplace her, or worse.

Her father would never forgive her for that.

"Stick close to me, okay, Bunny?" Meg insisted.

The little girl sighed as if to indicate her vast experience in subway travel—knowledge to which Meg, a transplanted Californian, could only aspire. However, she did grip Meg's hand tighter when the crowd pressed up against them, as well as when they boarded the train, which made Meg smile.

Meg and Nate and Bunny's mother, Robin, had all come

to an agreement: after ballet class, every week, Meg would be paid a not-unreasonable sum plus reimbursement of her expenses—MetroCard, snacks for herself and Bunny, a taxi from Borough Hall if the weather was especially wretched—to deliver the child safe and sound to her very doorstep. In a phone call, Robin had insisted—warily, it had seemed to Meg—that there be no detours, no smoking, and no other children. Bunny was to be Meg's only charge.

None of those caveats was a problem for Meg.

Robin, the anxious mother, also required an additional reference—her husband's apparently wasn't adequate—so Meg gave her Nikki's number in the principal's office. Speaking not as a friend or sister of Meg's boyfriend but rather as a rising star in school administration, Nikki confidently vouched for Meg as a top student who truly stood out among her classmates as a mature, responsible teenager.

Robin appeared to be satisfied with Nikki's appraisal, and that was the end of the inquisition. Meg thanked God Robin hadn't asked to talk to her parent or guardian. She hadn't yet told Alma or Lonnie that she had met Nate Holland. Lonnie would only worry for her, and Alma would be sure to screw it up somehow, determined as she was to make life miserable for those around her.

No, Meg realized, it would be best if she kept this particular item tightly under wraps.

"Did you know, Bunny, that the 6 train is a local, but the 4 and 5 are express? They go really fast in Manhattan, and they skip the small stops."

Bunny stared up at Meg blankly. *Okay,* Meg thought, *maybe that was a boring thing to say to a four-year-old.* Perhaps she should try again.

"So, do your mommy and daddy take you places, like, I don't know, the movies?"

Bunny's face lit up. "I love movies."

"You do? What movies do you love?"

"I've seen *Cinderella* a billion times. She's my favorite princess of all the princesses."

"Are there lots of princesses?"

Bunny became animated as she explained the inner workings of the princess empire. Her tiny pink mittens punctuated the air with every point she made. "There's Snow White and Sleeping Beauty and Jasmine and Ariel, and they all have their own movies, and I've got a Cinderella dress that I wore at Halloween, but Mommy says I can wear it for my birthday too, and I'm gonna have Cinderella come for my birthday party and she's gonna tell princess stories and play games, and I'm gonna be five on my next birthday. You can come if you want."

Meg was moved by the invitation. "I can?"

Bunny nodded. "But you can't wear a Cinderella dress because I'm wearing a Cinderella dress. You can be . . ." The little girl stopped, considered. "You can be Aurora. That means Sleeping Beauty."

"When's your birthday?" Meg asked.

"July eighth. That's my birthday. July eighth."

Meg clapped her hands. "That's like mine!" It was easy

to exaggerate gestures in the presence of a four-year-old, she noticed. Everything big: big smiles, big frowns, big hand movements. She felt self-conscious about it at first, especially in a train filled with business types in suits and dour expressions, but after a little while, she didn't even notice them. It was really just Bunny and Meg, two sisters together in a magical world of princesses.

Bunny's eyes went wide. "Really? Your birthday is July eighth, too?"

"It's actually July twelfth, but we were born in the same month. That makes us both pretty special, huh?"

"Yeah." Bunny, the young skeptic, had a look of pure adoration on her face. "You can share my party if you want. And you can even have some of my cake."

"Well, thank you very much," Meg replied with a big smile.

Wow, she thought. Sharing with her sister—it was something she was practically born to do. And something she could definitely get used to.

Chapter
TWENTY

Dear Jen,

How are you? I am fine.

I've been kind of worried about all the lies I've been telling. I started out small—just to keep things moving and everyone happy. Then it snowballed. The lie I told Robin about Juny living in Brooklyn Heights has now turned into Robin wanting to meet Juny and see where he lives. So I had to lie again, and I just picked some random street address that I saw in the phone book and crossed my fingers that Robin didn't know the people who lived there. And I've been telling my grandmother that I tutor a kid once a week so she doesn't bug me about being gone till supper, and then I was late one day when the subway broke down and now she wants to call the kid's parents and tell them when we eat and how important it is that I be home to cook for her. I thought fast and told her the kid's parents are deaf and couldn't talk on the phone, so she backed off that one. Whew.

   Lies beget lies. . . . I never lied before, not even to Lucie. But God knows Lucie lied to me my whole life. And her mother lies all the time too.

   I wonder if it's hereditary. I hope the Hollands aren't liars so at least I'll have some genetic balance.

   Do you think the ends justify the means in my situation? I thought so, but the weight of it all is kind of killing me. I think I need to come clean—and soon.

Love,

m

Meg vowed never to take the sun for granted again. She had done that when she lived in SoCal—everybody did, unless they were from the East Coast. Winter in New York really made her appreciate the warm caress of the golden globe.

   One day in early February, a day when the sky was especially gray, the air was obscenely gloomy, and Juny was required to stay late to talk to his counselor about colleges, Meg dragged her butt out the front door of the high school. She found Lonnie standing on the sidewalk at the base of the steps, holding a pair of to-go cups in his hands.

   Meg stopped in the middle of the steps and smiled. Suddenly, it seemed, the day got a little brighter.

   "Hey," he called.

   "Coffee?" she asked, nodding toward the cups.

   "Hot chocolate."

She walked toward him then, took a cup from his out-stretched hand, took a sip. The cocoa was heavenly and thick, like a pool of melted Hershey's Kisses.

"Thanks." Meg slurped, blissed out on cocoa goodness. "What brings you here?"

"I hardly ever see you now." Lonnie shrugged. "I miss you."

"You do?" Meg was touched.

"Yeah. I mean, it's great hanging out with Toni and the boys every night, but I like spending time with you. And I feel like I was just getting to know you."

Meg noticed he didn't make mention of Alma. "Same here," she said.

"Hey, you want to go somewhere? Just you and me?" He pointed to a late-model minivan parked at the curb with a sign reading *Toni's Furniture Emporium.* "I've got the car today."

"I didn't know you did deliveries."

Lonnie nudged her with his elbow. "Why? You wanna buy a couch?"

Meg laughed. "No–"

"Free delivery in Queens and Brooklyn," Lonnie said, as if he were trying to make a sale. "Extra for the Bronx and Manhattan. And don't even talk to me about Staten Island."

"Do you get good tips?" Meg wanted to know.

"You'd be surprised at the people who *don't* tip. I get crap from the people who buy the five-thousand-dollar leather sectionals. But the lady who orders a bed for her cats gives me ten bucks—plus coffee and pastries."

Meg wondered if her dad was a good tipper. Would he have offered Lonnie a cold drink or a hot coffee? She hoped Nathaniel Holland was more like one of those cat ladies than one of the sectionals.

"Remember when you first got here and we took the subway all over Manhattan?" Lonnie asked. "It seems like only yesterday."

"Well, it was just a few months ago."

"I know . . . but that was fun, wasn't it? It was a good start to your adventures here."

They had seen the Empire State Building and Central Park, stood at the rivers Hudson and East, crossed the Brooklyn Bridge, and ridden the Roosevelt Island tram. It *had* been fun. Lonnie had gone out of his way to introduce his only niece to the city.

"Yeah," Meg said truthfully. "I'll never forget it."

Lonnie smiled. "Good."

"Hey, Lonnie . . .you know you can always give me a call some night. Just to say hi."

He shrugged. "I called a few times, but *she* always answered, and I didn't know what to say."

"Ah, yes."

"Hop in. I'm gonna take you to my favorite diner in Brooklyn. It's called Kellogg's, and it's in Williamsburg, and they serve the best coffee."

"Better than Starbucks?"

"Star-what?" Lonnie asked. "I have no idea what you're talking about."

Meg laughed and got into the van. "Never mind. Must be a California thing."

She was late getting back; she and Lonnie had been talking, not realizing the time, and suddenly it was six. He drove like a madman, but still, she was half an hour past due at home.

"Where were you?" Alma demanded as Meg walked through the front door and straight into the kitchen. "This isn't your tutoring day."

Lonnie wouldn't come in, so she was forced to invent a story. "The kid needed an extra session," Meg said. "He has a test this week."

Alma grumbled. "You are going to give me that boy's number."

Meg ignored her grandmother and began cooking dinner. Pasta, she decided, or better, mac-n-cheese like Aaron made.

"I've been here all day," Alma said. Her voice was like a thousand needles pricking Meg's skin, making her flinch. "Don't you have any concern for *me*?"

"You could go out," Meg said pleasantly enough. "We both know you're capable of doing many things on your own."

"I am an old woman," Alma insisted. "I could break a hip on that ice. My blood could become infected. I could die."

"You won't die from a broken hip." Meg found a glass dish and began greasing the sides with butter. What else was in the recipe? Bread crumbs, cheese, pasta.

"You are rude and ungrateful," Alma said. "And you need to go to church more often."

"We already go once a week."

"We will be attending Mass in the mornings from now on. I have made a decision."

"I have to go to school in the mornings. I don't have time to go to church."

"Then you will go to parochial school."

"What?" Meg grimaced. "No chance."

Meg's grandmother gripped the back of one of the kitchen chairs. "Those public schools are filled with the wrong sorts of people. Bad influences. Drugs. Alcohol. Sex."

Meg put her foot down. "I'm not going anywhere. I like my school."

The phone rang then, and Meg was thankful for the distraction. Her grandmother would probably go on a tear for a while about the sorts of people who hung up on other people, but at least she wouldn't be yelling at *her*. For a few minutes, then, Meg could cook in peace. What was the sequence again? Melt the cheese in a pot and then add the pasta or the other way around?

"No, you may not talk to her," Meg heard Alma say. "You may never talk to her again, and you will never see her again. You are a filthy boy, and your family is disgusting!"

Meg froze in fear. Alma couldn't be talking to Juny,

could she? Belatedly, she dropped the cheese into the saucepan and charged the living room waving a wooden spoon. She grabbed for the phone in her grandmother's hand, but it was too late; Juny had hung up. "Alma! What the hell did you say to my boyfriend?"

"Nothing that he doesn't already know," her grandmother said with a smug grin. "Nothing that *you* don't already know."

Meg struggled to keep herself calm. Juny was a very understanding person. He wouldn't hold Alma's craziness against her.

Still, it was a hell of a thing to do.

"Juny never did anything to you," Meg said. "And neither did I. So why—*why* are you so mean?"

Alma raised a tobacco-stained forefinger to Meg's face. "*You* drove my boy away. It's *your* fault he's never here."

"Lonnie is thirty years old, and he's in love." Meg marched back into the kitchen and turned the gas on under a pot of water. "Deal with it."

"He doesn't love her," Alma said. She stood at the edge of the doorway, her nails digging into the door frame. "He loves me. He's *my* boy." Then she turned and walked away. "This is all *your* fault," she muttered again.

Meg felt tears spring to her eyes as she took down a box of pasta from the cupboard.

My grandmother is old, she told herself. *She's old and frail, and it isn't her fault that life didn't work out the way she wanted.*

Meg sat heavily in a kitchen chair.

Yes, her grandmother was old, but she knew exactly what she was saying.

Chapter
TWENTY-ONE

"Tell me again why I'm coming with you to your dad's house," Juny said as he and Meg walked the two short blocks from Astor Place to the Lafayette School of Dance. A light snow swirled about their heads, melting before it could make an impression on the ground.

"I need to prove to Robin that you exist and that you live in Brooklyn Heights," Meg repeated.

"But I *don't* live there," Juny said, pointing out the obvious.

"I know," Meg whispered. She had been telling lies to Robin for the past few weeks, but this would be her last, she promised herself: a final lie to put the previous lies to rest. "You'll just . . . have to trust me on this one."

They walked in silence for another half block, gloved hand in gloved hand, scarves commingling in the wind.

"I'm sorry about what happened the other night with my grandmother," Meg said.

"You don't have to apologize," Juny reassured her. "I know it had nothing to do with you."

"She hates me," Meg blurted.

"She doesn't hate you."

"No, I really think she does."

"She's your grandmother. Grandmothers don't hate. They bake chocolate chip cookies and knit ugly sweaters." Juny smiled. "Making people fat and unattractive is how they show their love."

Meg laughed and shook her head. "You don't know the Shanleys. We are so screwed up."

"Messed-up families are great inspiration for a creative mind. Maybe I'll write about you someday."

"Okay," Meg said. "Just give me perfect teeth, would you? And make me taller."

Juny leaned down and kissed her. "Nope. You're just the right height."

They stopped walking.

"Is this the place?" Juny asked.

They were outside the dance school. A pair of little girls came barreling down the steps followed by their mothers.

"Yeah," Meg said. "You can tell by the tutus."

Bunny thought Juny was about the greatest thing since the invention of princesses. And he knew just how to handle her, his experience with Mariela having prepared him. He wasn't afraid to get down to her level or to hoist her onto his shoulders so she could see down the street. He told her silly jokes and made weird faces and generally looked the fool but without a trace of embarrassment.

Where Juny really turned on the charm, though, was with Robin. He praised her home's architecture, her decorating skills, and her child-rearing abilities. And the way Juny called the view from the back patio "breathtaking," Meg would have thought Robin herself had hand-painted the Manhattan skyline.

In the end, it worked like a charm. Robin offered them sodas and cookies, and she gave in to all of Bunny's demands with a smile.

And then, a miracle occurred, one that Meg had been hoping for from the moment she took the job: her father walked in while she was still there.

Everyone who belonged in the Holland home was present. They were all there—together.

"Robin? I'm home," Nate called. Meg heard a set of keys jingle as they were hung up, a rustle of overcoat and gloves. She resisted the urge to run to her father and throw her arms around him as she knew her sister would.

Robin invited her husband into the kitchen. "We're in here, honey," she said. She accepted a kiss on the cheek from Nate. "You know Meg, of course, and this is her boyfriend, Juny Hernandez."

"Good to meet you, sir," Juny said politely as he offered his hand for a shake. "I've heard a lot about your family."

"Oh, really?" Nate smiled at Meg. "We hear a lot about Meg too. Meg likes chocolate and Meg flies on planes and Meg doesn't brush her teeth."

"What? No, no," Meg stammered. "I brush my teeth."

The grown-ups laughed. "That's the way little kids are," Robin said. "When you're around them often enough, you become a part of their vocabulary."

"My baby sister, Mariela, used me as her excuse not to take naps or eat her vegetables," Juny told Nate and Robin. "She thought she was pretty clever too, but she never got away with anything."

"Didn't your parents tell her not to lie?" Meg asked.

"Oh, they're just little white lies," Nate said. "No harm, no foul."

Exactly. Meg smiled to herself.

"Can you both stay for dinner?" Robin asked.

Wow, Meg thought. She was about to accept the invitation when—

"Sorry, Mrs. Holland," Juny said. "I have to get home. Lots of homework tonight."

Meg had an urge to elbow Juny in the ribs. *Wrong answer!* But it was too late.

"Oh, right, homework," she said. "I should go too."

"Maybe another time," Robin said, and Nate nodded in agreement.

"You're welcome whenever you like."

Meg's heart fluttered at the open invitation. Everything

she wanted—everything she had ever dreamed—it was all
finally happening.

Juny and Meg were silent as they walked to the Court Street
station, silent as they waited on the N, R platform.

While Juny periodically peered down the tunnel, Meg
sat on a wooden bench and stared at the ground. There
were hundreds—no, thousands—of gray and black blobs on
the concrete platform. Blobs of chewing gum, as gross as
that sounded. She couldn't imagine that there were that
many people in the city who simply spat their gum onto
the ground and continued walking, but there was the evi-
dence staring her right in the face.

"Okay, what'd I do?" Juny asked. He stuffed his hands
in his pockets.

Meg sighed. "Do you really have a lot of homework?"

"Yeah. Don't you?"

"Maybe. But who cares? We were invited to stay, and
you said no. How could you say no?" Exasperated, she
leaned forward and rested her chin in her palms.

"He said you had an open invitation," Juny argued.
"Just go back next week and tell them you want to eat with
them."

"Just like that?"

"Yeah, just like that. What's the big deal?"

"The big deal is that it's *next week*!" Meg's voice echoed
underground. "This is all taking too long, and he doesn't
even know who I am!"

She stopped and heard her voice fade from the air.

"I have to tell Nate Holland that he's my father."

Juny turned to her. "Meg, I know you're going nuts about this. But think about it first. Think about how you're going to do it. Whatever you say is going to change this guy's life forever."

"Really? Well, what about *my* life?" she snapped. "When does *it* change forever?"

Meg could feel herself growing impatient with Juny, but it wasn't *him*. It was the situation.

"Just . . . don't jump into anything," Juny counseled. He bent down to kiss her lips. "I don't want you to get hurt."

Meg appreciated Juny's worry—his concern.

But it was time. Time to change *everyone's* lives forever.

Chapter
TWENTY-TWO

Dear Jen,

How are you? I am fine.

Last night I watched that "Phoebe" episode, the one where she and Joey and Chandler drive to see her father and they sit outside while she figures out what she's going to say, but she can't do it.

She keeps trying, but she can't. She doesn't want to break the illusion of him she had built up in her head, so she never goes in. Remember that one? Anyway, I kind of feel like Phoebe—except I never had any illusions. I didn't even know I had a dad.

I wonder sometimes, why isn't my life filled with romance and crazy mix-ups and misunderstandings that get solved in thirty minutes?

They should make a show about my life. I bet it would get good *ratings. It'd be like a train wreck you couldn't not look at.*

Okay, here goes. Cross your fingers and wish me luck.

The brokerage firm where Nathaniel Holland worked was guarded by two stone sculptures: a bull and a bear. Symbols, Meg knew somehow, of the fluctuations in the stock market. Exactly what they symbolized, she wasn't sure, but they reminded her of the lions outside the Public Library on Fifth Avenue. She had imagined those lions coming to life, springing into action should someone or something threaten the precious books inside. What would *these* animals protect?

Last night, Meg had tried on nearly every item of clothing in her closet, modeling each outfit in a full-length mirror until she finally came up with the perfect one: a pair of gray wool slacks with two-inch cuffs, a navy blue turtleneck sweater, and a paisley scarf. She had practiced what she would say, sitting in a chair in front of Lonnie's old desk.

As she spoke, she imagined Nate Holland in a cavernous wood-paneled office filled with expensive antiques, mahogany and leather furniture, and a stuffed raven on the bookshelf.

She didn't know why her brain insisted on the dead bird. It wasn't like her father was Edgar Allen Poe or something.

She would be ushered in alone, perhaps offered an espresso or a cup of tea—which she would decline because she would be nervous and might spill it on herself.

Her father would be finishing up some sort of important

international sale, a call to Paris or London on the speak-
erphone, and indicate she should take a seat in a plush
leather chair. And when he turned his full attention to her,
as she knew he would, he would do so with a smile, letting
her know he was all hers.

All hers.

Then she would tell him what she had to tell him, and
he would rise from his chair and come around the desk and
take her in his arms and welcome her, welcome her to her
family.

Now, inside his office building, Meg's elevator passed
floor eleven, on its way to twelve.

Soon, Meg thought. *Very soon.*

She stared at the numbers overhead: after twelve, the lift
rose to fourteen, which was the highest floor in the building. But since there was no thirteenth floor, the fourteenth
was the thirteenth. One could call it fourteen, call it fifteen,
call it ninety-nine and a half, but it was still the thirteenth
floor.

The elevator doors slid open, and Meg faced two receptionists and a wall of windows that looked out over New
York Harbor and the Statue of Liberty.

"Can I help you?" asked one of the receptionists.

"I'm here to see Nate Holland," Meg replied.

"Do you have an appointment?"

"No."

"Will he know what this is regarding?" The woman
reached for a list of phone numbers.

"Um, no."

The woman put down the list. "Then who are you?"

"I'm his daughter's dance teacher's assistant. Bunny's."

"You're Bunny?"

"No, I'm Meg Shanley."

"And you're . . ."

"His daughter's dance teacher's assistant."

"Daughter's . . ."

The woman trailed off. Meg wondered, was she being deliberately obtuse?

"Just tell him it's Meg Shanley, the babysitter."

The woman punched four numbers into the phone and waited a moment. "Mr. Holland? There's a Meg Shanley to see you." A pause. "Babysitter." Another pause. "Meg." She pressed a button on the phone. "Room 1208 down the hall on your right."

Meg walked past the reception area and made her way down the corridor.

Okay, so the walls were not paneled with wood but rather made of thick glass. And Nate's office was not cavernous, but more of a nine-by-nine square.

He was on the phone when she came in and staring at a PC screen.

"Yes, sir, of course we can do that. . . . Uh-huh, okay. No, I wouldn't advise that, sir. . . . All right, if you insist." He caught Meg's eye and motioned for her to sit in the single vinyl-seated chair in front of his chrome-and-glass desk. He held up his forefinger as if to say, one minute.

Meg slid her knapsack to the carpeted floor and looked around at her father's office. There were a few photo frames on his desk: pictures of Robin and Bunny, no doubt, although she couldn't see them from this angle. On the wall was a reproduction of a Wyeth painting—Andrew, not N. C., she believed. Against the glass, it looked like it was suspended in midair.

The transparent walls made it possible for Meg to see through to the other offices: a woman to her father's left, another man to his right, several more men beyond that, each office nearly identical in its design, each computer in the same place on the desk, each phone, each chair, each framed reproduction of American art.

She had not been offered an espresso or a cup of tea or even a glass of water. And there did not appear to be enough room in the tiny office for Meg's father to come around his desk and gather her in a hug.

No matter, she told herself. She heard Juny's voice in her head, reassuring her: *Unexpected, but not unwelcome.*

"Now, Meg, how can I help you? Is Bunny okay?" Nate's forehead creased with worry.

"It's not Bunny, Mr. Holland." Meg felt her thighs begin to quiver, on the verge of shaking uncontrollably. She pressed her knees together to stop them. "It's . . .well, there was something I wanted to talk to you about."

"I'm kind of busy this morning. Can it wait? Give me your number and I'll call you later."

Meg shook her head. She had to continue—had to or

else she might never. "This will only take a minute, Mr. Holland. I swear."

Nate sneaked a peek at his colleagues, who were all deep in their work, hands on keyboards, phones to their ears. The Plexiglas muffled the voices, but Meg knew that everyone could hear her if they chose to.

"Okay," Nate Holland said. "Shoot."

Meg placed her hands on her shaking knees and took a deep breath. "You were a graduate of RFK High in Astoria in 1992."

"Excuse me?" Nate sat up straighter in his chair.

"And in that year, your senior year, you met and dated a girl named Lucille Shanley. Lucie Shanley, she was a freshman."

Nate's face twisted in confusion. "Wait a minute, wait. What are you talking about?"

Meg reached for her knapsack and pulled out a yearbook—the one from Lonnie's blue trunk—with Nate's photo in it.

"Where did you get that?"

Meg flipped to a photo of the cheerleading squad on the football field and pointed to Lucie, who was standing on top of another uniformed girl. She had one foot on the girl's back, the other in her hand stretched out in a sort of vertical split. She had a huge grin on her face, like she had no idea what was to become of her, like she had the world by a string. How could she have known that *this* would be the best time of her life? That this was her peak?

"You were on the football team, and Lucie was a cheer-leader, and you guys met at a party. You . . ." She swallowed hard and couldn't look at her father. "Hooked up a few times."

Nate's hands were now trembling like Meg's knees. His voice was thick, as if his tongue had swollen and filled his mouth. "May I?" He took the yearbook from Meg and flipped through the pages, slowly easing himself into the past. He found his own photo, his own words, his own accomplishments, and he smiled a small smile to himself. "This was my best friend in high school," he said, pointing to a square black-and-white photo. "I wonder whatever happened to him."

"Mr. Holland."

"And this was the girl who asked me to the Sadie Hawkins dance in my sophomore year. High school was one of the best times of my life."

"Mr. Holland . . ."

Now is the time, Meg thought. *Now is the best time. Now is the best time of your life. . . .*

"Hmmm?"

Meg leaned over the desk and turned the page back to the cheerleaders in their pyramid pose. She pointed to Lucie again. "This girl? Lucie Shanley? That's my mother."

"Okay."

"And you, Mr. Holland, you're my father."

There. It was out. It was out in the world—out of her head, finally!

"I'm . . ."

All the color drained from Nathaniel Holland's face in that moment. Meg could actually see the rosiness of his cheeks drip down past his chin and into his neck, where it pooled, bright red, above his collar.

"I'm . . ." he said again.

"You didn't date. Not exactly. But you and Lucie were . . ." She closed her eyes. She *really* didn't want to look at Nathaniel Holland at this moment. "You were . . . you know . . . *together*, and Lucie got pregnant, and then she got sent away to California, where I was born. Your parents knew, because they paid her, they paid us, to stay in California and not come back or contact you." By the time she had finished, her voice was no louder than a whisper, but it didn't matter. because Nate Holland had apparently ceased breathing. "As soon as I found out about you, I had to find you because you're, well, you're my father, and I thought you should know because, well, I wanted to know you."

Nate stared at the yearbook on his desk, and his hand went to Lucie's face. He rubbed his thumb against the photo. "I don't . . ." He looked up at Meg, then back down at the yearbook. "You . . . look like her."

"Yes. I just—"

"But you don't look like me."

"What?"

Nate closed the yearbook and slid it across his desk toward Meg. "You don't look like me because you're not my daughter."

Meg blinked once–twice. "Of course I am."

Nate glanced from side to side at his colleagues, who were still engrossed in their work, unaware of the conversation in his office, unaware that the vice president of international sales was causing Meg's world to crumble around her.

"In my senior year I dated a girl named Madeline Swenson. Maddy," he said. "She was the president of the student council."

"Yes, but you broke up with her to date my mother."

Nate shook his head and continued as if he were reading off a teleprompter, as if someone had written his life's story and he was merely reciting it, not actually remembering it. "Maddy and I went to the senior prom together, and we were homecoming king and queen. We rode on a float. She went to William and Mary and I went to Columbia, and we broke up because we were too far from each other. Long-distance relationships are hard."

No. No, no, no. This wasn't how it was supposed to go.

When Meg was in Lonnie's room, in the chair across from his desk, she told her father who she was and she showed him the yearbook and he hugged her and welcomed her. Hugged her and welcomed her, damn it!

"Mr. Holland, Nate . . . D–"

"No!" He held up a hand to stop her from finishing. "No. You are not my daughter. I have a daughter named Beatrice, and we call her Bunny. She is my child, not . . ."

He leaned back in his chair. "Frankly, I don't know why

an obviously bright young woman would want to come
here with this fabrication—"

"It's not a fabrication!"

"Are you in trouble, is that it? Are you looking for
money?"

"In . . . what? No, of course not."

"That house is my wife's, you know, not mine."

"I don't care," Meg insisted. "I don't care about that!"

"Someone has lied to you."

Meg's hands balled into fists. "No one has lied to me!"
Aware that she was in a glass box, her actions visible to all,
her words muffled but audible, she stopped to take a deep
breath, to properly compose herself. She smoothed down
the front of her turtleneck.

"Okay . . . okay. I know it's hard to believe that what
I'm saying is the truth, but it is. Your parents, who live in
Florida now, they set up an account that would wire a certain amount of money to my mother, Lucie Shanley, each
month. That money was to prevent us from coming back
here and contacting you. But they knew, and my grandparents knew, and my uncle Lonnie knew, and Lucie, of
course, she knew." She rubbed her temple with two fingers. "The only people who didn't know were, well, you
and me. Isn't that funny? I just found out a few months
ago. I came out here from California to meet you. Just
meet you. I don't want any money from you. I don't want
anything."

Nate Holland drummed his fingers on the top of his

desk and let out a long breath. "Good guess on the Florida thing, by the way."

"Good . . . ?"

"Or did Bunny tell you about that while you were supposed to be taking care of her?" His lips parted to reveal his teeth, but it wasn't a smile. Not even close.

"I *was* taking care of her. She's my sister—"

"And another thing—my parents didn't have money to 'pay off' anyone." He snorted. "They barely had enough money to pay for me to go to college. I had to get a football scholarship, which I hated."

"So you didn't want to be Jack Kerouac, huh?"

Nate stopped short. "What?"

They both sat staring at each other, staring at the desk, at the floor, at the phone, out the window. They listened to the sounds of Nate's colleagues talking in their offices. Several rooms down, a man and woman laughed as if at the most uproarious joke they had ever heard.

"Meg . . ."

Her eyebrows lifted.

"I'm sorry your dad . . . left you and your mom—"

"He didn't. You didn't know—"

"But it's not me. I never met a girl named Lucie. I never had sex with anyone besides Maddy before I went to college." He leaned forward on his elbows as if he were a stockbroker about to give a client bad news about her mutual funds. "It's a story, that's all. A story your mom made up, maybe so she could feel better about the way things turned out."

"But why . . . why would she do that? And my uncle, why would he . . ." She shook her head. "If it's a story, why pick *you*?"

Nate laced his fingers together, placed the tips beneath his chin. "I was a very popular kid in high school. I played football, had a lot of friends. It's natural for people to want to claim a little piece of that."

A lyric from one of Lucie's albums ran through Meg's head: *This is not my beautiful life.*

At the thought, she almost laughed out loud. Because truly, if you didn't laugh, you'd want to slit your wrists.

"I should probably leave." Meg rose and shook out the pleats of her wool slacks. It really was a nice outfit she was wearing.

Nate rose as well and held out his hand, stockbroker to departing client. "I'm sorry things didn't work out for you, Meg."

Meg laughed ruefully. "They've certainly worked out for you."

Nate placed his hands lightly on his gym-trimmed waist and smiled, obviously relieved that she was leaving, that he had dodged that bullet. "You'll understand why we can't have you babysitting Bunny anymore."

If it was at all possible for Meg's heart to sink further into her chest, it did so now at the mention of Bunny. No more subway trips. No more princess games. No more little sister.

She nodded as she walked toward the door. "Yeah, I

understand." She kind of half expected him to follow her, to politely hold open the door for her, then have a change of heart and call her back.

But he didn't.

So she paused with her hand on the knob and said without looking at him, "If it were true, you know, if you found out I was telling the truth—"

The intercom buzzed. "Mr. Holland, you have Mr. Reynolds on line three."

"If I could prove it, would you be my father?"

Another buzz. "Excuse me, Meg, I've gotta take this call." She could hear him arranging papers on his desk. "Very important client."

Her hand was still on the knob. She could see it there as if it weren't a part of her body. She watched as it turned the handle and pulled open the door, marveled at how it gently let the knob go, watched it roll counterclockwise in her palm.

Why, she wanted to know, didn't that hand return to Nate's desk and pound on it until it was black and blue? Why didn't it grab his fat red neck and squeeze? Why didn't it brush those important client papers off the desk and pull down the faux art and make rude gestures to Nate's colleagues through the glass walls?

That's what *she* would have done—if she were in control.

"Meg?"

She turned, not too anxiously, she thought. "Yes?"

Nate Holland reached into his wallet and withdrew a sheaf of bills. He held it out to her.

"Don't . . . I didn't come here for–"

"Take it. You might need it."

She could feel every fiber of her wool pants brush against her skin as her legs carried her back to the desk. She saw her hand–that insubordinate hand!–reach out and take the money. Her head nodded.

Her father returned to his call.

She waved goodbye to the interrupting receptionist, then walked right up to the reception area windows. She stepped up on the low sill and placed her hands by her sides. She leaned forward so that only her forehead was touching the glass pane. She had done this once when she was visiting Lucie in an office building in Bakersfield. It induced vertigo almost instantaneously and felt . . . *dangerous.* Here, Meg could look down onto a small park, empty except for a knot of homeless men sharing a bottle and some workers taking a late lunch. A mile away, Lady Liberty sternly held the harbor in check. Meg closed her eyes and imagined herself passing through the pane as through a sheet of water–falling over the edge of a cliff.

"Catch me," she whispered.

She wondered if anyone could.

Meg lay curled up, fully dressed, under Lucie's eyelet bedspread until the sun cast long black shadows across the carpet and the temperature in the room dropped by fifteen degrees. Despair consumed her past the point of sleepiness. Besides, if she slept, she might dream, and she didn't trust her brain anymore.

It had imagined her down a path of disaster; it had projected hope and love and a life that could never be hers into her waking thoughts. It had concocted an utter fantasy and made her believe in it. It had created the cruelest of lies.

No, she didn't trust that brain any farther than she could throw it.

God, what a long day this has been, she thought.

She heard slow, heavy steps in the upstairs hallway and smelled smoke drift toward her. "Lonnie?" she croaked. "Is that you?"

The bedroom door swung open: there stood Alma with a glass ashtray in one hand and a white-filtered cigarette—its ash nearly an inch long—in the other.

"Would you please not smoke in here?" Meg asked.

"Lucie hated cigarettes too." Alma blew smoke toward the ceiling. "But it's my house, my rules. And one of my rules is no boys before you're eighteen."

"I wasn't with a boy."

Alma sucked in smoke with a wheezing breath. The fingers gripping her cigarette trembled as she tapped its ashes into the ashtray. "Your school called. Said you were truant. Absent without a valid excuse. I want to know where you were."

Meg's head pounded and her stomach churned. She couldn't handle her grandmother. Not today. She had to leave. Maybe she could go to Juny's—it was movie night there.

If she could just motivate herself enough to change her clothes . . .

Meg crawled out from under the covers and stood at the open closet door, staring at her options. She remembered a book from her childhood—*The Lion, the Witch, and the Wardrobe*?—in which the kids pushed through their closet and discovered a magical land while the grown-ups remained oblivious back at home.

Meg wished there were a magical land through this closet. But wishes, she had discovered, simply didn't come true.

"I know what truant is," she answered her grandmother. "I wasn't truant." She fanned a hand along the back of the closet, searching for a secret passage—just in case.

She pulled out a pair of jeans and another turtleneck sweater and began to undress.

"Then where were you?" Alma asked. "Who were you with?"

Did it matter at this point? Meg wondered. What would happen if she told her grandmother the truth? Might she finally be offered compassion, support, love?

"I went to see my father."

It was quiet in the room, save for the raspy exhale of smoke from Alma's mouth. Meg thought her grandmother might actually be considering what she said, but then she saw her upper lip lift in a sneer. "You're no better than your tramp of a mother, chasing after a man who never wanted you."

Meg pressed her lips together and turned back to the closet.

"There's a reason he didn't know about you," Alma persisted. "Why couldn't you leave well enough alone?"

"He told me," Meg muttered to her boots, "that he's not my father."

"Oh, he's your father." Alma dragged hard on her cigarette with withered lips. "It was his parents. *They* didn't want him to know. They had plans for their son—college on a football scholarship, Wall Street, marriage into a good family. *I* had plans for my child too, you know. She wasn't supposed to have a baby at fifteen."

Alma leaned against the door frame. The ashtray was heavy in her liver-spotted hand, dragging her arm down, spilling ashes all over the carpet. "She wouldn't get rid of you. 'Too late,' she said. But it wasn't too late. It's never too late."

Meg's stomach tightened as Alma's words assaulted her—as their meaning bruised and beat her. Her own grandmother would have preferred it if she had been "gotten rid of."

"She tried to keep it from me, but you know how I found out? She told Lonnie, and Lonnie told me." Alma smiled slyly, and a wisp of smoke escaped from the corner of her mouth.

Meg sucked in a breath. *"Lonnie?"*

In that moment, she pictured fifteen-year-old Lucie, scared and in trouble, confiding in her brother—maybe here in this very room. She imagined the hurt Lucie must have felt—the betrayal she'd experienced at the hand of her twin, the person she was supposed to be closest to in the world.

No wonder she was angry when he showed up in LA, Meg thought. *She probably never forgave him—never spoke with him again.*

Maybe that's why she never told me about him.

But he was young, she reasoned. *He didn't know any better. He probably thought he was helping. . . .*

Alma scowled. "It was for her own good. If it hadn't been for me, you would have died in poverty years ago. It was because of me—because *I* talked to his parents—that they supported you."

Meg could feel her anger growing, rising up in her chest and threatening to explode her lungs. "Because of *you?*" she cried. "Because of *you,* Lucie could never tell my father about me even if she wanted to. Because of you, she had to keep me a secret."

Alma scoffed. "Who did you think was going to pay for everything? Me?" She shook her head. "Lucie was a high school dropout with nothing going for her—"

"But *you* made her leave school! You sent her away!" Meg's fingers curled into her palms, forming fists.

"I fixed things!" Alma insisted.

"No," Meg fired back. "You ruined *everything!*"

She grabbed her jacket and tried to push past her grandmother, but Alma stopped her with a bony hand on her arm.

"They look at you," she rasped. "People look at you like you didn't raise your child right, like you didn't teach her manners and proper behavior. And I was not going to have people look at me that way."

Meg couldn't bear to be near her grandmother for one second longer, to see her dried-up cheeks and neck, her hateful eyes. Meg shook her grip loose. "All you care about is yourself." She tore her gaze away and took the stairs two at a time.

"Where are you going?" Alma demanded.

Meg shook her head. Her hand reached for the front door. "I don't know."

"If you go," Alma yelled from the top of the stairs, "don't come back."

Meg stopped. The last time she heard those words, they chilled her. Maybe it was because she cared then—cared that they had come from Lucie, her sister for all of her life.

But Meg didn't care this time. Alma deserved what she asked for.

She deserved, more than anything, to be finally, utterly alone.

Chapter
TWENTY-THREE

Dear Jen,

When you grow up in Southern California, you're acutely aware of the ground below you, probably more so than other people in the world. There are no warnings for earthquakes, no predictions or forecasts. There's no such thing as earthquake season or earthquake weather, although some people like to pretend there is. These things just happen. You might be in bed or watching your favorite show on TV or, God forbid, you're in the bathroom, and the whole world just starts shaking, like it got hit by a giant truck. They always tell you to find a doorway to brace yourself in or to hide under a sturdy desk or table, but no one ever has time for that. It takes a second or two to realize what it is, then another to wonder if it's the Big One and the state's going to fall into the Pacific, and by the time you figure out that table from IKEA isn't made *of real wood and probably won't hold up under the weight of the ceiling, the whole thing is over.*

When you grow up in Southern California, you know the earth can start shaking at any moment, through no fault of your own.

But I thought I would be on solid ground in New York.

You can't do anything for me, Jen, I know that. You can't wave a magic wand and make things better, and maybe it was naive of me to think you ever could. That's okay. You were a friend when I needed you. And I just want you to know that I appreciated it.

Meg remembered Lonnie's words and hopped the F train to Coney Island. The F was one of those orange lines like the B, the D, and the V. The N and Q trains also went to Coney, but they were yellow lines, and yellow felt too upbeat and sunny for Meg's grim mood.

Late afternoon before rush hour, the train was nearly empty, although Meg still chose her seat wisely. During one of her first subway rides alone, she had ventured onto a crowded A train and struggled to keep herself upright. When she noticed an open seat at the back of the car, she had lunged for it. Within seconds she knew why the seat was still available: Hobo Jones was the seat's companion, and if she breathed at all, she would get the smell of him up her nose and in her mouth. She quickly retreated, but alas, the overpowering urine/booze/sewage stench clung to her, and she had to rush home and take a long hot shower.

She didn't make a mistake like that twice.

The F train dead-ended at Stillwell Avenue in Coney,

where Meg exited the subway and headed straight for the water. The wind coming off the Atlantic bit clear through her jeans and sweater and numbed her to her bones. She looked sharp, though, which was a bonus.

There was a color to winter on the East Coast that didn't exist in Southern California. The sky took on a grayish white cast, and the patinas of the buildings, cars, trees, water, and sand were muted, as if a thin netting had been tossed over the landscape to protect it until spring.

All of the rides at Coney were shut down for the season, and the concession stand doors were closed and padlocked. The pier was empty save for a handful of Chinese fishermen who were using raw chicken bits as bait.

Meg wondered what sort of fish would be attracted by the bloody flesh of poultry—and what sort of person would eat that fish.

The sand was barren as well, and while the rumors of washed-up hypodermic needles were clearly exaggerated, Meg still didn't want to put her butt down.

But despite all the negatives—and there were an awful lot of those—Coney Island in the winter had one thing going for it: it was the perfect place to be sad.

I'm sorry things didn't work out for you, her father had said.

If you go, don't come back, her grandmother had said.

And so had her mother.

Meg exhaled. All she had wanted was to be on solid ground. Was that simply too much to ask?

She stared out over the water. Nary a wave to be seen on this winter's day. No roar of surf against sand, no cries of seagulls, no boat motors or lifeguard whistles or children shouting or people laughing. Nothing but flat, murky brown sea and the echo of silence. She sat down on the edge of the boardwalk and didn't care if the wet sand got into her jeans. The salted wind stung her eyes, but she let them water, let fat blobs of tears leak out the corners of her eyes. Soon her mascara would run and she would look like a raccoon, but she didn't care about that either.

What had she expected—instant love? Instant acceptance?

No.

Maybe.

No, no, of course not. She hadn't *expected* anything. She had *hoped*. There was a difference. She had *hoped* her father might be the sort of person she could depend on, the kind of guy who took responsibility for his actions, no matter how many years had passed. Surely it wasn't possible that Lucie the flake—*her* Lucie—had been more mature than Mr. Vice President of International Sales?

Of course it's possible, and stop calling me Shirley, Meg heard in her head.

A tickle of nervous laughter bubbled up from inside her chest, rising to the back of her throat and out her nose. The absurd sound cut across the empty boardwalk, and the Chinese fishermen turned their heads.

Meg laughed even harder. *"Crazy white girl," they must be thinking, "laughing with herself."*

Crazy white girl.

God, she was tired.

She heard footsteps on the boardwalk and looked up. Walking toward her was Juny, handsome and strong in his varsity jacket. She felt a profound relief on seeing him. It was the relief that came from knowing that someone, somewhere, cared for her.

A comfort in the knowledge that she was not unlovable.

Juny knelt beside Meg and gently brushed a lock of hair off her face before he kissed her.

"Most people visit Coney in the summer," he said with an easy smile.

"Thank you for coming when I called. I didn't know where else to go, and this felt right."

Juny nodded. "Now you're a real New Yorker."

He took her in his arms, placing a layer of warmth between her and the biting wind. She buried her face in his chest and didn't let go—couldn't. She felt tears spring to her eyes—how could she have any more left? Great big sobs convulsed her chest. Juny guided her to a patch of sand beneath the fishermen's pier that was soft, clean, and dry and where they were blocked from the wind.

"I . . . I feel so stupid. He just . . . ignored it all, ignored *me*. I mean, I was standing right there, right *there*, and he pretended I was some stupid girl off the street.

"I should have done something," she said, her voice growing fierce. "I should have said something. But I just left like it was okay that he didn't care, okay that he bought my silence with a stupid pile of cash." She reached into her jacket pocket and withdrew the money.

She hadn't even looked at it, certainly hadn't counted it when he gave it to her. It looked to be around three hundred dollars. It was more money than she had ever held in her life.

"Here. Want it?"

Juny folded her fingers around the bills. "No, I don't."

"Well, I don't want it. I don't want anything to do with it. I don't want anything to do with *him*."

Without warning Juny, she let out a skull-penetrating scream.

Juny clasped his hands over his ears.

"Sorry," she said when her voice was spent. Under the boardwalk, her tone was deadened by the wood, but she could still feel the scream echo in her head. "I never should have come here. Lucie was right." She shook her head and snorted a laugh. "Can you believe that? *Lucie* was right. She told me my father was a jerk. She told me he'd only hurt me." She looked up into Juny's eyes. "And you were right too. Oh God, everyone was right except me."

Juny frowned. "How was I right?"

"You told me to wait and to think about it. But I didn't. I couldn't."

When she stopped speaking, Meg could hear nothing but the rush of ocean against shore.

"Alma told me I wasn't supposed to be here," she

whispered. "I thought she meant Queens, but she meant—"

"She's crazy," Juny said, folding her into his arms again. "She's old and crazy. You can't listen to her."

"This was all a waste of time," Meg said. She pulled away from Juny and dug the heels of her boots into the sand.

"A waste of time? What are you talking about?" he asked, sounding angry now. "What about Nikki and Mariela and Lonnie? What about Bunny?"

"Bunny . . ." Meg softened. She thought of her amazing half sister, waving pink-mitten-covered hands in the falling snow, playing with the princesses, clinging to Meg's arm in the subway.

Her sister. Her real sister, not like Lucie.

"Bunny will never forget you. She'll miss you and ask about you. She'll hound her parents night and day. Where's Meg? When's Meg coming? Why isn't Meg here? Trust me. Mariela's the same way."

When Meg met Bunny, she had felt an instant affection for the girl, an immediate desire to protect her and keep her safe. She'd assumed Bunny's extreme cuteness was to blame, but maybe it was more: maybe it had been a sisterly bond she had never really experienced before.

"Maybe I can get in touch with her when she's older," Meg suggested. "I can be the cool older sister from Hollywood."

"See?" Juny smiled. "That's what I'm talking about."

"And then, of course, there's you." Meg pulled Juny close by his jacket lapels and kissed his lips, tasted salt air on his tongue. "Thank you."

"For what?"

"For being a great boyfriend."

Juny opened his jacket and held her tighter to his chest. She could feel his heart beating through his sweater, wondered if he could feel hers.

As they kissed, Meg felt the gloom of Coney Island fall away. The biting wind and the Chinese fishermen dissolved, leaving only the two of them in a cocoon of tenderness and longing.

Oh yes, tomorrow her face would be red, scratched by the spiky ends of Juny's late-afternoon beard, but that worry was a lifetime away. In this place, they were far removed from the rest of the world. Here, Meg felt like she could escape the ugliness that surrounded her.

Under this boardwalk, in Juny's arms, she felt . . . worthwhile.

She wanted to be lost in that feeling, to drown in it. She didn't want to think about anything else.

Meg's fingers found the waistband of Juny's jeans as his found hers. It was hot under the boardwalk, humid beneath Juny's jacket. Juny laid her back on the soft, cool sand, caressing her, covering her with his kisses.

Meg closed her eyes. Her head swam. With the sound of the waves crashing at her feet, it was as though she were underwater. She didn't fight the current—didn't want to find her way to the surface. She let it take her.

And then, in the delicious darkness, a picture began to swim before her.

It was Lucie—at *her* age—at fifteen.

Lucie, living in Astoria with Alma, a mother incapable of real love.

Lucie, desperate and longing to get out.

Lucie, finding a boy, tall and handsome. A football player who made her feel special . . .

Meg had sworn she was nothing like her mother. And yet—

No. No, no, no.

She wouldn't follow the path Lucie had chosen. Like mother would not be like daughter.

"Juny?" Meg pulled back from her boyfriend and took his hands in hers. "Stop. I—I can't do this."

"What?" It took Juny a moment to understand what she was saying, but in seconds, he returned to his senses. He nodded and said, "Yeah, okay. Okay."

He rolled over onto his back. Meg laid her head on his chest and listened as his heartbeat slowed. She didn't need to explain to him. The way she felt was enough.

Juny stroked her hair softly. "You want to go now?"

Far off at the end of the pier, the fishermen were packing up their bait, heading in for the night.

Meg sighed softly. "Let's stay here for a few minutes. Just like this."

She wanted to enjoy the moment.

For the first time in as long as Meg could remember, it was a moment of peace.

●　　　●　　　●

After Coney Island, Meg couldn't go back to Alma's house, certainly not right away. When Mrs. Hernandez invited her to stay for dinner, she accepted gratefully.

She hadn't eaten a bite of food since breakfast, she remembered; she was ravenous and light-headed from hunger. She could hardly wait for Mariela to finish saying grace before she inhaled a giant plate of chicken and rice and plantains. It was, without a doubt, the best dinner she had ever tasted in her entire life.

Dessert was even better: chocolate cupcakes decorated with vanilla frosting and M&M candies, served in front of the Hernandezes' fireplace in the den.

"I made them," Mariela told Meg.

"You mean you put the M&M's on the tops," Nikki said.

"Yeah. I *made* them."

"Well, they're the most delicious cupcakes I have ever had," Meg said. It was like talking to Bunny, she thought, a slightly older Bunny with an interest in horses rather than princesses.

Mariela smiled appreciatively. "I'll make you another one," she said, and ran back to the kitchen.

Meg turned to Juny, who sat beside her on the couch. "She's gonna eat all the M&M's off the top, isn't she?"

Juny laughed. "Pretty much."

Meg sighed, content and drowsy. Her head felt so heavy; every muscle was exhausted. She wanted to be nowhere else but here: beneath Juny's arm, in front of the warm fire, her belly full of food. The comfort Juny's family offered made her feel like one of their own. Here, in this home, she could finally, *finally* relax.

She awoke sometime later. A hand gently stroked her face.

"Meg," Juny whispered. "Your uncle's on the phone."

She blinked the sleep out of her eyes and sat up. Someone had given her a blanket while she slept and arranged a pillow beneath her head. The room was dark.

"Hello?" she said into the phone. "Lonnie?"

"I'm at the hospital, Meg," Lonnie said in a solemn voice, so far away. "How fast can you get here?"

Chapter
TWENTY-FOUR

She had survived chemotherapy, but smoking got Alma Shanley in the end anyway. The fire department said she had probably fallen asleep with a burning cigarette. The place was ablaze in minutes.

Thank God no one else was hurt, the fire chief had told them.

Aside from Meg, Lonnie, and Toni, no one attended Alma's funeral at St. Ambrose's Catholic Church. Father Flammia said some very nice words, Meg thought, about her grandmother's selflessness as a wife and mother, even if he was making it up as he went along.

The mortician had prepared Alma well, adding some rouge to her leaden cheeks, a hint of lipstick and eye makeup, and swapping out her pink wig for a more natural-toned brunette one. She looked more alive than Meg had ever seen her.

At the cemetery, there were a few simple prayers, a little "ashes to ashes" business, and then Alma Shanley's mahogany casket with white satin pillow and double-stitched lining was lowered into the ground. Lonnie slipped the priest some brand-new twenties, and it was over.

"Father, this probably isn't the best time to talk about this," Toni was saying to Father Flammia as Meg watched them walk away, "but Lonnie and I would love it if you performed the ceremony for us."

Meg looked over at Lonnie. "You're getting married," she said softly.

Lonnie nodded.

"Congratulations."

"Thank you."

Lonnie took Meg's hand as the two of them stared at the neatly dug grave and the coffin sitting smack in the middle. Once they had left, the cemetery workers would come and begin filling in the empty spaces with shovels—but not yet. As long as the family was still present, mourning was officially in session.

"Maybe I shouldn't have waited till she passed on," Lonnie said. "Maybe she would have come to my wedding."

Meg glanced at him, and the two shared a secret smile. "Yeah, I'm sure she would have loved that."

Lonnie chuckled. "And hell would have experienced a cooling trend."

"I'm sorry you lost your mother, Lonnie."

He nodded. "And you lost . . . well, you lost a place to live."

"And my clothes and my books and—"

The letters, Meg thought. *Jen's letters.* They were all gone.

"Are you okay?" Lonnie asked.

"Yeah." All of Jen's words of wisdom, her love and support, the only love and support that had ever been *real* in her life, had vanished. Through bad times and *very* bad times, they had sustained her. Meg had carried them three thousand miles from one side of the continent to the other. What would she do now—without them?

"I'm sorry, Meg."

Lonnie pulled her into a hug. Meg looked up at him and then over at Toni with the priest. They would be happy together, she thought. An instant family for Lonnie: wife and two kids. Just add water and shake.

Funny. She'd thought *she'd* be the one with the instant family.

"You don't have to leave. Toni and I want you to live with us for as long as you want. Till you finish school or whatever," Lonnie said.

"With you?" Meg asked.

"Sure. Toni's always wanted a girl around the house. Me and the boys give her a lot of crap."

Meg tried to picture herself in a two-bedroom apartment with her uncle and his new family. "Where would I . . . ?"

"I know it's small, but the foldout couch has been okay

so far, hasn't it? It'll just be until we can find a larger apartment."

"You'd move to a new apartment for me?"

Lonnie smiled at her as if she were slow. "We're family, Meg. That's the sort of thing family does."

"Thank you," Meg said, and wrapped her arms around her uncle's neck. As it turned out, he was the only solid and dependable Shanley of the bunch. "I really appreciate the offer. Please tell Toni thank you, okay?"

Then she stepped back from her uncle and offered a self-assessment. "I did exactly what I said I would do, you know? I found my father and I met him. And I got to know my family—Lucie's family. I think I understand Lucie a little better now, knowing where she came from and what she went through." She paused. "I think—I have to give her another chance." She smiled at her uncle. "But I will definitely come back for a visit very soon. Like, how cool will it be to say, 'I have family back east.' Right?"

Lonnie stood up straighter. "I have family out west." He grinned. "Yeah, that does sound cool."

"Yeah."

They stared at Alma's grave for another moment.

"Was she always like that?" Meg asked. She hesitated to add "cold and cruel," this being a sacred site and all.

Lonnie's gaze followed the clouds shifting and reshaping themselves up above. "I think she loved us, but she wanted to control us. Lucie never wanted to be controlled." He shrugged. "I didn't mind so much, most of the time."

Meg's uncle squinted against the bright sun. "She never once mentioned me? Not once in fifteen years? Not even a slip of the tongue, like, 'My brother, Lonnie, used to collect action figures' . . . or whatever? Nothing like that?"

"I'm sorry."

"No big deal," he said, although Meg could tell that it was. It hurt him deeply. He was a very different Lonnie than the one Lucie left fifteen years ago. "Outta sight, outta mind, I guess. Mother never talked about her either, so I suppose we're even." He held Meg's gaze in earnest. "You'll tell her about me, won't you? About Toni and everything? How we're happy?"

Meg nodded. "Most definitely." She waited as her uncle joined Toni a short distance away, then she knelt at her grandmother's tombstone, so new the edges of the engravings were still sharp.

Alma Grace Shanley, 1939–2008
Beloved Wife and Mother

"It was only a hundred dollars," Meg said to the gray marble. "A hundred bucks once in a while, and we called it a happy envelope because it made us happy, but it didn't make us rich." She stood and stared down at the grave of her grandmother. "Was it worth it?"

She wanted to believe that her grandmother had died peacefully in her sleep, that her last dreams were pleasant ones, that maybe, just maybe, her thoughts had turned to forgiveness in her final moments of life.

"I'm sorry you never got to know me," Meg whispered to the earth.

It was hardest to say goodbye to Juny. He simply couldn't understand why she was leaving.

"My parents would let you stay with us," he insisted. "We have plenty of room."

They were at JFK airport. Nate's go-away money, plus the cash Meg had made babysitting Bunny, gave her enough for a one-way ticket to LA.

"I have to go back. I have to see Lucie." She couldn't say much more than that because she didn't know much more than that. She had to set things straight with Lucie, had to finish what had begun years ago. Alma's death was a sign—if nothing else, it forced Meg to go home, to find out if Lucie *was* her home.

"This isn't forever. I'll come see Lonnie and Toni and the boys. . . ." She smiled at him. "And you."

Juny looked so obviously forlorn. "I'm really gonna miss you."

Meg's heart just about broke into song hearing that. She wanted to shrink Juny down to G.I. Joe size, stuff him in her pocket, and bring him back to LA with her. *"A Confederacy of Dunces,"* she said. "Read it? John Kennedy Toole."

Juny thought a moment and then smiled. "No, I haven't."

"Gotcha!"

"Very nice, Hollywood, very nice."

"So you'll read it—"

"I'll read it."

"And maybe you can write me something about it," she suggested.

"What, like a homework assignment?" But he smiled when he said it.

They kissed then, and it should have been like an on-screen kiss with a slow, lingering embrace, but a security guard hustled them along so other people could pass through the checkpoint.

Meg smiled and waved as she headed toward her gate, but she didn't cry. She would be back, she knew. Things were not over with Juny.

Chapter
TWENTY-FIVE

Not much had changed since Meg was in Hollywood. The stars were still in the sidewalk, the handprints in the cement. Palm trees swayed on the boulevard, and luxury automobiles cruised Sunset.

She wasn't sure what she would find at the old apartment, who she would find. Lucie's battered Spectra in the car hole gave her a moment to rethink her decision to come here. Why had she returned? What did she really want?

She already knew the reason Lucie left Queens—she had experienced it herself. Was she hoping to hear "I love you" or "I missed you" or some other nonsense from Lucie? No. That was simply a ridiculous notion. There would be no tears of joy, no sustained embraces. She wasn't Rachel; this wasn't *Friends*. It wouldn't be like on television at all.

There was just one question Meg needed to hear the answer to—and then she would know where her home truly was.

She pressed her finger against the bell, heard nothing for a long moment, and then came the click of the dead bolt and the dull rattle of the chain. There was still time to cut and run! But no, Meg stayed put. The door opened, and a rope of red hair fell across a pair of startled eyes. "Hi, Luce."

Lucie's hand brushed the hair out of her face, and in a split second, so brief that Meg would have missed it had she blinked, a mixture of relief, surprise, and happiness flooded Lucie's face.

"Can I come in?"

Lucie's blank stare returned as she appeared to consider the request. Just like Alma, Meg thought. Lucie was just like her, hiding her emotions.

The door opened wider. Meg took a step in and looked around. Not much had changed here either. Same sofa, same chair, same television and VCR. "How are you, Luce?"

Personally, Meg thought she looked as battered as her Spectra: older, tired, a little rusted.

Lucie shrugged.

"You working?"

She nodded.

"How's Aaron?"

"He's good."

"You're together?"

"Yep."

They stood in silence for what felt to Meg like an eternity.

"Aren't you gonna ask anything? About me? About my trip?"

Lucie crossed her arms over her chest. "How's the house?"

"Burned to the ground."

Again, a flicker of surprise. Then Lucie nodded and said nothing.

Meg didn't know whether to reach out and throttle Lucie or to take her in her arms and sob. Instead, she slipped a finger into the front pocket of her jeans and held her hand out to Lucie. "I'm returning this to you."

Lucie stared down into Meg's palm. "My ring? Thought I lost that in the move." She frowned and walked into the kitchen.

Meg followed, placing the ring down on the kitchen table. It was the same table as before. And *that* was the same coffeepot, and the same dish rack, and the same microwave and the same crappy Wal-Mart chairs.

"Coffee?"

"Sure."

While Lucie made herself busy, Meg took a look around. "Did you paint?"

"Yep."

"Looks good."

"Thanks."

"New curtains?"

"Yep."

"Nice."

Lucie kept her back to Meg while she worked. "Are we finished with the small talk, the how are yous?" She cast a quick glance back at Meg and then shook her head. "Go ahead and speak. It's obvious you came a long way to say something to me."

Meg crossed her arms and watched the water drip through the filter and become coffee. *Be careful what you wish for,* she told herself. *Ask and you will receive, but you might not like it very much.*

"Why didn't you tell me the truth?"

"It's complicated."

"So explain it to me. I'm pretty smart."

The back of Lucie's head shook, and her hair swung from side to side. "I can't. You'll hate me."

"Oh, come on." Meg made a big show of pulling out a chair and settling herself down onto the hard surface. "We've covered that ground already, haven't we? I've got all day, Luce. No place to go, no one to see."

Lucie remained silent.

Fine, then she would continue. "Lucie, did you ever care about me? Did you ever think about *me*? All those years you told me I had no parents—*we* had no parents—all the lies . . . did you ever think about how they would affect me?"

"No."

"No?"

"Not the way you'd expect. I never thought you'd find out."

Meg was dumfounded by this answer.

"Of *course* I cared about you," Lucie said as her fingers gripped the edge of the counter. "Everything I did was for you. Every move, every school, every crappy job I took. It was all for you."

"And the guys?" Meg asked bitterly. "Were they all for me too?"

"I wanted something stable for us, Meg, and I couldn't do it by myself. I never could." With a shake of her head, Lucie flipped her hair off her shoulders. "I did my best. I loved you . . . as much as I could. I was young and scared. You met my mother. She wasn't much of a role model."

"You're blaming your mother now?"

"No—"

"Why don't you blame me while you're at it?" Meg said, her voice and temper rising. "If I hadn't been born, everything would have been fine for you!"

"No! No!"

"Then what are you saying?"

"I never wanted to be a mother!" Lucie yelled. "Okay? Is that what you wanted to hear? I never wanted that. I was too young. Too young to be responsible for myself, let alone another human being. And I had failed at everything. I was a crappy student, a crappy daughter. I couldn't be a crappy mother too." Lucie paused. "So I became your sister. That, at least, was something I knew I could do."

"But you weren't even that," Meg said. Her heart was pounding so hard she could feel it in her head, could feel her temples pulse and her eyelids twitch. "You weren't even a sister I could count on. You were never there for me, Lucie."

"That's not true. I was always here."

"You gave up on me. I had to write to a TV star for advice and compassion. How insane is that? Thank God I could at least count on *her*."

Lucie finally turned around and stared at Meg. Her eyes were big and soft, and the liner around them was smeared in the corners. She made not a sound as she left the room. The only noise in the kitchen was the wet steam of the coffee as it finished brewing.

In a moment, Lucie returned to the kitchen and placed a shoe box on the table. "Open it."

Meg lifted the lid. Inside were dozens of envelopes—*her* letters to Jennifer Aniston from the earliest days, when her handwriting was a childish scrawl. She pulled out one of the letters. "'Dear Jen,'" she read, "'how are you? I am fine. Today a big girl pushed me off the bleachers in gym class, then stepped on my hand. It hurt really bad. I don't want to go to school there ever again! But Lucie's making me. This is so unfair.'"

She had been eight when she wrote this—her hand had been throbbing at the time from the girl's sneaker—and it had been the first day at that new school. What had Jen written in return? "'Trust Lucie,'" Meg remembered. "'She'll talk to the principal about it, and everything will be okay.'"

The letters, *her* letters. *Lucie* . . . was Jennifer?

Meg looked up from the shoe box. "Why did you do this?"

"You needed a friend," Lucie said. "And you deserved someone better than me. Jen was beautiful and perfect, and she knew just what to say."

Meg felt her head nod on its own. That letter she had shown Aaron months ago? The one about the boy who liked her, that Jeff kid?

(*Smile at Jeff,* Jen had written. *Be your charming self.*)

She hadn't told Jen his name, but Jen knew . . . because Lucie knew.

"I used to get so excited when you finished a letter," Lucie said. "I'd take it from you to mail, and then I'd sit in my car and read it, and sometimes you just broke my heart. You were lonely and funny, and you had the sweetest little stories. I couldn't wait to write you back. I knew it would make you happy."

"The sunglasses," Meg remembered. "Were those yours too?"

Lucie nodded. "Cost me a week's pay. Man, when you broke those, I said never again. Jen can send letters but no gifts." She gave a small laugh, shaking her head.

"Why did you stop?" Meg asked quietly.

"I wanted you to talk to me instead of her. I hoped it might make us closer."

"I kept writing, you know. Even after you stopped, I wrote and wrote. I wanted to hear more from her. She had some good advice." Meg's head felt so heavy. She looked out the kitchen window to the sun setting over the far-off Pacific.

Those letters had been her lifeline for so long—she'd even carried them across the country with her. Had the words meant so much because she thought they were Jennifer Aniston's? Or because they were from someone who loved her and cared about her?

"I'm not a very smart woman, Meg. I did stupid things, and I'll probably do more stupid things, but I promise I will never lie to you again. I'd really like another chance."

Out of the corner of her eye, Meg saw movement on the linoleum. She jumped back when she saw the giant roach.

"Looks like Gregor's back," Lucie said matter-of-factly. She sprang into action, swiftly capturing the insect under a glass and sweeping him onto a magazine. Then she opened the back door and flung the roach into the wilds of Hollywood.

She learned something from me, Meg marveled, *she remembered that was important to me.*

Lucie shrugged. "You named him. I didn't have the heart to kill him."

Meg's gaze slowly circled the small kitchen: the stove, the sink, the fridge with a pair of finger-pointing magnets that said, "Don't forget!" then landed it on Lucie.

"Lucie," she said softly, "I don't want to cut people out of my life anymore. Your mother did it and you did it and my father did it. You discarded people when they didn't fit, and that really hurt them. It hurt me." She sighed. "You can't just keep moving and starting over again. It's not like pressing the reset button on a video game."

To Meg's surprise, Lucie agreed. "You're right. I won't run away again."

Meg frowned. "Really?"

"I bought curtains, didn't I?"

Meg nodded. "Good."

"So . . . does this mean you'll stay?"

Meg thought for a moment. Was this her home, then? Was Lucie her home? She searched deep inside herself for an answer to the contrary, but she searched in vain. Every bone in her body told her the same thing. "Yes, I'll stay."

"And you don't hate me?"

Silence in the kitchen. Outside, it had grown dark.

"No," Meg said at last. "I don't hate you."

Lucie's head bobbed up and down, and she smiled with apparent relief. "Good, good." She pointed to Meg's sweat-shirt, a hand-me-down from Toni with *Princess from Queens* written in glittery gold letters on the front. "We should probably get you some new some clothes, huh? Looks like that sweatshirt has seen better days."

Meg gently clutched fistfuls of fabric. "We can go shopping, sure. But I'm keeping this. It reminds me of people I'm going to see again."

Not long after Meg arrived back in Hollywood, a package came from Lonnie. She remembered the promise she had made to him. "Lonnie's getting married to a really nice girl," she told Lucie. "He wants you to know that. He's a good guy, Luce."

"That . . . that's great," Lucie said. Meg noted it was without the rancor she would have expected in months past. Maybe Lucie *was* learning. "What'd he send you?"

Meg opened the box and found three items inside. The first was a mini–snow globe with a mini-Manhattan under falling white flakes. This was a souvenir, Lonnie wrote, of her first real winter. There were also two envelopes. The first was from Juny. Meg tore it open.

Dear Meg, she read to herself. *Things just aren't the same without you around. Guess what? I talked my dad into looking at some California schools. We're coming for a week. Maybe I can ditch the family for a while so you and I can—*

Meg felt Lucie's eyes peeking over her shoulder. "I'll finish this one in my room."

The second envelope had a return address in Burbank, California.

"How did Lonnie get a letter from Burbank?" She pulled out a head shot of Jennifer Aniston. She was smiling coyly at the camera, her blond highlights framing her perfect face. "Okay, very funny, Lucie."

"I didn't send that."

Meg pulled out a sheet of paper. The header at the top of the page read: *Jennifer Aniston Club of Southern California.* She held the paper up ceremoniously as if she were reading a proclamation. "'Dear Meg Shanley. Thank you so much for your letter. I always love hearing from my wonderful fans. You can read more about my projects and what's going on in my life at my fantastic Web site. There's always something new! Stay beautiful! Love, Jennifer.'"

Meg and Lucie stared from the letter to the head shot in silence.

Finally, Meg sighed. "You were a much better Jennifer Aniston."

Lucie blushed. "Thanks."

"Now, if you'll excuse me . . ." Meg took her snow globe and mail into her bedroom, closed the door, and sat on the bed in a patch of sunlight.

She opened Juny's letter and pressed the page to her heart.

Dear Meg, she read again. *Things just aren't the same without you around.*

Acknowledgments

I am grateful to the following for their invaluable assistance in making this book possible: my editor, Kristen Pettit, whose insight and guidance helped me find my story and who loved Meg as much as I did; my agent, Faye Bender, whose wisdom and strength encouraged me every step of the way; my manager and friend, Adam Peck, whose support has never wavered and who will always be my first reader.

And my husband, Maurice Jordan, who sees all and still believes.

Thank you all so much.